Lake of Fire

Elements Supernatural Thriller Series, Volume 1

Katie McVay

Published by Katie McVay, 2023.

LAKE OF FIRE

First edition. January 2, 2023.

Copyright © 2023 Katie McVay.

ISBN: 978-0983885368

Written by Katie McVay.

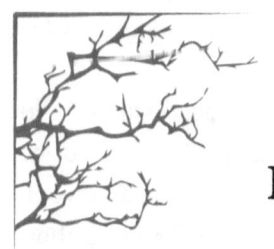

PROLOGUE

I DIDN'T KILL MY HUSBAND. I know that for a fact. But I did play a part in his death. That's not a fact, per se. Just something I know to be true.

My mother, Susan, would've called that kind of truth—my "knowingness"—intuition. Cognition. Extrasensory perception. Up until my husband's death, I would've called it some sort of fake sixth-sense bullshit.

But now? After everything I went through? I would've agreed with my mother, God rest her soul.

She had a gift, my mother, her own intuition, or clairvoyance, whatever you want to call it. She had visions, heard voices—the whole works. She didn't hide her gifts from the family, exactly, but she didn't talk about them either, at least not with me. She'd just say weird things, like how my spirit guides were always watching over me, or give me cryptic warnings about where not to go and what not to do, based on one vision or another.

Or, perhaps creepiest of all, she'd have conversations with invisible people in empty rooms. Like the time I overheard her one-sided chat with my deceased grandmother as she set the dining room table.

"Yes, mom," my mom was saying just as I was about to walk into the dining room. "Lilian knows you're looking out for her. I told her."

I ducked around the corner out of site for a minute, listening.

"I think she's a bit too young yet to understand what it all means, though. She's only thirteen." There was a pause and the sound of silverware clinking. Then, "Well, divine timing is always at play, right? Isn't that what you always told me? So Lilian will know when she's supposed to know."

For whatever reason (fear of ostracization? Social stigma? Not needing the attention?) my mother shrugged it all off as normal behavior, and didn't encourage questions or conversation. So I would follow her lead, not press for information, shrug it off and go about my day. Ashamedly, I grew up knowing my mother was different, but I never understood it or appreciated it until long after she was gone.

And sadly, because of her reticence, it wasn't my mother, my own flesh and blood, who made me believe in the supernatural.

It was The Property, as I came to call it. The Property made me believe. It was also responsible, partially, for my husband's death. That goddamn house. And me, of course.

"The Property" was an old house by a lake. It was a remodeler's dream. *This* remodeler's dream, anyway. For a time.

The house was built in 1900, in the Queen Anne style that was popular at the time. It sat on ten acres, and featured oversized bay windows, a steeply pitched roof (many steeply pitched roofs, in fact), a round turret, a large wraparound porch with decorative railings, and lots of colorful paint: red, yellow, pale green. You can see it, right? Its flamboyant façade, its beautiful asymmetry, all its complicated irregularities?

It was a long-neglected charmer in need of some TLC. I was chosen to bring her back to life, to remodel her inside and out.

The lake was another story. My client, an old woman named Emma, called it a lake. But it was a pond, really. Not large enough to boat on (there was no boat launch) but large and deep enough to swim in, and skate on—both regular occurrences in its hey-day, apparently.

The lake was in the front yard, about fifty paces from the house, its murky water blackish green and spotted with scum. They had a symbiotic relationship, the lake and the house. I felt it even back then: they fed off each other. You couldn't, in fact, talk about one without mentioning the other.

So, while I had free reign of the house, the lake, apparently, was off limits. Leave it alone, Emma said. Don't clear it of algae. Don't aerate it to get the oxygen flowing. Don't vacuum it or pump out the water. Don't go near it, in fact. Stay away.

I obliged her, of course, because it wasn't my property and I wasn't in charge.

Soon enough, I found out she wasn't in charge, either. The old woman hadn't chosen me to remodel her ancestral home. The Property had. Emma was just there to do its bidding. She was the one who was obliged to obey. Because The Property was in charge, and it would have its way. It always did, until the bitter end.

CHAPTER ONE

I WAS ON MY KNEES IN the first-floor powder room, toilet brush in hand, when Emma called me.

A doozy of a headache had come on moments before, right as I started cleaning the bathroom. I'd experienced many in the two weeks since burying my husband, Kevin.

My cell phone rang from the kitchen counter. I put the brush down and stumbled toward it.

Caller I.D.— *Unknown.*

On a normal day, any given day, I would've ignored an unknown number. Let it go to voicemail. This, though, was anything but a normal day. This day was the start of it all.

And yet, something made me answer. Despite the white-hot pain ripping through my skull, I wanted—needed—to answer that call. At the time, I thought it was the guilt I'd felt over ignoring so many other calls: my sister, in Denver, calling to see how I was doing; my mother-in-law, ditto; our hippie neighbor, Stella, who'd brought food on several occasions so I wouldn't have to cook, and sage so I could clear the air of any negative energy roaming around our house; our financial accountant, Jake, wanting to discuss the future of the business.

Every well-meaning human in my life, I'd either ignored or cut short. So maybe if I answered this call, and gave it everything I got, really made myself present for whoever was on the other end, known or unknown, all my guilt would go away. Hell, maybe even the headaches would go away.

I answered the phone and hit the speaker button so I could pop a pill and talk at the same time.

"Hello?" I said.

"Yes, hello? Is this LB Remodeling?"

Her voice was soft, yet steady and firm.

"Oh, yes. Sorry." The headache had temporarily made me forget that I usually answered every call, unless I could tell from the caller I.D. it was personal, with an official salutation. "LB Remodeling, this is Lilian." I swallowed two Advil with a gulp of water and pushed the bottle off to the side. A wave of nausea hit me and I sat down to let it pass.

"Hello, dear," said the woman, who sounded elderly. "My name is Emma Becker."

"What can I do for you, Mrs. Becker?"

"Miss Becker," the woman clarified. "Please call me Emma. I'd like you to remodel my home."

"Remodel your home. Okay, well, I ... I'm sorry. You've caught me at a bad time."

"Should I call back later?"

"No, that's not what I mean. It's just that I'm not taking on any work at the moment."

"Of course you are, dear," she said. She was direct, insistent. She seemed like the type of old lady who didn't take shit from anyone, and I instantly liked her.

Emma lapsed into a quiet, dry coughing fit that left her breathless.

"Are you alright?" I asked, when I sensed she was able to speak.

She swallowed a few sips of something, then said, haltingly, "I'm fine."

"I can refer you to some other contractors I recommend."

"I don't want another contractor, Lilian."

"I'm sorry, Emma. My business partner, my husband ... recently passed ... and well, I'm not quite sure I'm ready ..."

I stifled a sob, then cleared my throat to compose myself.

Emma sighed. "They do have a tendency to do that, don't they, dear? Die on us. Such a terrible thing. I'm very sorry for your loss."

In his final moments, Kevin asked to be cremated. But I felt obligated to use the pre-paid funerals my in-laws had gifted us as a wedding present. They were funeral directors and wanted us to be taken care of, and so they thought a death package—caskets, burial plots and a memorial service—was a totally appropriate gift for newlyweds.

I felt guilty not heeding Kevin's last-minute wish to be cremated. It was his final wish, after all, the first of three things he said to me as he lay dying in our driveway.

"Lilian," he struggled to say, his voice a strained whisper. "Listen to me."

"Shhh, Kevin. Just lie still." My hands were shaking. I could tell he was seriously injured.

"No, listen. I need..." he coughed and winced in pain. "I have to be cremated."

"What? No, Kevin. Don't talk like that. Just stay still for me. I'm going to call for help."

I pulled my cell phone out of my back pocket and dialed 9-1-1.

I put my hand on his chest and smiled at him.

"9-1-1 what is your emergency?"

Kevin smiled back, a line of blood trickling from his mouth. He said, "I love you, Lil."

I gave the dispatcher the information. As I was hanging up, Kevin's body relaxed and seemed to melt into the pavement. He locked eyes with me and, with the faint sound of an ambulance siren whirring in the distance, he uttered his final words. Four little words that made no sense at first, and were soon eclipsed by more immediate needs than the request of my dead husband: Finish the basement remodel we'd started. Cancel the other two projects we had on the books. Plan a funeral. Host a memorial service for our closest friends and relatives. Decide what to do about the business Kevin and I had spent twenty years running together. Drug myself to sleep every night. Distract myself with menial and meaningless housework, thinking—hoping—it would ease the grief.

So, while my house was spotlessly clean, my mind was a goddamn mess.

Now, after two weeks without Kevin and no backlog of work, I had no idea what to do. Sure, I was dealing with his estate, but that took up only a fragment of time in what felt like really long days. Most days I had absolutely nothing to do. Most days it was just me and the empty house.

So I cleaned. A lot. I scrubbed and mopped and dusted and washed. The whole house, top to bottom. Everywhere was up for grabs. Everywhere, except Kevin's closet. I couldn't bring myself to clean it out. It was simply too soon.

In the moments in between distractions, I felt empty and lonely, desperate to see Kevin one last time. It was during those moments when his last four words came back to me.

His urgent plea would start rattling around in my head. Then the pounding headaches would start. Sometimes they'd last for hours, accompanied by a noisy, persistent buzzing and clicking. And always, floating in the background, was Kevin's whispered four-word plea.

When I didn't respond to Emma's condolences, she continued, "Listen, Lilian. I'm old. I don't have a lot of time. I need your help. Please."

The old woman fell into another quiet fit of coughing. Although I didn't think I wanted this—or any job—right now, how could I possibly turn away an elderly, sick woman in her time of need? Guilt prodded me.

"I can't make any promises," I said. "But I'll at least take a look at it. What's the address?"

"Hilldale Avenue, off Route 7. It's the only house on Hilldale. It's not hard to find."

"You mean the Queen Anne that sits back from the road? That's the Becker estate."

"You're familiar with it?"

Yes, I certainly was. I'd been admiring it for twenty years. Kevin and I had gone for a Sunday drive on the outskirts of Pennsgrove, through neighborhoods we weren't overly familiar with. On a whim we'd turned off Route 7, turned right onto Hilldale and there it was: that stunning Queen Anne home of my dreams.

I didn't realize at first sighting all those years ago that the famed Becker clan owned that property. In the ensuing years I came to learn more about the family and their business.

And now I was on the phone with a member of the famed Becker clan of Pennsgrove.

"How's the day after tomorrow, Miss Becker?" I said.

"Wonderful, Lilian. I'll make sure my nephew, Eric, is there."

"Eric. Got it."

I got off the phone and ran to the toilet to vomit. I cleaned myself up and looked in the mirror at my pale face. Then I took another Advil and crawled into bed. Within minutes I was enveloped in the warm embrace of a sweet, dreamless oblivion.

Had I known that night would've been one of the last of its kind, I would've cherished it more. Would've cherished the peace. The dreamlessness. Because it wasn't much later that the dreams came, and the fear began.

CHAPTER TWO

I'VE ALWAYS LOVED QUEEN Anne homes. It's something I got from my dad. Even though he was in the new home business, his dream had always been to completely renovate, top to bottom, this style of Victorian home. He'd hadn't been given the opportunity, but now I had. This project had fallen in my lap. And for once, there was no one to tell me no.

Kevin had favored newer-type construction: ranchers, Cape Cods, split-levels, colonials. Much easier and cheaper to fix, he'd always said. So those were the projects we took on. I'd argue with him every now and again, say we needed to mix up our portfolio, to give us a sense of more well-rounded experience. He was right in that they could be tricky projects—not too many contractors wanted to take them on, which was all the reason I thought we should. But Kevin's opinion usually prevailed, and the vast majority of the projects we accepted were ones he approved. So, with every newer home that went on the books, I secretly pined for the chance to take a hammer to an older one.

Even the house we bought together in Pennsgrove was a Neo-Colonial style home, in a development chock full of other Neo-Colonial style homes that were re-popularized in the late-20th and early-21st centuries. Drive through any subdivision in America and you'll likely see these types of homes: two-story vinyl-sided boxes, with nothing much in the way of exterior decorative features. They were plain and boring, but quick and easy to construct—a win-win for the builder and the buyer.

But the Becker place? There was nothing plain or boring about that house—let alone quick and easy. I thought about this while driving to the Stop and Shop late the next morning. I'd been too busy needlessly cleaning the house that I hadn't noticed the fridge and kitchen cabinets were nearly empty. And without much of an appetite and no other mouths to feed, grocery shopping had fallen by the wayside.

I parked my car and grabbed a cart from inside the grocery store vestibule, already deep in thought about the feasibility of the Becker project.

A renovation job for Kevin and I could be a few days, a few weeks, or a few months, depending on what we were doing, time of year and the availability of materials. We'd waterproofed a basement in a day, built a deck in a week, and remodeled a large kitchen in a month. But that was with the pedal to the metal. The Becker project would need to be slow and steady, and could easily take many months.

I could do that, right? Devote the next six months of my life, or more, to renovating a large, old house all by myself? Well, I wouldn't be all by myself. I'd be without Kevin, is what I meant. I'd have help, of course. Crews of electricians, plumbers, demolitionists and other assorted laborers.

And I'd have Sam. Sam would be my foreman. He'd be the best man for the job. It had always been his dream to renovate a Queen Anne, but, like me, he'd never gotten the opportunity. He'd want to do this, though he'd probably be hesitant. But we still trusted each other. I know we did. I'd just have to feel him out.

I zipped from aisle to aisle, mindlessly throwing cans and packages of food into my cart.

Yes, I could do this. I *should* do this. After all, the project had fallen in my lap, it had always been a dream of mine, and I could do it in my dad's honor. Not to mention that it really was an opportunity of a lifetime. The Beckers had been one of the founding families of Pennsgrove. Their family business had put the town on the map, making us synonymous with quality baked bread. If you were a Pennsgrover in the market for a loaf of bread, it was almost a sin to buy anything other than Becker.

Back in the 70s, the Beckers donated millions of dollars to the construction of a much-needed community center. It was named in the family's honor: the Becker Community Center of Pennsgrove. Everyone in the community knew it as the BCC, and we all benefited from its forty years of events and programs.

Indeed, the Becker name loomed large in Pennsgrove. So, despite my initial reservations about taking on the project, despite wanting to take a break from the business, I recognized this opportunity for what it was: a fresh start, if that's indeed what I wanted. An opportunity to prove to friends, family, and colleagues that I could continue on in the face of tragedy. A way to prove to myself that I could do it. Not to mention the credibility the project would give me.

It would be an honor, really, to renovate the Becker family estate. So I had to get a hold of Sam. If I could convince him to—

Bam!

In turning the corner into another aisle, my shopping cart collided with the front end of another's. It was Debbie, of all people—Sam's ex-wife. Her six-year-old daughter Carly, sitting in the cart holding a Barbie, startled and looked at her mom for reassurance. A second girl, eight-year-old Becca, stood at her mother's side, silently staring at me.

Debbie wore pink sweatpants and a white tank top, and her dirty-blonde hair was pulled back into a messy ponytail. She'd always had beautiful blue eyes, but now they were overshadowed by dark rings underneath that turned them more murky-blue rather than ocean-blue.

I looked at her and she looked at me, and her eyes went big and then her face faded into a furrowed-brow look of disdain. It was the first time I'd seen her in two years.

"Hey ... Debbie ..." I said, maneuvering my cart out of the way.

Carly made a noise and Debbie said to her, "It's OK, baby."

"Hey, Carly. Hey, Becca," I said. "Do you remember me? I used to work with your dad."

"Hi Lil-lian," Carly said, struggling to pronounce my name. She looked at me sadly with her blue eyes, which she'd inherited from Debbie, then returned her attention to her Barbie, stroking and braiding its hair.

Becca looked at me but spoke to Debbie. "Mom, where's the bread?"

"Next aisle over, baby," Debbie said.

"I'll get it," Becca said and started walking away.

"Wait!" Debbie called after her. "You got to get this kind." She held out a book of food stamps and pointed. "This one." Becca glanced at the book, nodded and disappeared around the corner.

No Becker bread for them, I thought sadly. Only government-approved, cheap generic bread.

Debbie made no attempt to leave, but she made no attempt to talk, either. I couldn't tell if she wanted to be friendly or throw a can of soup at my face.

She'd left Sam the night she found out. Packed a few suitcases, threw the girls in the back of her car, and took off to her mother's. Sam came home that night to an empty house, which didn't help his situation. Made it way worse, in fact. Another domino had fallen in the long line of dominos that was Sam's life, this one—partially—on account of me.

Debbie was now a single mom with two mouths to feed, living on a waitress' salary. Last I knew she was receiving Sam's alimony and child support, but it wasn't enough. It could never be enough. I knew that just by looking at her.

The guilt came back as I looked at her pale face and thin frame, sensing her utter exhaustion.

"How you been, Debbie?"

She shrugged. "You know."

"The girls are beautiful. They must be in what, first and third grades?"

Debbie glared at me a moment, her lips pursed. "Thought you'd want to know more about Sam, since it's been so long."

"I wasn't ... going to," I stammered. "I'd rather know how you three are doing."

"We're fine," Debbie said quickly. "But Sam's a goddamn mess. You should know that in case, you know ..."

I knew what she was getting at, and I didn't know if I should laugh or be insulted.

"He's broke," Debbie continued. "Can barely afford child support. Can't find a decent job to save his life ..."

"I'm sorry to hear that," I said. "Is he, is he ... currently working?"

"Still sending me money here and there, so yeah, I guess so."

"That's good," I said. "It sounds like he's trying, Debbie."

The tension in Debbie's shoulders loosened, and she released her grip on the grocery cart handle. She stared off into space for a minute, contemplating. After a brief pause, she seemed to snap to. She narrowed her eyes at me once again—angry, bitter, accusatory.

"You know, a man with his talent shouldn't be slinging shit for crap wages," she said.

"I agree."

"He was co-owner of a construction company, for Christ's sake. Now look at him."

She adjusted her purse on her shoulder, gripped the cart handle and started to maneuver around me.

"Goodbye, Lil," she said with a huff.

"Debbie, wait!" I said, and she paused. "I think I can help you. I mean, I can help Sam. Which in turn will help you, and the girls."

"A little late for that, ain't it, Lil? I mean, isn't this all your fault?"

I shrank back. That was only half-true, but it didn't make it sting any less. Clearly, Debbie wasn't ready to let it go. But perhaps by seeing me for the first time in two years, and finally confronting me about it, would allow her to move on. If that's what it took, I was more than willing to offer myself as the emotional punching bag.

"Do you ... do you want to get together sometime and talk about it?" I asked.

"No, I don't."

"Mommy, I'm hungry," Carly whimpered from inside the cart.

"I know, baby," Debbie said, still looking at me. "We're leaving now."

Just then Becca emerged from around the corner, holding two welfare-approved loaves of bread. .

"C'mon, baby," Debbie said to Becca, who put the bread in the cart.

Becca looked at me, then took her place beside her mom.

"Shame about Kevin," Debbie mumbled, adjusting her purse on her shoulder again. "He was a good guy." Then, with a glare in her eye she said, "Guess we both know now what it's like to lose a husband."

Becca turned to look at me one last time, sadly, silently, before the three of them disappeared around the corner.

CHAPTER THREE

THE PROPERTY LOOKED like I felt: really fucking messy.

Maybe that's why I took to the house immediately. We were both falling apart. I could feel her pain.

Sagging front porch, splintered spindles, peeling paint. Broken sash windows covered in ivy. Missing slate roof tiles.

And on the inside: loose plank flooring. Dangerously spliced knob and tube wiring. Small "water closet" bathrooms with outdated plumbing and cracked ceramic.

But, as they say, the house had good bones.

Kevin and I each had our job descriptions, specific roles we filled in the renovation company we owned. He was the salesman and lead foreman; I did the marketing and business development. He was front and center; I was behind the scenes. We were both equally involved in client communication: answering calls and emails, booking appointments, and generally staying in touch with clients.

It was a decision we made early on, and it worked. We both had our own irreplaceable strengths. He didn't know how to build a website from scratch, like I did, and I didn't know how to install an HVAC system from scratch. I got us the leads, and he made them into customers. I kept them as clients for repeat business, and he kept them in awe with his reputable, quality work.

Kevin was the perfectionist, the person willing to put in the extra time and work to ensure everything was just so. I was the one willing to let little details go, so long as the quality wasn't affected. I mean, if the homeowner didn't care that our supplier ran out of ¾" crushed gravel for underneath their deck and we had to switch to 1" crushed gravel, then why should Kevin care? But he did.

Sometimes he'd give me guff for it, harp on me about my willingness to accept anything less than perfection. I'd let it go most of the time, laugh it off, because I understood where that came from.

Kevin was never supposed to go into construction. As an only child, there was an expectation that he would take over his parents' mortuary business when they retired. They saw him working for my father as a way for Kevin to pay for college, something he'd give up once he had a degree.

But their son had other plans. He wanted nothing of the funeral industry. He didn't go to college, and continued swinging a hammer for my dad well into his mid-twenties. Construction, it turned out, had been his true passion.

For years, resentment brewed between father and son. Kevin's father took it personally, because, well, what son wouldn't want to follow in his father's footsteps?

This caused Kevin to continually try proving to both of them that he'd made the right decision. That he'd be a success in his chosen field, perhaps even more successful than had he become a funeral director. So he worked harder and longer, climbed his way up, and by the time he was twenty-four, he was the company's youngest ever lead foreman.

Marrying me two years later sealed the deal for Kevin, because when I left my father's company to start my own, Kevin decided to come with me. He proposed that we'd start, own and run the company together. That was a win-win, of course, but I surmised it was also yet another middle finger he could give to his parents, something else he could rub in their face. For once, LB Renovations gave him ownership of something, a thing that was his, that he'd created. Not something that had been handed to him. And it gave him a sense of control he'd lacked his entire young-adult life.

I knocked on the door and rang the doorbell, unsure if Eric was already there. Mine was the only car in the driveway. I tried the door—unlocked.

"Hello?" I called out, as I entered into the front hallway. I stood there a moment to get my bearings. The kitchen was to my right. There was a parlor to my left, and a long, wide wooden staircase just in front of me. The entire first floor looked unfurnished: no carpets on the herringbone parquet wood flooring, inoperable chandeliers in the entryway and dining room, no lamps or any form of lighting at all, in fact. And not even a single utensil in any of the kitchen drawers.

I climbed the stairs. The second floor was similarly empty. Three bedrooms, two bathrooms and not a single trace of life. Not even mouse droppings. There was, however, dust on the windowsills and a layer of grime on the floors, but nothing more. The third floor had two more bedrooms and one more bathroom, all empty. Not a single article of clothing, not a lonely toothbrush. Nothing.

Absolutely ... nothing.

I inspected the basement and noticed two large puddles of standing water, for which foundation cracks seemed to be the culprit. There was a sump pump, which I assumed took care of whatever flooding had occurred. A dehumidifier purred away in the corner, doing its best to dry out the moist air.

I made my way back into the kitchen to take some notes and review my measurements. I placed my tool bag and my notebook on the counter and gathered my thoughts.

Two people immediately came to mind:

My dad. He would've loved this house. Old home renovation was his passion. He would've known exactly what to do about fixing up this house, where to start, which materials to use and how to bring it back to life.

And Sam: he used to love to talk to my dad about old homes. They even dreamed of one day finding a Queen Anne just like this one and fixing it up together. Had my dad been alive, this could've been the house they chose. If I took this project on, I knew Sam would be the perfect candidate to help me breathe life into her again. But I still wasn't sure I could bring myself to reach out, after all that'd happened.

I finished up my notes, double checked my measurements, and decided I had everything I needed. As I turned to leave, I collided with a man I hadn't heard arrive, who seemed to appear within steps of where I stood. My notebook and tape measure clattered to the floor. I gasped as I caught a glimpse of him, apologized, and took a step back to collect myself.

"Kevin?" I whispered.

His hair was styled differently and his eyes were a different shade of blue, but Jesus Christ he looked just like Kevin. Maybe ten pounds lighter and a year or two younger, but the same height, the same build, the same almost everything else.

He bent over to retrieve my dropped items, then handed them back to me. My hand trembled as I took them.

"Hello," he said. "Didn't mean to startle you. You must be Lilian."

He didn't sound anything like Kevin. Their voices were completely different, which was somewhat of a relief. He reached his hand out for me to shake but I hadn't composed myself enough to reciprocate, nor had I convinced myself that I wasn't seeing a ghost. I just stood there, and he lowered his hand.

I finally snapped to, and put my notebook and tape measure on the counter with the rest of my things.

"Sorry about that," I said. "Who are you?"

"Eric Becker. Emma's nephew. I was supposed to meet you here today."

"Right. Sorry," I said,

"Nothing to apologize for."

We stood there for a few minutes, awkwardly staring at each other. Finally, I offered my belated handshake.

He held my hand and my gaze a few seconds longer than the situation called for. He released my hand, smiled softly and, with a tilt of his head, asked, "Who's Kevin?"

"Oh, he's my ... husband. Kevin O'Shea. He actually ... passed away recently."

As Eric and I stood staring at each other, my brain tried to make sense of why this guy was a spitting image of my dead husband. Coincidence? Perhaps the Beckers and the O'Sheas were related somehow? Or did I miss Kevin so much that I was somehow projecting his face onto that of a complete stranger?

"I'm very sorry for your loss," Eric said, gently squeezing my shoulder.

His touch was comforting, and made me lose focus for a moment. What did I want to talk to him about specifically, in addition to the whole house in general?

Oh, yes. The basement.

"Thank you," I said. "So, the house. Let's start with the basement. There was a flood recently?"

"Two weeks ago. The hot water heater burst."

"Is that why the main water line is shut off?"

"The main has been shut off for awhile, luckily. Otherwise, I would've had an even bigger mess in the basement."

"So, no one currently lives here," I said, more to myself than to Eric. Which would explain why the house was empty, and appeared to have been for some time. Emma hadn't told me that on the phone, and I hadn't thought to ask.

"I haven't lived here in many, many years," Eric said, looking off into the distance behind me, as if in a trance. After a few seconds, he refocused on me. "I moved Aunt Em out about four months ago. I look after the house now, and I stay over sometimes."

"You did good to shut the water off at the main and not just at the toilets and sinks," I said. "Plumbing is usually a vacant home's weak spot. And I'd recommend an inspector do a walkthrough, just to see what you're dealing with."

"I had a building inspector out after the basement flood," Eric said.

"Do you have a copy of his report on you? I'd like to see it before agreeing to take on the project."

"I don't." He took a step closer, looked me deep in the eyes, and lowered his voice to a whisper. "Listen, Lilian. We don't have much time. I want you—Aunt Em and I really want you—to restore this house."

A chill went through me. "Why the urgency? If you don't mind me asking."

Eric took a step back and suddenly looked pensive. "Aunt Em is dying. Stage four lung cancer."

"Oh. I'm ... I'm so sorry. I didn't know. Emma didn't mention that."

Eric nodded as if he wasn't surprised and kept going. "She started treatment two months ago, but it really is pointless. Doctors say all it is doing is prolonging her life."

"Then why do it?" I said impulsively, as an image of my mother flashed into my brain. "Why willingly put yourself through all that pain?" There was a moment of silence as my words hung in the air and Eric eyed me curiously. I was surprised by my sudden outburst and felt, in turn, embarrassed and ashamed. "I'm sorry, Eric. That's none of my business."

"It's alright," Eric said, smiling warmly. "It's a valid question. Aunt Em doesn't want to die in some sterile, unfamiliar environment like a nursing home or a hospital, surrounded by strangers. She wants to die in this house. This is where she belongs. That is her dying wish, and I want to make that happen. We need your help." Eric stepped forward again. "Please, Lilian."

For Christ's sake. Why did it have to be cancer? It could've been any other disease, one I was less familiar with, one I had less intimate knowledge of. How could I possibly say no now? How could I deny the wish of an old woman dying of cancer?

Fuck.

"I'm going to need the building inspector's report," I said, sighing.

Eric's lips curled up into a grin—even that reminded me of Kevin.

"But listen, Eric. This project is going to take months. I don't know if we have that kind of time."

"We have faith in you, Lilian. You'll get the job done in time."

"Just out of curiosity," I said, as he walked me to the front door. "And this is none of my business, and you don't have to tell me but ... what's the plan for afterwards? Once she passes?"

"Aunt Em wants to keep the house in the family. But there's really no one to will it to, other than me. And I don't want it. I want to sell it."

Eric opened the door and allowed me to pass in front of him. My left shoulder brushed against his chest as I walked out onto the porch and another chill went through me, a pulse that tingled my scalp and my extremities.

"Thank you so much, Lilian," Eric said. "Aunt Em and I are so happy you're willing to help."

I nodded. "I'd like to bring my foreman by, give him a walk-through before we start."

"Of course," Eric said, taking a step towards me, closing the gap between us.

I felt flushed. "We'll start soon after that."

Eric took another step. I was doing my damnedest not to step toward him. Then he reached into his front pocket and held up a key.

"What's this?" I asked.

He motioned to the front door. "Come and go as you please." I took the key from him and put it in my own front pocket. As I turned to go, Eric smirked and said, "One last thing, Lilian."

"Yes?"

He leaned in. "I'm going to need your phone number."

"Oh, right," I said, still in a daze. I pulled out my cell phone, he pulled out his and we exchanged numbers.

As I was turning around in the driveway, with Eric waving at me from the porch, I allowed myself a proper exhale. It was a loud and heavy sigh that said, *What the hell did you just sign up for?*

CHAPTER FOUR

I DIALED THE NUMBER and squeezed my eyes shut as the phone rang, wondering what the hell I was doing. I thought about hanging up, but realized that he'd know who was calling anyway. Hanging up, too, I realized, would make me feel like an even bigger copout than I already did for not giving us closure two years ago.

His voice was calm, but confused. "Lil? Is that you?"

"Sam. Hey."

"I, um, I ... how you doing?"

I'm not big on small talk. I prefer to get right to the heart of the matter. It's one of the things Kevin loved about me, and something Sam got used to. So to spare each of us the discomfort, I decided to push right past the bullshit.

"Did you hear about Kevin?"

"Yeah, Lil. Hell of a thing. I'm so sorry. I meant to call but ... you know ..."

"I know you did, Sam."

"And the service ... I wanted to. You know what he meant to me. And I wanted to be there ... for you ... and him ..."

"It's okay."

"People are talking, Lil. They're worried about you. You, uh, you doing okay?"

"I'm getting by. I got some sympathy cards. From the old crew. You know. Murph and his wife. Stew. Big Al. The usuals."

"The usuals, yeah. I bump into them sometimes at Donovan's. We buy each other a round, shoot the shit, then don't see each other for another six months."

23

"How they all doing? Still a bunch of pricks?"

Sam laughed, and I could tell, by the way he sighed at the end, that he was two or three deep into a six pack. He liked to drink, but it had never been a problem. More like an intermittent habit. It wasn't something that had been longstanding, or inherited. None of us thought he'd become a true alcoholic. Until he did.

"Yeah, Lil. Still a bunch of pricks. But you know, they're all doing fine for themselves."

My dad had been threatening to retire for years, and he knew his brother would need a new business partner. My uncle was younger by six years, and would want to keep going. Dad had been grooming both Sam and Kevin, best friends since high school, for one—or both—of them to take over the business. My father, in fact, had hired them out of high school and taught them everything he knew. That's how the three of us met. Sam and Kevin were eighteen-year-old apprentices, and I was a sixteen-year-old office assistant. And since I was underage and the boss's daughter, I was off limits.

It took me and Kevin two years to break one of the company's policies of not "shitting where you eat." We dated off and on until I graduated college, and we became official when I came home with a fancy marketing degree with which to help my dad and uncle grow the business. By then both Kevin and Sam were supervising foremen, in charge of a ragtag team of carpenters and plumbers and electricians, including Tim "Murph" Murphy, Stewart "Stew" Watson, and Donald "Big Al" Albertson.

Neither Sam nor Kevin were family, but to my dad, they were the sons he never had. And then, soon enough, Kevin *was* family, and he left my dad to help me start LB Renovations, leaving Sam as the one who would eventually take over as my uncle's new business partner when my dad retired.

Given the circumstances, he did a hell of a job for as long as he could.

On Sam's end, I heard the cheer of a crowd and some rustling in the background.

"Did I catch you at a bad time?" I asked.

"Nah. Just having a few, watching the game."

"Good. Listen. There's something else."

He was quiet a moment, and I didn't know if it was because he was waiting for me to continue or he was distracted by the game.

Then, in a soft, faraway voice, he said, "I can't believe he's gone."

"What?"

"Kevin. He's gone. I mean ... it's been a long time since ... you know. But still. I miss him."

"Me too."

"What the fuck happened, Lil?"

"It was an accident."

"I know. Read that in the paper. And I heard a few things from people who went to the service. But ... shit like that doesn't happen to people like Kevin."

"It happens more than you think."

Sam exhaled. "Lil, you know the dangers we all faced every day on job sites. Broken bones, deep cuts, and mangled limbs. We dealt with the possibility of that shit every day for twenty years yet none of us ever got a scratch. And then he goes and falls off a ladder in his own goddamn driveway?"

He was louder now, as if competing with the TV. I wondered if time hadn't been kind to Sam in the two years since I'd seen him. Maybe guilt and shame had taken a bigger toll on him. Maybe his drinking had become a problem again.

"I know, Sam," I said. "I don't know what to tell you. It was an accident. I can't believe it either, but there's nothing more to tell."

"I know, Lil. Sorry." I heard him take another swig of beer. "There was something else you wanted?"

"Yeah, Sam. I found you a Queen Anne."

"What?"

"I don't know what you're up to these days, if you're working or what not, but ..."

"I'm doing side jobs here and there. Got a few interviews lined up."

"Good for you, Sam. I don't want to interfere with whatever work you've got for yourself, but do you at least want to take a look at her?"

"Where is she?"

"Hilldale Avenue, off Route 7."

"You mean the Becker place? Large property with a lake?"

"That's the one. You're familiar?"

"Yeah, your dad and I drove by it once or twice, daydreaming about it."

"Oh," I said, as Sam took another long swig of beer. "I don't think I ever knew that..."

Sam seemed to ignore my confusion. "So, you went and snagged yourself the Becker place. Well I'll be goddamned!"

"Yeah, so what do you say, Sam? She's a bit rough and pretty banged up but ..."

"Eh, you know I got a soft spot for broken things."

"I'll have an inspection report soon that'll tell me how broken she is. But if anyone can fix her up, it's you."

"Your dad and I never got the chance ..."

"I know. It was both of your dreams. I'm sorry."

"Not your fault, Lil. Even though you think it is. It's not."

"Yeah, Sam. I know."

We were both quiet a moment, probably reliving some private thoughts.

"You sure about this?" Sam finally said. "It's a big project. You think you're ready? So soon after, you know ..."

"I don't know, Sam. I think so. I know I could use your help. At the very least, I could use a second opinion."

"Okay, Lil. Tell me when and I'll be there."

I hung up, then grabbed some Advil for the headache that was starting to blur my vision. I realized that I didn't want the Queen Anne project for myself.

I wanted it for Sam.

CHAPTER FIVE

I WAS TWENTY-FOUR AND Kevin was twenty-six when we got engaged. I knew something was up the minute he told me one Saturday night he'd made reservations for the two of us at the more upscale Don's Steakhouse Grille. I'm not a fancy restaurant kind of girl. Kevin knew that, so the choice was suspect. Expensive steak places weren't his family's thing, either.

Nonetheless, there he was: at my door, wearing a charcoal-colored Brooks Brothers wool suit.

"Nice," I said. He kissed me hello,

"Even nicer," he countered, scanning me head to toe and smiling.

"Didn't think I owned a dress, did you?" I said, winking.

He led me to the car and held the door open for me.

It was all unnecessary, of course—the clothes, the restaurant, the bottle of fancy wine Kevin ordered for us. I knew the proposal was coming the minute he told me about the reservation, and I would've said yes no matter how he proposed. I didn't need the suit or the wine or the steakhouse. He could've taken me to Donovan's and popped the question over a shot of tequila at the bar for all I cared.

But he'd gone the extra mile, so all I could hope for was that he wouldn't wait all night to ask me the question to which I'd been prepared to say yes. So when he pulled the black box out of his suit jacket pocket after dinner, before dessert, I said "Yes!" before he even had a chance to put it on the table.

He smiled. "I didn't need to do any of this, did I?"

"Nope."

"Knew it was coming?"

"Yep."

Kevin sighed. "I should've known. And Don's? What was I thinking?"

I smiled and said nothing.

"Want to get out of here?" he said.

"Yes, please."

Kevin put the black box back into his pocket and paid the bill. We drove to Donovan's for dessert: tequila shots at the bar, in our fancy clothes. Kevin finally put the ring on my finger and we slowly got drunk, the rest of the patrons helping us celebrate our engagement with rounds of free shots and shared toasts.

Presently, I found myself standing before our closet, holding that Brooks Brothers suit in my hand. The closet was nearly empty of his clothes. I looked down and saw two piles on the floor, on either side of me. Had I fallen asleep standing up, and dreamed about that night?

Admittedly I wasn't getting much sleep, so I guess it was possible. But it felt more like a daydream, because while the images of me and Kevin were clear as a lucid dream, I was aware of my current self, as if I stood at a safe distance, watching the whole thing unfold.

I didn't have time to think about my waking dream or daydream or whatever the hell it was because the doorbell was ringing. I looked at my watch and realized that I also didn't know how much time had passed since I'd started sorting Kevin's clothes, but that didn't matter either, because my financial accountant was here for our scheduled 2 p.m. meeting.

I opened the door. "Hi, Jake, I—"

It wasn't Jake the accountant. It was my next-door neighbor, Stella.

"Lil, honey," she said, smiling warmly, head tilted to one side.

I looked at her, at the image of perfection that was Stella
Matthews, at the glow that seemed to always surround her, and,
finally, at the casserole she was presenting to me.

"Oh, hey Stella," I stumbled, embarrassed. "I'm sorry. I wasn't
expecting..."

"No, I'm sorry. I know you must be busy. Just wanted to say hi
and give you this." She held up the casserole dish.

"Thank you, that's very kind," I said, taking the dish from her.

"Chicken tetrazzini. One of my favorite comfort foods."

Kevin and I had always loved being invited over to the Matthews'
for dinner. Stella may be eccentric by normal standards, and the way
she made a living could be classified as ... *different* ... but I didn't care.
I liked Stella, and the woman could cook like nobody's business. Her
lasagna was out of this world—and, some would say, so was Stella
herself.

She'd brought a beef and cheddar casserole to Kevin's funeral,
and it was such a huge hit several people asked for the recipe. Ever
since, every few days Stella had shown up on my doorstep with a new
comfort food casserole.

"I finished off the breakfast casserole you gave me a few days ago,"
I said. "I'll get the dish back to you soon."

As I spoke, Stella's gaze casually left mine and focused over my
left shoulder towards the kitchen. Her smile slowly melted, and her
eyes fluttered closed for a few seconds. She swayed gently from side
to side, as if moved by some invisible force. I sensed she must be
"having a moment," doing whatever it was that Stella does. So I
stayed silent, giving her the time she needed to finish whatever it was
she was doing.

I'd known Stella for ten years, but never knew how she did what
she did. For the longest time I didn't understand the things that she
saw, couldn't comprehend the things she felt. I had friends who were

clients of hers, but their stories and experiences weren't something we talked about as part of our everyday conversations.

So I didn't know, I didn't understand—not then, anyway.

After about a minute, her eyes opened and refocused on me. She smiled warily.

"I hope that's okay," I said slowly, wondering if I needed to give her time to recover. "That I get the dish back to you later?"

"That's fine, honey," she said, sounding exhausted. She paused a moment, cleared her throat, then straightened her back and smiled wide. "Okay, I should go." The moment was over, she'd shaken it off. The regular Stella was back.

"Oh, well, do you want to come in for a few minutes?"

"No, but thank you." She looked over my shoulder again and then back at me. "I shouldn't leave those precious little lambs of mine alone for another minute."

"Are you sure? My financial accountant is due any minute, but—"

"I'm sure," she said, placing her hands on my upper arms and giving them a gentle squeeze. "Enjoy the casserole."

Just then Jake pulled into the driveway and Stella gave both my arms a final tender caress.

"Listen, Lil," she said, looking intently at me. "Call me if you need anything. Anything ..."

"Okay, Stella," I said, a little confused—and somewhat frightened—by her insistence to help. "I will, thanks."

She walked down the steps of the front stoop, greeting Jake as she walked past his car towards her house.

I ushered Jake inside and motioned for him to sit at the dining room table.

"Coffee? Tea? Chicken tetrazzini?" I offered, lifting the dish briefly before retreating to the kitchen to put the casserole in the fridge.

Jake chuckled. "Just some water, Lilian. Thanks."

I'd known Jake Campbell just as long as I'd known Kevin and Sam, and even after almost thirty years of friendship and twenty years as our financial accountant, he still insisted on calling me Lilian. He did little to break the stigma of accountants being stuffy, boring, and professional sticks in the mud. He ate, breathed, and dreamt numbers. But once you got to know him, he was a hell of a nice guy. Plus, he always did right by Kevin and me.

"You know Stella Matthews, right?" I said, returning to the dining room with a glass of water for Jake and a cup of coffee for me. "My next-door neighbor?"

"Sure, sure," Jake said. He opened his briefcase and pulled out some manilla folders. "Barb's a client of hers."

"Oh, I didn't know your wife was into... that kind of thing. No offense."

"It's not my cup of tea," Jake said, shrugging, "But Barb likes her, so that's good enough for me."

"Happy wife, happy life, right?" I said playfully, not knowing in that moment how right I was.

Jake smiled and nodded and put three Excel spreadsheets in front of me. He wasn't one to waste time getting down to business. He respected brass tacks as much as I did.

"Got a couple of things for you here." He pointed to the first piece of paper with his pen. "First is the balance sheet for Q1. You know, your assets and liabilities ..."

I laughed. "I know what a balance sheet is, Jake."

"Right," Jake said, pointing to the next two documents. "And here's your Q1 income statement and cash flow statement."

He nodded and took a few sips of water as I reviewed the documents.

We were silent a moment as he sipped his water and I drank my coffee and reviewed the documents. Finally he said, "Everything alright, Lilian?"

"Sure, Jake. Why?"

I looked up at him and he was pointing at me with his pen.

"You're rubbing your temple pretty hard. It's all red."

I hadn't noticed. It must've become a subconscious thing I started doing when I felt the headaches coming on, because when I stopped rubbing I could feel the dull ache on the right side of my head.

"Oh, yeah. I, uh, I've started getting these headaches."

"Well, you're under a lot of stress ..."

"Stress. What's that?" I said, and Jake smiled. A small one, but a smile nonetheless.

"So, any questions? Anything you need clarification on?"

"No, Jake. Not really."

I must've started rubbing my temple again, because Jake was staring at a spot just above my right ear. He lowered his eyes and looked at me, and I mean *really* looked at me, dead in the eye, like he was trying to figure out where I was emotionally, so he could figure out how to proceed professionally.

Preferring shop talk, Jake didn't like to get overly personal. He didn't discuss his own private matters, but he'd listen if you talked about yours, because he knew your personal life could affect your financial life. And since your financial business was his business, he knew he had to help you with your uncomfortable life shit, as well. So if you were struggling with death or divorce, he wanted to know about it, but stopped short of giving you personal advice. He gave you the professional, financial advice you needed to help you sort out the personal bits yourself.

"This can't be easy for you, Lilian," he said.

I shook my head and drained the rest of my coffee.

"But your business is doing fine financially," he continued. "That's the good news."

"Is there bad news?"

I pointed at his empty glass to see if he wanted more water, and he shook his head.

"From my perspective as your accountant, no. I just meant that I'm sure you're dealing with a lot, and you might be unsure what direction you want for your business."

"You mean, if I can keep running the business without Kevin?"

"You can run the business without Kevin. I know you, Lilian. You have it in you. But do you want to?"

"I don't know, Jake. I really just don't know."

He folded his hands on the table and looked at me. That was Jake's way of saying he was going to shut up for a bit so that I could get some personal shit off my chest. Was there such a thing as financial psychologists? If so, I think Jake had missed his true calling.

"I have one more job on the books," I said. "It'll take a couple months. I figure that would give me time to figure out what I want, while bringing some money into the business in the meantime."

"That's great, Lilian. That tells me you're open to options. Keep going solo, partner up, sell the business outright ..."

"Sure."

"I can help you with all those options. Whatever you decide."

"I know, Jake. And I'd be grateful."

"Then there's just one more thing we need to discuss." He pulled a large manilla envelope out of his briefcase and placed it on the table.

"What's this?" I asked.

"Another option."

He opened the envelope, pulled out two stapled packets of paper and placed the thinner packet before me, keeping the other, thicker packet closest to him. I scanned the front page quickly and looked up at Jake, confused and angry and surprised.

"A life insurance policy?" I said.

"Judging by your reaction, I'm guessing you knew nothing about this?"

"No! Kevin never told me."

"He took it out for himself three months ago."

"How much is it for?"

"Five hundred thousand."

"Half a million dollars? Jesus, Jake!"

"Kevin and I met with the same insurance agent who set up your whole life policies twenty years ago when you started your business. He helps a lot of my small-business owner clients."

"And you didn't question why Kevin wanted a second life insurance policy?"

"I assumed he had his reasons. And I assumed you knew, or that he'd tell you."

I started rubbing my temple again, remaining silent as Jake took the opportunity to do what he did best: guiding a client through their emotional private baggage so they can get to a happy financial ending.

"I'm sorry, Lilian. I honestly thought you knew. And of course, not in a million years did I think you'd be using it so soon. But look, put aside for a moment the reason why Kevin did this, and look at the bigger picture. You have even more options than you originally thought. You're a wealthy woman, Lilian."

"The bigger picture, Jake, is that Kevin intentionally kept this from me, and I'll probably never know why."

Jake knew I was right, and there was no amount of money that could fix that. So he offered a suggestion instead.

"You're still working with your estate attorney, figuring out Kevin's will?"

"Yes. None of the estate needs to go to probate. The assets will transfer directly to me. It's all just paperwork at this point."

"That's great. Because as you probably know, life insurance policies aren't subject to probate either. They get transferred directly to the beneficiary for payout."

"I think I knew that. Maybe I didn't remember. I don't know." I was rubbing my temple harder now, the dull ache quickly becoming a throb.

"What's the other packet?" I said, motioning to it.

"Nothing you need to worry about right now." He took it and the thinner packet in front of me and slid them both back inside the envelope. Then he put the envelope into his briefcase. "You've got enough on your plate. Let me handle this. I'll get you a copy of it at some point. In the meantime, I'll start the paperwork process. You don't even need to think or worry about it."

"Thanks, Jake. I appreciate it."

He nodded a silent *You're welcome*, stood to go, and I walked him to the door.

"Oh, wait," I said. "I know you'll get me a copy at some point, but can you email a copy of the policy to Helen? You know my estate attorney, Helen, right?"

"I know Helen."

"I don't know if she has it already, if Kevin gave it to her. But just to be safe. She's going to want it for her records, and I want her to have it in time for our meeting."

Jake paused, then laughed. "I suppose your estate attorney is going to want to know about an extra million bucks, isn't she?"

"A million?" I said, confused. I knew my head was pounding and I was starting to not think clearly, but I'm pretty sure Jake had just told me the policy was for half a million. "I thought you said ..." I looked at him quizzically, and the smile melted from his face.

"Did I say a million? I meant half a million. Sorry, Lilian. I might've been confusing you with another client."

"Oh. OK."

"When's the meeting?" he asked.

"In two days."

"Sure, Lilian. I can get Helen a copy. No problem."

I had one final request for Jake, a question, really, and as the question formulated in my brain, so too did Kevin's four-word plea, whispered to me as he took his last breaths.

"Hey, do you think, um ..."

Jake suddenly looked uneasy. His shoulders tensed up. "What is it?"

"I don't know ... I can't help but have this feeling ... that Kevin knew he was going to die."

Jake let out a long exhale. "OK..."

"What other reason would he have for a second life insurance policy? Did he ever say anything in your support group? Talk about death or dying or ...?"

Jake looked at me as if I should know better than to ask that question.

"I know, Jake," I said. "Everything the guys talk about is confidential."

"Right."

"But Kevin's gone. You're no longer betraying his confidence. If there's something I need to know ..."

"If Kevin thought he was going to die, or if he thought his life was in danger, he never said anything to any of us. Does that help?"

"Yes, but ... then why the second life insurance policy?"

"Listen, Lilian. I think you need to focus on *you* right now. What's best for your personal, professional, and financial future."

Easy for him to say, I thought. His spouse wasn't hiding secrets. His wife didn't spurt out a cryptic message, then die right in front of him before she had a chance to explain. With such things left unresolved, it was kind of hard to focus on the future.

Jake said he'd be in touch, and we waved as he got into his car and drove away. I closed the door and walked into the living room, exhausted. As I collapsed on the couch and closed my eyes, I made a mental note to contact Helen, just as soon as I got rid of this goddamn headache.

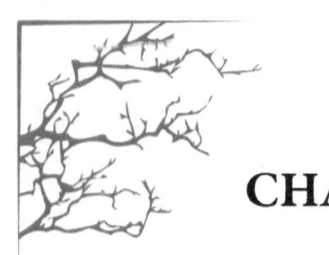

CHAPTER SIX

I STOOD ON THE FRONT porch of The Property, waiting for Sam. I had a mental image in my head of what he looked like then, and I compared it to what I thought he looked like now. Two years really isn't a long time, but it can look and feel like twenty when you've been through as much shit as Sam had been through. So I imagined that that short amount of time had taken its toll.

Back then, after the shit had hit the fan, I had been concerned about the toll on our marriage, which is why I had suggested couple's therapy to Kevin. He'd refused, but he did join a men's support group. He didn't want to. I think part of him thought it was beneath him, sitting around with a bunch of other men discussing their feelings. His biggest objection, though, was being vulnerable. He rarely let anyone see his soft side, even me. Kevin was always stoic and steady, in control of his emotions. For the most part, I appreciated that. It meant I could be the one to lose control. It meant we hardly ever fought. But it also meant I didn't always know when he was sad or upset or angry or jealous. It meant that we couldn't have deep, emotional conversations in which we laid bare all our feelings.

It was fear, I suppose, that prevented him from being vulnerable. Fear of rejection, fear of judgement, fear of appearing weak. So that side of him remained hidden, tucked away, unreachable.

That bothered me at first, when we started dating. Not being able to "go there" with the man I grew to love. But as the years went by and we got married and started the business together, it was something I just got used to. I couldn't change that about Kevin, I could only love him in spite of it. And besides, we were happy and healthy and successful, so who was I to push for more?

Jake had been having problems of his own (I never knew what they were) when he found out about me and Kevin. He found this local support group for men online, and started going. I never knew anything about the group—their official name, other members, what they talked about. I only knew they met once a month, at night, at our local YMCA. Jake went a few times, then encouraged Kevin to go.

One meeting, Jake said to Kevin. If he didn't like it, he didn't have to go again. So Kevin went and, much to my and Jake's surprise, kept going every month.

It bothered me at first that he suddenly found it so easy to pour his heart out to relative strangers (if that was indeed what he was doing) after having dismissed my suggestion of couple's therapy. Wouldn't it be easier, I thought, and less stressful to talk to two people (your wife and a licensed professional) than a room full of Joe Blows? But I figured, hey, at least he was talking to someone, and, in the succeeding months, it actually did seem to help. I was seeing a therapist, and our marriage seemed to be getting back on track.

I was still talking to Sam at that point, and he got to calling Kevin's support group his Fight Club. "Kevin at his Fight Club?" he used to say. Or, "How's Kevin's Fight Club going?"

That is, in fact, the last memory I have of seeing Sam: two years before at Donovan's, when we sat at the bar, Sam draining the last sips of his Bud Light and asking about Kevin's Fight Club. I laughed, paid both of our tabs, excused myself to go to the ladies' room, then never came back.

I texted Sam later that night that we shouldn't talk or see each other for a while. I didn't know how long. He understood and I cried myself to sleep. It was hard, but it got easier day by day, and the next thing I knew, two years had passed.

I heard his truck now as I stood on the porch. Butterflies rose in my stomach as he drove his pickup slowly up the driveway and came to a stop. He slid out and made his way up the steps. And then there we were, face to face for the first time in two years.

Turns out, I had been wrong. Time, it seemed, had been very *good* to Sam.

Even through a couple layers of clothes, I could tell Sam had gotten into shape. Not that he was ever out of shape. He'd always been of average height and weight. Last I saw him, that night at Donovan's, he had that extra fifteen around his belly that most middle-aged men have, and his longer hair only accentuated the growing bald spot. He always wore jeans, flannels, and boots because, you know, he was a blue-collared construction worker who preferred comfort over fashion. Still, he wore his middle-age well, comfortable in his own skin. More than anything else, that's what made him sexy.

The Sam that stood before me had lost some fat and gained some muscle, cropped his hair close to the skull so the bald spot was undetectable, and seemed to stand taller and more confident. And he was wearing a casual button-down shirt tucked into khakis and sensible work shoes. It struck me just then that his outfit was something Kevin would've worn.

"Good to see you, Lil," he said, looking at me, then the ground, then out at the lake.

"Yeah, Sam. You too. You look good."

"Thanks. I'd gained a few pounds when Debbie left. Stress and all. Well, you remember ..."

"Of course, Sam. I was there. I remember."

"Right, sorry. It was a tough time for all of us back then, huh?" He paused, shook his head. "Back then? Listen to me. It's only been two years. I'm making it seem like all that shit happened forever ago. So anyway, I started boxing to take out my negative emotions, right? Next thing I know I'm a fitness freak. Go figure."

Sam truly was Kevin's polar opposite. Where Kevin had both feet planted firmly on the ground, with plans and goals that he stuck to with fervor, Sam often had his head in the clouds, and let life take him where it may. Kevin could be distant and aloof, coming across as cold. Sam was emotional and upfront with his feelings, and you always knew where you stood with him.

I adored that about Sam. And that adoration made Kevin nervous. I never knew, of course, that Kevin was bothered by my affection for Sam, because he was always so buttoned-up. It took a few drinks for me to find out.

A week before we got married, while sitting at the bar at Donovan's after a long day at work, Kevin said to me: "You know, Lil. I'm not just marrying you because I love you. I'm marrying you because Sam loves you, too."

And I laughed unintentionally, at the preposterousness of his comment, at his drunken insecurity, at his jealousy. And I laughed at the revelation of it, too: that Kevin O'Shea felt that way at all, and took so long to tell me.

I assured Kevin that, while Sam was adorable, he wasn't my type. Then I drove us both home, guided him to the bedroom, and continued assuring him of my love and fidelity.

Turns out, though, Kevin was right to worry.

Kevin felt the need to prove to his parents that, although he'd chosen a field they didn't initially agree with, he could—and would—be successful. This led to him not showing his vulnerable side, bottling up negative emotions, never letting anyone see when he was hurting or struggling. Because any ounce of weakness could be used against him, thrown in his face, held over his head.

In spite of this, Kevin was still practical and grounded in a way that made him seem dull and boring—but dull and boring was exactly what my twenty-something self needed. In an unstable time when I was still figuring out what I wanted, Kevin was exactly what I needed. I needed emotional and financial stability, and Kevin could give that to me.

So never mind the fact that, physically, I was more attracted to Sam, who could only give me what I wanted. He was flighty, but that made him creative and imaginative. He could change his mind at the drop of a hat, but that spontaneity could be fun, and led to some great adventures. He was emotional, but that allowed him to love you deeply from the inside out.

I could've had my pick between Kevin and Sam and, at the end of the day, Sam would've made one hell of a boyfriend. But I needed a husband, and, simply put, Kevin was the better choice.

"What?" Sam said, noticing my grin. "What's so funny? I see you laughing at me, Lil. What'd I say?"

My cell phone started ringing, interrupting my bittersweet nostalgia.

"Nothing, Sam. It's nothing," I pulled out my phone. The caller I.D. said *Unknown* and I thought it might be Emma, so I motioned for Sam to start without me. Sam started walking around the house, snapping pictures on his cell phone and making measurements as I stepped off the porch to take the call.

"Hello?" I said.

"Lilian? Is that you? It's Emma."

"Yes, hi Emma."

"I'm so glad you've decided to accept the job."

"You're welcome. What can I do for you?"

"Just calling to see when you can start."

"I'm at the house right now with my foreman Sam, and—"

"Oh, good!" she said, and I could hear the sudden, excited inhale which quickly became a loud coughing fit. Her breathing settled into a gentle wheeze. "You've started the job."

"No, Emma. We haven't officially started. My foreman and I are here to walk the site together. I haven't gotten the inspector's report from Eric yet, and we have design ideas to run past you. Then I'll need to work up an estimate ..."

"We don't have much time, Lilian."

"I know, Emma. Eric told me. I'm so sorry." I'd had my back to the house. I turned to see where Sam was, and saw him standing at the lake's edge, motionless, staring down into the water. The sight of him, how he appeared to be in a trance, reflected sunlight dancing across his face, gave me a full-body chill. Something about it—the image of someone standing at the lake's edge—seemed familiar. A sense of déjà vu crept up on me.

"Emma?" I said when I realized she hadn't responded. "I know it sounds like a lot, but everything I mentioned should only take a day or two, depending on how quickly we agree on design ideas."

"Listen to me, Lilian. Do whatever to the house you think is best. We don't need to discuss design ideas and I don't need an estimate because money is no object."

I let her comment sink in a moment.

"So ... so you're saying I can do whatever I want to the house?"

"That's exactly what I'm saying. Eric and I trust you implicitly."

"And I can bill you for whatever, because money is no object and you don't want an estimate in writing?"

"That's right. I just want you and—Sam, is it? I just want you and Sam to start."

Christ, she sounded exhausted. Exhausted and in a hurry—to start the project and, perhaps, to die.

"And Eric will agree to all that?"

"It's my house, Lilian."

I laughed at her tenacity, in spite of everything she was facing. "OK, Emma. We'll get started in a few days."

"Great," she said, coughing one last time. "I have to go now, Lilian. Thank you so much. Goodbye."

As the line went dead, I pointlessly mumbled goodbye and shoved the phone into my back pocket. I called out to Sam. He looked up from the lake, and I motioned for us to meet on the porch.

"That the old lady?" Sam asked.

"Yep, that was her. Emma."

"And?"

"It's a sad situation. What's so interesting about the lake?"

"Huh?"

"I saw you staring into the lake. Deep in thought or something?"

"I don't know," Sam said, looking confused. "My mind went completely blank. And my eyes were open but all I saw was black. Like I was awake and asleep at the same time. It was weird." He seemed to shake it off. "Eh, maybe I was just staring off into space..."

"You sure, Sam? Everything alright?"

"Yeah, Lil. I'm good." But he still looked confused and unsure of himself.

I nodded and then motioned to the house.

"OK. Well, ready to go inside?"

"Beat you to it." He pulled out his phone and started scrolling through the photos he'd taken.

"I didn't even see you go in," I said, more to myself than Sam. I'd only been on the phone five or ten minutes. There's no way he'd been able to walk the house and ponder lakeside in such a short amount of time.

Sam shrugged and kept scrolling.

"You saw the entire house?" I asked. "Basement, too?"

He stopped scrolling, looked up from his phone and gave me a funny look. "Yeah, Lil. Look." He motioned to his phone, as if I hadn't been paying attention the first time.

"I believe you. So, what'd you think?"

"She's a beaut. I have a lot of ideas. Hey, wanna discuss it over a couple of beers at Donovan's? You know, for nostalgia's sake? That could be fun, right?"

There was that spontaneity I both adored and feared.

I must've been making a face because Sam froze, his eyes wide. "Oh, shit, Lil. I'm sorry. Is that a bad idea?"

"No, Sam. It's fine. It's a good idea. But can we eat, too? I'm starving."

Goddammit, I didn't want this job. Something deep inside was telling me to walk away. Kevin would've said no without a second thought. His decision would've been based on practical purposes—too costly, too time consuming. But me? Mine was an emotional decision.

It was for Emma's sake, to give a sick old lady her last dying wish.

And it was for Sam's sake, to give him redemption and an opportunity he was denied—not to mention the money I'm sure he needed.

And for my sake, to appease my sense of altruism, and to clean my slate.

But for fuck's sake ... what the hell had I been thinking?

CHAPTER SEVEN

I PLACED THE FLOWER on the ground in front of the headstone. I'd chosen a single red rose, because that's my middle name, and because that's what was on the bar at Donovan's the night Kevin proposed: a single red rose, in a white plastic vase. The vase was between us when we first sat down at the bar, and was partially obscuring our view of each other.

"A rose for my Rose," Kevin had said, as he plucked the flower from the vase and offered it to me. Then he moved the vase to his other side, out of our way, so we could continue what we'd started back at the restaurant. Later that night, I went home with a ring and a rose, and the thought that a girl really could have it all.

Standing now at Kevin's grave, I cried at the memory: bittersweet tears for the happy girl with her rose and her ring, and angry tears for the naïve girl who thought her life could be perfect. I glanced to my right, at the open patch of green next to Kevin where I would one day rest. I decided not to linger. I'd had enough of death in the past two years, and didn't even want to fathom my own. Best move along.

I started walking across the grass to the narrow gravel road where my car was parked. Nearing the road, I saw a car to my right, slowly driving towards me. When it stopped, Helen Whitman, my estate attorney, climbed out of the car.

"Lilian," she said, taking off her sunglasses and approaching me. "I thought that was you."

Helen was in her mid-seventies but didn't look a day over sixty. She and my dad had been high school sweethearts. Dad had gone on to marry my mother, and Helen had moved on and married as well, but they stayed in touch.

I met her when my mom died of cancer, when she became our family's estate attorney. I got to know her pretty well over the subsequent years; unfortunately, it was because people in my family kept dying.

By the time my mom was diagnosed, it was already too late to save her. But she insisted on treatment, knowing it would make her ever sicker, just so she'd have more time with me and my father, however short that time may be. My father and I disagreed with her, but it wasn't our body and it wasn't our life, so it wasn't our decision to make. I won't go into any more details about any of that because if you know someone who battled and/or died from cancer you already know how ruinous the disease can be, on so many levels, for everyone involved, so there's nothing more I really need to add.

Just know that my mother and I had a good relationship, she got breast cancer when I was twenty-eight and had been married to Kevin for two years, and her death came quickly and mercifully six months after her diagnosis.

After mom passed, Helen became a sort of surrogate mother to me. Mostly I think that, being childless, she needed to mother something, or someone. But she was also single, and might've been looking to rekindle a spark with my dad. That didn't work out, my dad stayed single the rest of his life, and Helen went on to remarry a proctologist named Larry.

Helen and I stayed in touch, sent Christmas cards and whatnot, and I worked with her again when my dad died. That was two years ago. Heart attack. Also, quick and merciful. Dad worked ridiculously long hours, didn't take care of himself physically or mentally, and thought stress was a natural state of being. Like there was something wrong with him if he wasn't sleepless or anxious or irritable. He probably worked himself to death, but of course, because of what happened, I thought his death was my fault. Just like I thought Kevin's death was my fault.

So now here I was again. Another death, this time my husband's. This one was also quick and merciful, if not wholly expected. But unlike the others, I hadn't seen this one coming from a million miles away.

But I was beginning to think Kevin had.

Helen sighed, looking out toward Kevin's grave. "I know what it's like to bury a husband so young, how gut-wrenchingly awful it is."

"You mean your first husband, Henry?" I said, confused.

"Yes, he's buried over there," she said, pointing slightly behind her to her left. "Not very far from Kevin, actually."

"Henry died? I thought ... I thought you divorced him."

"He died of a brain aneurysm. It was long ago, and you were newly married and starting your business, so maybe you remember it as divorce."

"I'm sorry, Helen. I don't know why I thought that."

Helen looked at me with a look approximating pity, then suddenly seemed to remember something. "Oh, since we're here together, can I give you the packet of info we spoke about on the phone? The forms you need to sign? I have them in the car. Save you a trip ..."

I said yes, and Helen walked back to her car and rummaged around in the rear passenger seat, speaking as she did so.

"As you know we'll be able to avoid probate because your company was joint ownership and the detailed survivorship ensures that everything transfers directly to you, the co-owner, negating the need for probate."

"Right," I said.

She closed her car door and walked back over to me.

"The process itself is straightforward, but there is a lot of paperwork." She handed me a thick manilla envelope. "This is all the business-related paperwork for you to sign."

"What about the individually owed assets? Like the house and our cars?"

"They exist outside of the jointly owned business, so as executor of the will you'll be closing out accounts or transferring them to yourself, the main beneficiary. The titles to the house and any vehicles will need to be transferred. Health insurance will need to be cancelled. Final tax filings ..." She trailed off, then looked at my sympathetically. "It's a lot to deal with, Lilian. If you need any help ..."

"I'll be fine, thanks." I opened my driver side door and tossed the manilla envelope onto the passenger seat.

"OK." Helen furrowed her brow at me for the briefest of seconds. "Oh, and I know Kevin had some retirement accounts and a whole life insurance policy that—Lilian, honey? Are you alright?"

"Just a little lightheaded," I said. "I'll be fine."

Helen smiled. "I'm here for my monthly visit. Would you like to join me? I could use the company. And you look like you could you use a little more fresh air."

"OK, sure," I said reluctantly, and we started walking on the gravel road.

Helen knew just about everyone in Pennsgrove, or knew at least one person from every family that lived here. Par for the course, I guess, when you're one of the few estate attorneys in town and have been in the business for fifty years. So as we walked she pointed at various headstones along the way, or in the general direction in which a certain family was buried together, all while spouting some interesting factoid or another—even little bits of hearsay were within her reach. Safe to say, Helen Whitman could've doubled as the town gossip.

"Did you visit your parents while you were here?" Helen asked as we made a right from the gravel road and into the grass.

"Today was the first time I've visited since dad died."

"Two years ago, right?" Helen said, and I nodded. "You're just like him, you know."

I smiled and said nothing, and Helen felt the need to keep going.

"That work ethic, and wanting to help everyone. You, especially. Trying to help your uncle with the business after your dad died, and run your own company with Kevin at the same time. I don't know how you did it. And then add on top of that, what happened with Sam and—"

Helen suddenly froze, her eyes becoming wide and unblinking, the result of what she must have felt was a verbal faux pas.

"Lilian, honey, I'm sorry," she said. "I didn't mean to bring that up. I wasn't thinking ..."

"It's okay, Helen."

"No, it's not. It was terrible, what happened, and I'm sure you want to forget all about it and focus on rebuilding yourself now that Kevin is gone. It was careless of me."

"Honestly, it's fine. Actually, Sam and I saw each other last week for the first time since, well ... then."

"Really?"

We started walking again, through the grass and around headstones.

"We're going to be working on a project together," I said. "Renovating the Becker estate."

"The Becker estate! That's quite an honor, Lilian. No one has touched that house in years."

"Based on the interior and exterior conditions, I'd say decades."

"How did that come about, if you don't mind me asking? The Beckers are such ... mysterious people. And so private! I've done some work for them in the past. They never did take too kindly to outsiders."

I didn't want to burst Helen's bubble, because it seemed like she was itching for some juicy story about how I'd gained access to the Becker inner sanctum. And I didn't want to reveal the reasons for the renovations; if the Becker family was as private as Helen claimed, I didn't think Emma would appreciate me spreading the news of her failing health. Getting this project had been quite simple, so I decided to stick with the simple truth.

"Emma Becker called me and asked me to do the job," I said.

Helen paused at first, then seemed to accept that story. "Well, I'll have to tell some of the others at the Historical Society. They'll be tickled to know about this."

"You volunteer at the Historical Society?"

"Two days a week. As a favor to Frank. We go way back, as you know." Suddenly Helen got serious. "But listen, Lilian. Do you think this is a good idea?"

"Renovating the Becker estate?"

"No, honey. Working with Sam."

"Oh. Um ... I do, actually."

"I know you probably don't care because you seemed to have moved on but ... there are some people who still remember ... you know ..."

"You're right, Helen. I don't care."

There were several people in my social circle who, upon hearing what had happened two years ago, didn't bother trying to hear both sides of the story. Kevin, obviously, was one of them. So was my dad. And Helen, whose usual partiality was, in this case, affected by her unrequited love for my dad, naturally took his side.

The only ones who knew the truth were me and Sam. And once we gave up talking, trying to control the situation, convince people of that truth, well, that left everyone to their own devices. And you know what people do when left to their own devices? Whatever the fuck they want.

So as far as Helen was concerned, Sam was a monster who deserved everything he got. He deserved to have Debbie walk out on him. He deserved to lose his partnership with my uncle. He deserved to lose his reputation. Time, obviously, hadn't changed her opinion.

And time hadn't allowed some people—Debbie, Helen—to move on.

There are some people who still remember ... you know ... Helen's words rattled around in my brain for a moment.

I wasn't sure who Helen was referring to, exactly, because to me it seemed like most people had gone back to focusing on their own lives, instead of poking their noses into mine and Sam's and Kevin's. I'd bumped into several of my dad's workers, both current and ex-employees, and they were, for the most part, happy to see me. They wished me well, told me they missed seeing me around the shop, gave their condolences on Kevin's passing.

"I didn't mean to sound rude," I said. "But if people see me and Sam together, let them talk. We're working together on a project. End of story."

"Oh, Lilian. I know it's none of my business. I just don't want to see you get hurt again. But if Sam's involved ... well ..."

"I appreciate that, Helen. Really. But this could be good for us. Allow us to bury the hatchet. Let him regain some confidence and redeem himself. And who knows, this project could be just what I need."

Helen let out a long breath of air. "Well, I wish you luck, honey."

We'd reached Henry's grave. It didn't feel right to watch Helen pay her respects; it felt too intimate a moment for me to be involved in. Plus, I had a minor issue that I felt would become a major issue if I didn't deal with it soon. So I started to make my leave, say my goodbyes, when Helen said, "Still lightheaded, Lilian?"

"I'm good, thanks."

"You sure? You've been rubbing your temples almost the whole time we've been walking. And your face is flushed."

"Just a little headache."

The first throb had hit when Helen mentioned Sam. From there it'd become a dull ache. But I knew that was just the beginning. More pain was coming.

"Listen, Helen. I might need help with one other thing. Did you know Kevin had a second life insurance policy?"

"I knew about the whole life insurance policy. But a second life insurance policy? No."

"I asked my financial accountant Jake Campbell to email you a copy, in case you didn't know about it or have it."

She laughed, more out of annoyance than humor. "Well, I certainly didn't know about it, and I didn't get an email from Jake yet. When did Kevin do this?"

"It's a term policy he took out three months ago. And he never told me."

"Oh, goodness. Well, he was under no obligation to tell me. Although having a copy of the policy would've been helpful for record keeping and having a complete picture of his entire estate. But he obviously should've told *you*. And given you a copy of the policy."

"Yeah, I know. When's the last time you spoke to Kevin?"

She exhaled loudly, looked up at the sky and thought a good long minute. "I want to say when the two of you came in together two years ago, to settle the last few things for your dad. I haven't spoken to him since."

"So you're saying there shouldn't be any surprises in his file?"

"No, Lilian. The will hasn't been changed. You're the executor and main beneficiary of everything."

"Thanks, Helen. Listen, I should go."

"Okay, Lilian," Helen said, giving me a hug. "Please take care of yourself."

As I walked briskly back to my car, I could hear Helen's voice as she began speaking aloud, presumably to Henry, or maybe God, or perhaps whomever was willing to listen.

So as I got into my car, I did the same: spoke aloud to whomever I thought might be listening.

"Please let me make it home," I muttered. "Please let me make it home. Please let me make it home."

I made it home, with about ten seconds to spare.

CHAPTER EIGHT

DAYS LATER, SAM AND I found ourselves in the kitchen of The Property, reviewing a copy of the building inspection report Eric had given me. Sam was slurping from a thermos of coffee and cutting up an apple with a pocket knife he'd pulled from his back pocket. I grinned when I remembered that Sam always had a pocket knife, or a Swiss Army knife, or a utility knife in his back pocket at all times. Always. He never went anywhere without one. He sliced off a chunk of apple and offered it to me, which I declined.

"Evidence of structural movement of foundation," Sam read as he chewed. "Vulnerable areas of roofing system. Signs of insect infestation, water leakage, and rot resulting from significant wood or soil contact around perimeter of house. Evidence of small attic fire from knob and tube wiring. Above average levels of CO from heating system. Lead water and sewer lines ..."

"About what you were expecting, Sam?"

"It's a lot, but I'd say so."

"I wouldn't worry about most of it. We're going to be replacing almost everything, anyway. Plumbing, electrical, windows, the roof, HVAC ..."

"It's the foundation issue that scares me."

"Me too. Think we'll need a structural remodel?"

"I'll call Don, my structural engineer buddy."

I nodded. "How'd your search for blueprints go?"

Sam had been on the hunt for blueprints of the house. His first stop had been the building inspector's office at Borough Hall. Their archived building permit records only went back fifty years, which

Sam had anticipated. So while they may not have the original 120-year-old building permit on record, if renovation work had been done in the last fifty years—which it looked like it had—a permit, and perhaps blueprints, should be on file.

Yet the search had come up empty. The office had no record of the house ever being built or renovated. The clerk, however, did leave a tip for Sam: "Talk to Frank Jones at the historical society. That guy knows everything about this town and everyone in it. If there's a history to this house, Frank will know it."

"So I go to see Frank," Sam was saying, finishing the last of his apple and washing it down with a few swigs of coffee. "You know Frank, right?"

"I know Frank. Not really well. We see each other around town sometimes. He helped me and Kevin do historical research on several of our renovations over the years."

"I tell him I'm renovating the old Becker house."

"Is he familiar with it?" I asked.

"After he picked his jaw up off the floor and asked if I really wanted to get involved in that *hellhole*, I got to thinking he was familiar with the house."

"Hellhole?"

"His words, Lil. Not mine."

"What'd he say?"

"Says he knows Emma Becker. Known her since grade school in the 1950s. Lost touch with her after high school. Never married and never had kids, as far as Frank knows."

"The house, Sam. What about the house?"

"Right. Sorry. Built in 1900 by a member of the Becker family and—"

"It was built by my great grandfather," a voice cut in. "Oskar Becker."

We both turned, Sam's thermos slipping from his hand onto the kitchen counter. "Jesus Christ!" he hissed, startled.

Eric had appeared out of thin air and was standing in the kitchen doorway.

"Who are you?" Sam said. He looked at me. "Who's this?"

"This is Eric," I said.

"Lilian," Eric said, approaching us. "Nice to see you again."

"I hope you don't mind we let ourselves in."

"That is why I gave you a key, remember?" he said teasingly. "So that you may come and go as you please."

Eric held his hand out to Sam, who was staring at Eric as if he'd just seen a ghost. "Eric Becker, Emma's nephew."

"Holy shit, you look just like—"

I grabbed Sam's arm, squeezed and shook my head slightly as if to say, "Yes, I know, but not now."

Sam jerked when I grabbed him, looked over at me, at my hand squeezing his arm, then focused again on Eric. He let Eric's hand hang there for a good ten seconds while he looked him over. I can only imagine Sam was doing the same thing I did when I first met Eric: figuring out how the hell he looked like Kevin.

Slowly, cautiously, Sam took Eric's hand. He introduced himself: "Sam Hunter. You the guy looking after the place?"

"Yes, but I'm not the one in charge."

"That would be your aunt?" Sam said.

"Aunt Em," Eric said. "Yes. And she is so pleased that you've accepted her offer."

Sam nodded. "We were just reading the inspection report."

"Any surprises?" Eric asked.

"Not really, not for a house this old."

"But it will probably add to our ... *timeline*," I added, eyeing Eric and hoping he would catch my drift. Emma's health was precarious, and she wanted to die in this house, but that depended on how quickly we could make it livable again. Making it livable again would take just a tad bit longer now that we knew what we were dealing with.

"Understood," Eric said, with a subtle head nod. "How long will it take?"

"Three or four months, total?" I said. Eric's eyes darted back and forth as he looked at me, as if he were processing my statement, working something out in his brain.

"It takes as long as it takes," Eric finally said, glancing over at Sam, then back at me.

"We're going to be starting in a few days," Sam said. "That alright with you?"

"That's fine, Sam. Start as soon as you can."

"I know you stay here sometimes," I said to Eric. "It's probably best if you didn't while construction is ongoing."

"I thought you might say that, which is why I'm here, actually. Packing up the few things I keep here to take back with me."

"You live around here?" Sam said.

I adored Sam for his directness, but tact was not a skill he'd ever acquired. Sam was all rough and jagged edges, while Kevin had been filed down to a smooth finish. It was that polish, that social savvy, that differentiated them. And probably one of the things that made them best friends and eventual enemies.

"I live close by," Eric said in response to Sam's question, without further explanation. Then he craned his neck, looking at the counter behind Sam and me. "I see you have blueprints."

"On loan from the historical society," Sam said. "Apparently copies of the originals."

"You should've said something. I have the original set from 1900. I could've saved you the trouble of tracking them down."

"No trouble," Sam said, his brows furrowed as if still inspecting Eric's face.

"Who did you speak to at the historical society? Helen Whitman? She's terrific."

I wasn't aware Helen and Eric knew each other, so the comment struck me as both curious and ironic. She'd mentioned working with the Beckers, but she hadn't said when or with whom.

"You know Helen?" I asked Eric.

"We met several times," he said. "She's done some work for my family over the years. Executing wills, managing trusts, property transfers ..."

"She did mention that," I said.

"Wait," Sam said, looking at me. "Helen Whitman? As in your estate attorney?"

"She volunteers there part time," I half-whispered at Sam.

"Oh." He regarded Eric. "No, I talked to Frank."

"I'm sorry to hear that," Eric said.

"Eh, Frank's not so bad."

"He's been known to spin a tall tale or two," Eric said. He smiled at me, an openly flirtatious smile where his eyes thinned with suggestion. I smiled back, reservedly, bashfully, hoping Sam wouldn't notice.

"Isn't that his job as the town historian?" Sam said, his expression still guarded.

"His job is to know the town's factual history," Eric clarified.

Sam looked like he wanted to punch Eric in the face.

"Frank knows this town inside and out," I interjected. "I can attest to that. I've worked with him several times over the years."

Eric swung his eyes at me, then back to Sam.

"Aunt Em calls me the unofficial family historian," he said.

"That right?" Sam said, and Eric nodded.

"Any facts you need on this house, the property, any of the Beckers, feel free to ask me."

The two men continued to stare each other down. I could practically taste testosterone on my tongue.

"What we know so far," Sam said, "is that this house is in rough shape. And that
it ain't no catalog house from Sears, Roebuck and Co."

Eric laughed gently, which seemed to release some of the tension. "This house is very unique, built to my great grandfather's particular design specifications."

"Did the original design include the lake?" I asked.

Eric's smiled faded. "The lake?"

I motioned Eric over to the kitchen counter to show him the land blueprint.

"Here's the house," I said, pointing to where the house was situated on the blueprint of The Property. "And here's approximately where the lake is now." I pointed to a blank spot on the blueprint, what to a casual observer would look like an open field. "There's a change in topography in that spot, but no signs of a lake."

"Change in topography?" Eric said.

I sifted through the various blueprints and elevation maps until I found the topographical map. I pulled it out and placed it on top.

"See all these contour lines?" I said, pointing to the random circular patterns that filled the entire page. "All the contour lines on The Property are about equidistant, spaced apart evenly, meaning the land is pretty much flat."

"Except this area here," Sam said, pointing to an area on the map where the circular contour lines are spaced farther apart from each other. "Lines that are close together indicate a rise in elevation, like a hillside, slope or mountain. These lines are far apart, which indicates a depression of some sort."

"That's where the lake is now," I said. "These lines indicate to us that, before there was a lake, there was a pretty significant crater, or sinkhole, in that same spot."

Eric stared wordlessly at the blueprints, as if deep in thought. Sam and I curiously eyed each other as the atmosphere slowly grew thick with awkwardness. Had Eric not heard us? Was he simply processing the information? Or perhaps he thought a response wasn't necessary.

Finally, Eric said, "I'm not aware of anything that may've existed there before the lake."

"Maybe there was an unsightly hole in the front yard and the family was trying to cover up the eyesore," I suggested.

"With a lake? That's one hell of an expensive coverup, Lil," Sam said. "If that's the case, why not just fill it in?"

"I'd have to ask Aunt Em," Eric said. "She might know."

"No need" I said. "It doesn't matter at this point."

"When was the lake added?" Sam asked.

"The 1960s, I think. I was told it was my grandfather's idea. He thought it would be a nice addition to the property for swimming and ice skating."

"I couldn't find a permit on file for that anywhere," Sam said. "Or supporting documentation."

"Our building inspection archives only go back fifty years, to about 1970."

"I found that out when I was there today. But these countertops?" Sam reached behind him and knocked on the counter three times. "Corian. Invented in the 1970s but not popular until the 1990s and still very popular today. Second floor bathrooms have it, too. So there's been some recent renovation work done. No record of it though, with the inspector's office or the historical society."

"I'm not surprised," Eric said. "Archives get lost, damaged, misplaced. You've probably both worked on enough old houses to know that."

Sam was quiet—I could see him working it out in his head. Eric was right. Files get purged, lost, stolen, damaged. It was possible, and probable, to not have permits on file anywhere for a thirty-year-old kitchen upgrade, let alone the original or copies of a 120-year-old blue print. But a lake?

"A lake is a totally different animal," Sam said. "It's not like renovating a bathroom or kitchen. All you need there is a permit. But adding a large body of water to a property? That requires soil testing, land evaluations, watershed considerations, finding any existing water sources, possible tree removal ... That's months of work and a shit ton of paperwork. You mean to tell me none of that survived?"

The men stared at each other, the sheer sense of testosterone reaching a fevered pitch. I'd had enough.

I took a step forward, positioning myself between both men, as if preparing to jump in and break up a fistfight. "It's not a big deal, really," I said. "Eric, your aunt said we were to steer clear of the lake, anyway. We're asking more out of curiosity."

Eric slid his eyes from Sam to me and relaxed his position. "I understand."

"But we'd still like to compare the copy of the blueprints we have with your original," I added.

"When will you be here next?" Eric said to me. "I'll come by and drop them off."

"We start demo next Monday," I said.

Eric winked at me. "Good, I'll see you then."

I smiled in return, then glanced at Sam. It was apparent that only two of us were ready to leave. Sam's body language said he was still on guard, figuring Eric out.

"C'mon," I said to Sam.

Sam gathered up the remnants of his apple and threw it forcibly in the trash. "Yeah, okay."

As the three of us walked out together, I realized that Eric must live closer to The Property than he let on. There was only one car in the dirt driveway—Sam's pickup that we'd ridden in together. Eric must've walked. He waved to us from the porch, as Sam backed down the driveway and out onto the road.

CHAPTER NINE

OSKAR BECKER, DEVOTED Family Man and Business Owner, Dead at 73

Oskar Becker (1860-1933) succumbed Tuesday afternoon after a long battle with melancholia. He is survived by his wife Frida; two children, Anna and Oskar Jr.; two brothers, Walter and Karl; and numerous grandchildren, nieces and nephews. A celebration of Oskar's life will be held at St. Jude's Catholic Church on Friday, March 24th at 2 p.m.

It wasn't much, but it was a start. A small notice in our local paper, declaring the death of Oskar Becker.

I'd wanted to do some online research on the Becker family, partially for personal curiosity. Mostly, though, I was looking for pictures. Some explanation as to why Eric Becker bore a striking resemblance to Kevin O'Shea.

So one night, after a long day at The Property, I sat up in bed with a glass of wine, laptop at the ready. I typed "Eric Becker" into the search engine.

I'd decided to cast a wide net at first because it was possible Eric hadn't lived here his whole life. He could've gone to school abroad, or married and moved to another state, or taken a job somewhere else.

There were over fifty-one million Internet search results, including a surgeon in Los Angeles, a CEO in Manhattan and a psychiatrist in Houston. None of them were the Eric Becker I was looking for. Nor were any of the countless others I scanned page after page after page looking at.

Then I narrowed the search to "Eric Becker Philadelphia."

A few of those were around, but none that, based on their Facebook and Linkedin profiles, looked like Eric: mid-forties, blonde hair, blue eyes.

How about "Eric Becker, Becker Bread"? Can't get any more specific than that.

Zero search results.

I mean, that was technically possible, right? If you're not into social media you probably wouldn't be found online. If you haven't won any awards or donated to your alma mater or own a business, you might not be found online. If you don't have much of a life and keep a low profile, and if you don't have a criminal record, you probably won't be found online.

Unless, of course, you're already dead. Then, ironically enough, you might be found online. An obit. A news article.

Eric Becker, so far as I could tell, was most certainly alive and well. So I switched tactics and started with a Becker I knew was long deceased: Eric's great-grandfather, Oskar Becker, the family patriarch who'd built The Property.

Only 4.5 million search results.

I scrolled through and read a few articles, becoming so engrossed that I startled when my cell phone rang.

The screen said, *Sam Cell.*

It felt weird, but good, to see his name on my phone after two years. I'd never deleted him as a contact after the incident; we just stopped communicating, and I either forgot or didn't feel the need to delete him.

"Hey," I said.

There was silence at first, dead air. Then—loud, intense static, crackling and buzzing and hissing. Wincing, I pulled the phone away from my ear.

"Sam? Can you hear me?" I yelled into the phone.

But there was no Sam, only an incessant, wordless cacophony.

I was just about ready to hang up, thinking it was a bad connection or static interference or both, when I heard a voice...a low, gravelly, male voice, rising through the static:

"You—will pay—both—pay—for your sins—"

I'd never heard that voice before; it sounded angry and vengeful. It sounded evil.

Chilled, I quickly ended the call and threw the phone on the bed. My heart hammered in my chest as I wondered how something like that could happen—how a stranger could be calling from Sam's number.

The phone rang again.

I closed my eyes and willed myself not to look at the caller I.D. *Let it go to voicemail, Lil.* But something made me answer the call, just like something made me answer the day Emma called.

Again, the display: *Sam Cell.*

I reached for the phone with a shaky hand and braced myself. "H-hello?"

"That little shit has no right," he said. "I mean, what the hell, Lil?"

I sighed. "Sam. It's you."

"Of course it's me ..."

"What, um, who's...who's a little shit?"

"Eric Becker. He's a dead ringer for Kevin. Who does he think he is? He has no right looking like your husband and my best friend."

Sam had been drinking. I knew he had been working his way through a six-pack of something. He was slurring some of his words. And he hadn't called Kevin his best friend in three years, since that time we were all hanging out at Donovan's and Sam and Kevin were a little tipsy and Sam walked up to Kevin and threw his arm around him and called him his "bestest bud in the whole world," and all but planted a kiss on him. Kevin shooed him away but blushed all the same and when I teased him about turning red he'd blamed it on the booze and embarrassment. I knew deep down, though, that it was really because he loved Sam like a brother, even if he was a pain in Kevin's ass and was, according to Kevin, secretly in love with me. There's was a brotherly love, which made their fallout even harder to bear.

"What's the matter?" Sam said. "You sound upset."

Why did he have to be drinking? In my moment of weakness and vulnerability and fright, when I needed him to be clear-headed and rational and less emotional than usual, why couldn't he be sober? I wanted to tell him what had just happened, and I wanted him to comfort me. But in his own vulnerable state, he wouldn't be able to comfort me. He'd be overly emotional, probably angry. So I comforted him instead. No need for both of us to be freaking out about my mystery caller.

"Nothing, Sam. I'm fine. I'm just—just happy to hear from you."

Sam paused a moment before continuing. "Okay, Lil. So look, I don't think it's a good idea for you to be alone with him. Even if it is just looking at blueprints."

"We won't be alone, alone. Our demo guys will be there."

"Guess you're right, but still ..." There was a pause, and I heard a quick succession of swallows.

"Was there another reason you called?"

"Well, yeah. Sorry. So the demo guys are gonna rip out all three bathrooms first, then work on gutting the kitchen."

"Right. That will take, what? Week and a half, two weeks?"

"About. Give or take."

"And the flooring? What'd you find out there?"

"You and Kevin ever work with Bob Watson?"

"A few times."

"Your uncle and I used him a lot."

"I remember. He still have his flooring business?"

"Pretty close to retirement. But yeah, still getting down on his knees every day."

"Does he want to take a look at the house?"

"Already did. I met him there yesterday."

"And?"

Sam cleared his throat. "I had a hard time pulling him away from the lake. It was the weirdest thing, Lil. He walked right over to it and just stood there staring at it as I was telling him about the house. Hardly looked at me. It's like he went into a trance or something. Kind of like I did. How I blanked out. That's weird that we both did that, right?"

I'd thought Sam said he wasn't sure what had happened to him while standing lakeside, but now he seemed confident that he'd experienced more than just an innocent and momentary lapse of focus.

Either way, it was weird, and it gave me pause for a moment, but that was a rabbit hole for another time. Right now we needed to focus.

"Sam? The flooring?"

"Oh, right. So Bob said all the hardwood flooring throughout the entire house, even the herringbone parquet on the first floor, is actually in pretty good shape. Some loose planks here and there, but nothing major. And he thinks it's all original."

I took a sip of wine. "So we can refinish versus replacing?"

"He didn't see any type of finish on them, like wax or varnish or paint, so he thinks they've always been covered with large area rugs to protect them instead. Apparently that was the thing to do back then and future generations just kept doing it. In any case, Bob says he can refinish all the flooring rather than replace it. That'll save us a ton of money."

"That's good, because we'll need all the money to fix the structural issues."

"Oh, yeah. About that," Sam said. "Don said the horizontal cracks and slightly bowed walls aren't causes for concern. Easily fixed. There's no foundation shifting, from what he could tell."

"That's a relief."

"There's water management we need to address, which we already knew. Filling the cracks and voids. Re-sloping the soil around the perimeter. New downspouts and gutters ...."

"But the house is structurally sound?"

"According to Don it is."

"What a miracle," I said.

"If the floors don't get damaged during demo, *that* will be a miracle," Sam said, taking another swig. "So, what have you been working on?"

"Oh, well...do you remember the name Oskar Becker?"

"Eric's grandfather?"

"Great-grandfather. The one who built the house."

"What about him?"

"He killed himself. In 1933, just after the Great Depression ended."

"No shit. That's terrible."

"Apparently he shot himself. His wife Frida found his body floating in the lake."

"Jesus."

"Weird thing is, his obituary said he died from 'melancholia.'"

"What's that?"

"It's what we now call depression."

"Makes sense. If he killed himself."

"The family was probably trying to avoid scandal, save the family from embarrassment. So they skirted around the word 'suicide.'"

"Could explain why Eric's a little off. Maybe he's got the melancholia."

"C'mon, Sam. Eric is a little eccentric, but he's harmless."

"You're just saying that because he looks like Kevin."

Kevin.

I was quiet a moment, thinking. I had no worries professionally. Jake would help me with the business side of things. Could I or should I continue the business? Run it solo, find a new partner, sell the whole damn thing. No matter. It'd be hard, but I'd figure that out. I had enough money, and that money gave me options.

But personally? Being alone in our house for the first time in almost twenty years...*sleeping* alone for the first time in twenty years...it was strange and sad, and some days I felt like I was dreaming. Like at any moment I'd wake up and hear him in the shower or see him walk in the front door or smell the sweat of a rough day coming off him when he bent down to kiss me. In those anticipatory moments, I'd strain my ears and turn my head, but when there was absolutely nothing to see or hear or smell, I'd remember: *There's nothing left to anticipate, Lilian.*

No amount of money could solve that.

I knew I had to move on. Honor Kevin's memory, yet keep living my life. But Jesus Christ, how could I move on when I had a constant reminder of him staring me right in the face?

"Lil, you there?"

"Yeah, Sam. I'm here."

"I'm sorry. About what I said."

"It's okay."

"I—I've had a few beers. Causes me to say things I don't mean."

"I know. I remember."

Sam sighed. "Look, I'm just saying to be careful with Eric. I got a weird vibe about him."

Kevin's four-word death plea echoed in my ear, and I had a flash in my mind and somehow, in that moment, I knew what I needed to do next.

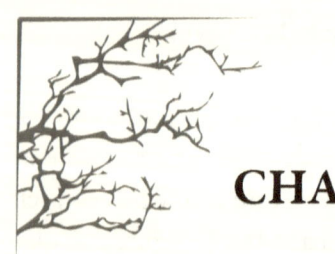

CHAPTER TEN

I RANG THE DOORBELL and cleared my throat. The plate of chocolate chip cookies I held was still warm, and I could smell them through the cellophane.

She answered the door, smiling ear to ear. "Lil, darling," she said, tilting her head.

"Hi, Stella."

"Please come in."

Once I was inside, she wrapped me in the tightest, most enveloping embrace I've ever received from, well, anyone. Not being the overly affectionate type, and not wanting to drop the cookies, I mostly just stood there and let it happen.

She released me, then placed both her hands on either side of my face. "How are you?"

"Fine. I'm fine."

She squinted, and gave my body a quick scan. "Well, we'll see about that, won't we?" I was quiet, confused by her comment. Suddenly her demeanor changed, and her frown brightened into another smile. "Are these for me? Did you bake me cookies?"

"Yes, cookies for you and the family."

"So thoughtful, Lilian. Are they gluten-free, by chance? I'm weaning the kiddos off gluten-containing grains. So bad for their tummies."

She took the plate from me, turned and glided through the foyer into the kitchen. Her long skirt billowed behind her, as did her long auburn hair, and the myriad of bracelets she wore on both wrists jangled as she moved.

Stella Matthews was thirty-five, and had moved in next door as a newlywed ten years before. In that time, she'd given birth to four children, two boys named Cosmo and Castor and two girls named Astra and Aurora. In previous decades, you might've called her a tree hugger or a hippie. Now it was more appropriate to call her New-Agey.

In other words, she had a large crystal collection. Shelves of self-improvement books. A kitchen stocked with organic and, now, apparently, gluten-free food. She practiced yoga and meditated. She read auras and energy fields. She balanced chakras. She had a Ouija board and twenty decks of tarot cards. After the birth of her third child, she decided to turn her passion into profit and became a full-time alternative and holistic healer. She turned a downstairs spare bedroom into her practice room and never looked back.

I was familiar with some of the things Stella practiced—Reiki, Qi-Gong, chakra balancing—but I didn't know when they were used, or how. And I knew some of the tools of her trade, but I didn't know how they were used. I simply didn't know how Stella did what she did. Hers was a world that was as completely foreign to me as construction was to her.

According to Kevin, who had been friends with Stella's husband, Joe (the most regular of non-New-Agey dudes you'd ever meet) she earned three times more money annually as a healer than she did at her previous day job as an executive secretary.

Stella was a psychic, too. She preferred the term clairvoyant, because that term, apparently, helped differentiate the particular way she was able to see things. Stella's clairvoyance allowed her to have visions, see signs, symbols, and messages, and they popped up in front of her as if projected on a movie screen. Other psychics could touch objects or people, like shaking a hand or touching a personal object, and see the story behind it. And still other psychics had strong gut feelings, what we'd call cognizance: knowing what had happened, or was going to happen.

People paid good money to have Stella tell them stuff, especially about their futures. I was here for another reason entirely. Not for her to tell me my future; I'd prefer to find out my future the hard way by actually, you know, living life, and finding out what happens when it happens. I was visiting Stella because I'd hoped she tell me a little bit about Kevin. I didn't want her to look forward in time so much as back in time. And I didn't necessarily need her clairvoyant skills for what I wanted to know.

"Not gluten-free. Sorry," I said, as Stella put the cookies on the counter.

"Still, so kind of you. Thank you."

"Thank *you* for all the casseroles. Which were all delicious."

Just then, two children came tearing through the kitchen toward the living room, where a small child-sized table and four chairs were set up, full of flash cards and coloring books.

"Castor! Aurora! What has mommy said about running through the house?"

Two children's voices rang out in unison, "Skip down the street and run against the wind, but always walk through the house."

"That's right," Stella said. She looked at me. "Sorry about that. We've had some discipline issues ever since I started homeschooling them last year."

"No problem," I said.

"Before we begin can I offer you something to drink? I like to make sure my clients are well hydrated before a session, since it can be very draining."

I declined her offer, and she started walking down a short hallway to a room at the end, which was her practice space.

"Session?" I said, as she led me into the space and closed the door.

"Yes, what are you interested in? A tarot card reading? Some reiki? Reflexology? You didn't say on the phone, but whatever you need, Lilian, I'm here for you."

"Thanks, but—"

"And can I just say," she interrupted. "I hope this isn't out of line but—" here she took my hands in hers, raised my arms out to the side and scanned me head to toe— "You look beautiful."

"Oh." I felt a blush rise to my cheeks.

She smirked and winked and gave my hands a final squeeze before letting go. "Absolutely gorgeous."

"Thank you."

She sat down at a little round table draped with a long, dark tablecloth decorated with yellow stars. She motioned for me to sit in the other cushiony chair across for her. I obeyed and glanced furtively around the small space. There were pillows on the floor and lit candles on the windowsills, and three or four silken tapestries hanging on the wall.

"I'm sorry, Stella. I ... I think there might've been a misunderstanding."

"A misunderstanding?"

"I'm not here for me."

"Oh, Lilian." She reached across the table and put both of her hands atop mine, her green eyes looking right through me. "The grief you must be feeling. The crisis you are experiencing must be so unbalancing for your soul."

"I'm dealing with my grief pretty well ... considering," I said.

Images of a dying Kevin, a drunk Sam and a flirtatious Eric flashed before me in quick succession.

"Of course you're coping," Stella said. "But your spirit is crying out for healing. I can sense it in your aura. That's what led you to me. I can help transform you from the inside out. As within, so without ..." She closed her eyes, took a deep breath and issued a long exhale.

"Really, Stella. I'm not here for me. I'm here for Kevin."

She opened her eyes, grinned at me and gracefully nodded her head. "Ah, I see. You must sense that his spirit is stuck between worlds, and needs help crossing over. That's very common when the nature of death is tragic."

"I really just want to talk," I said. "Ask a few questions. About Kevin."

"Do you want me to communicate with him? Allow him to speak to you, through me?"

"Well, no. Not really. That's not what I ... Wait. You know how to do that?"

Stella laughed softly. "I must admit I'm still learning. I'm not the best at mediumship yet. Three months ago, I thought I successfully channeled Joe's Aunt Barbara, who died of old age. But Aunt Barb was a nasty woman, and this spirit was so sweet that I don't think it was her." Stella leaned across the table and whispered, "Somebody else's Aunt Barb, I think."

I laughed uneasily. She sat back in her chair and said, "What would you like to know?"

"I know Kevin and Joe were friendly. Went out for beers a few times after work."

"They did. Which reminds me. Beer is full of gluten. I might have to talk to Joe about switching to gluten-free beer. Anyway ... go on."

"I was wondering if Kevin ever talked about our business to Joe."

"I'm sure he did. They're both businessmen, after all. They probably 'talked shop', exchanged stories, that kind of thing. Is there something specific you're wondering?"

I took a deep breath and went all in. "Three months before he died, Kevin took out a half-million-dollar term-life insurance policy on himself. And he never told me about it. I found out from my accountant while I was settling Kevin's estate."

"Oh my," Stella said, leaning forward and clasping her hands together.

"I was wondering if maybe he told Joe about it."

"If he did, Joe didn't tell me."

"I'm starting to think Kevin didn't tell anyone. I mean, why would he do that? Take out a huge life insurance policy months before he dies and not tell anyone? Not even his own wife?"

Stella thought a moment. She pinched her eyes closed and gripped the edges of the table. "He knew," she said.

"What?"

Through the doorway I heard soft voices, two children engaged in a conversation.

"Kevin knew," she repeated.

"What did he know?"

She paused, her eyes still closed and now fluttering, her head twitching. While still muffled, the children's voices grew louder. They were playfully teasing each other; the boy had taken something from the girl and she was demanding it back. They were laughing and threatening to tattle on each other.

"He knew he was going to die," Stella said.

I tried to tune out the children and focus on Stella. "That's what I thought too, but—"

"He had dreams," Stella interjected. "Night terrors."

Suddenly the children's voices escalated. There were squeals of delight and heavy footfalls, as if they were now chasing each other around the house.

"Did you say night terrors?" I asked, unsure I heard her correctly over the children.

Stella was undistracted by the noise, focused instead on whatever visions now swirled in front of her.

"He didn't want to sleep," she said, her voice cracking. "He was too scared." She sniffed. A few tears rolled down her face.

The squeals turned to screaming, as the two children continued chasing each other through the house, their incessant *thump thump thump* mirroring the sudden hammering of my heart. The noise reverberated down the hallway towards us.

"Do you need to quiet them down?" I asked.

She kept her eyes closed and ignored my question. She was lost in thought, wrapped up in a trance, unreachable.

"Intra ... cranial ... hemorrhage ..." she stammered.

Only a few people knew that was Kevin's official cause of death. Stella was not one of them.

She put both her hands on top of her head and winced, as if in pain. Her voice was still cracking, tears still rolling down her face. "Make it stop," she whispered. "Please. Make it stop."

Her children's horseplaying had reached such a fever pitch that I thought Stella was reacting to *them* at first. Asking for them to stop. I, too, winced as their shrieks tore through me, and covered my ears and begged silently for them to quiet down.

Suddenly Stella's eyes flew open, and she grabbed my arm and squeezed. Her eyes were wide. She was pale. "Beware the double walker!" she said.

In that moment, it felt like all the oxygen had been sucked out of the room, and I had to gasp for breath. And suddenly it got so quiet on the other side of the door, so eerily stone-cold quiet, that I thought I'd imagined hearing her children. Because how could there be screaming one moment, and absolute stillness and silence the next?

"Shhh!" I heard a muffled voice say. A third child. "Don't interrupt the spirits."

I ignored the new voice and focused on Stella.

"What did you say?" I said.

"He's saying, beware the double walker."

"Who, Stella? Who's saying that?"

"Kevin."

Little prickles of cold broke out on my arms, spread to my entire body. I was shaking.

"I have to go," I said, standing. I tried to steady my legs. "How much do I owe you?" I rummaged through my purse with trembling hands, pulled out a fifty-dollar bill and placed it on the table. "If it's not enough, let me know."

I tore out of that room, nearly pulling the tablecloth off in my haste.

"Lilian?" Stella called after me.

I sped down the hallway, through the kitchen, and came to a halt in the living room. Three angelic little lambs stood there, staring at me. I paused long enough to ponder how such tiny creatures could create so much commotion; then I smiled at the kids and dashed out the front door.

I rushed across the yard to my driveway, unlocked my own front door and ducked into the downstairs powder room. And that's where I sat, sobbing, for what felt like hours.

How did she know? I thought, sitting on the edge of the tub.

How could Stella possibly know?

CHAPTER ELEVEN

I'VE RENOVATED MY FAIR share of supposedly haunted houses. I spent twenty years kneeling in dirt-filled crawl spaces, working alone in dark, spooky basements, hunching over in dusty attics. All spaces that time forgot, and homeowners abandoned. They are as good a place as any for ghosts to hide, if you ask me.

But ghosts can appear anywhere, really. They traipse through the kitchen when you're watching TV in the next room. They appear in the bathroom mirror after you've stepped out of the shower. They slink out of your closet as you're lying in bed, trying to fall asleep.

They can manifest as dark masses, white circles, shadow figures, ghost animals, wisps of smoke. They make your hair stand on end, send chills down your spine, make you scream and run into another room, incite anger for invading your space. Sometimes they bring comfort. You may feel at ease in their presence, so you ask them to stay for a spell. Especially if the spirit is a departed loved one.

They touch your hair, whisper in your ear, call out your name. They mess with your electronics, make your lights blink, drain your batteries.

If you believe that humans are made up of layers of vibrating energy, and that our physical bodies are vessels for containing that energy, along with our soul, then believing in ghosts, the residue of that energy, is probably natural. And if you're familiar with the first law of thermodynamics, which says energy can neither be created nor destroyed, then you know that energy is constant. It's always swirling around us.

I had this client once, a retired physics professor who wanted me to remodel his three-level, 1700s-era farmhouse. He liked to invoke the first law of thermodynamics to explain the ongoing presence of a ten-year-old slave girl living in his basement. Her corporeal body had died centuries ago, he said. But her energy will live on forever. And so will all of ours.

Other homeowner clients have confessed similar stuff to me—seeing ghosts of deceased pets; witnessing objects mysteriously disappearing and, sometimes, reappearing somewhere else in the house; hearing disembodied voices echo up from the basement or down from the attic. They're the schoolteachers, the business professionals and the stay-at-home moms, wide swaths of people from just about every walk of life, who've admitted, in one way or another, that they share their home with some...presence.

Those people are in the minority. They're the few brave souls that confess because they think it's cool to live in a haunted house and want to have that story to tell. But sometimes they just want me to have full disclosure, since, you know, it might sway my decision.

"Before you accept the job," they would say, "I need you to know this house is haunted."

I nod and say okay, and accept the job, despite any cohabitating hobgoblins, cordial Caspers, or pesky poltergeists.

I believed every single one of my clients. I believed *they* believed. And I believe in the possibility. The problem is, I'd never experienced anything like that firsthand, ever. I never had personal experiences that couldn't be debunked, explained away by some science. I'd never seen supernatural phenomena, paranormal activity, ghosts, spirits, apparitions, phantoms, specters, shadow figures, whatever you want to call them. And I sure as shit had never heard of anything called a "double walker."

I hadn't known much about psychic ability, either. ESP, clairvoyance, precognition, mind reading, all the terms that basically mean the same thing: receiving information through some means other than your five senses.

That is, until Kevin died. And The Property fell in my lap.

And Stella uttered Kevin's dying words.

Beware the double walker.

It started happening after that. A stirring within me. All those external things that had happened to me seemed to activate something powerful internally. Something was changing, growing within. A deep sense of knowingness developed, a dead certainty about things I just knew to be true without knowing *how* I knew. How I obtained the knowledge defies all logic and reason. All I can say is, when it happens, it feels like something or someone (the Universe, a spirit guide, a guardian angel, take your pick) is downloading information into my head for me to process. Its onset is so sudden, and the information dumped so quickly, that it sometimes gives me migraines and nausea, and I feel fatigued to the point of needing to lie down. Especially if the message is big.

I know this ability now as *claircognizance.*

In the beginning, though, I chalked the headaches, the nausea, the fatigue, up to stress. Given everything I'd gone through, that explanation made perfect sense to me. Now I know that a quickly developing headache is a sign that my body is trying to tell me, warn me, even, that an important piece of information was on its way. Like an urgent email into my mental inbox.

Whether I liked it or not, I was developing a sixth sense.

My mother would've been so proud. She would've called it "my little intuitive gift." I guess you can say it's a gift, because most of the messages I receive are intended to help me, guide me, show me the way. And my precognizance allows me to figure things out. Like the identity of the double walker.

When Stella uttered, verbatim, Kevin's dying words, I knew...I knew who the double walker was. No headache needed. I'd already received that important download a few days before, when Sam and I were backing out of the driveway of The Property. Eric was waving goodbye to us from the front porch, and my temple had started throbbing as a wave of lightheadedness hit me. At first I thought it was hunger, because I hadn't eaten all day. But then I remember pushing that to the side because it didn't feel like the right answer. The right answer was that something felt off about Eric. Hell, even Sam recognized it.

I didn't know, right then, that I was getting information about Eric that would change the course of my life forever. Racing out of Stella's house is when I knew that I knew.

Beware the double walker.

Those four words that had been rattling around in my brain, unrecognized and misunderstood, for weeks.

Until I knew. Until I knew I'd found the double walker.

CHAPTER TWELVE

DONOVAN'S IS AN INSTITUTION in Pennsgrove, and is your prototypical Irish pub: lots of dark wood, Irish flags and shamrocks on the walls and ceiling, a low-key atmosphere, and a good collection of Irish whiskeys. Sam, Kevin, and I had been going there since high school. We'd grown up with the owners' kids, Sean and Sophie. The three of us liked to pop in after school sometimes, because the owners would give us free Shirley Temples.

Said owners, Patrick and Grace Donovan, had emigrated in the sixties from Kilkenny, Ireland. They bought the bar, had their kids Sean and Sophie, and ran the place for almost fifty years together. Grace died in 2010. Patrick decided he didn't want to run it without his beloved wife anymore, so Sean stepped up and bought it. And now a third generation Donovan was being groomed: Sean's twelve-year-old son, Liam, could often be found flitting around—sweeping up, wiping down tables, or sitting at the bar doing his homework.

Which was where he was when I walked in—sitting at the bar, sipping a soda, his schoolwork spread out in front of him. I hadn't seen him in two years and, boy, had he sprouted up. I didn't think he'd remember me, but he did; he looked up from his work when I entered, smiled and greeted me.

"Long time, no see, kiddo," I said.

I did a quick scan of the place. I didn't see Sam, and I didn't see any workers. There were about a half-dozen patrons spread about the small dining room area, only a few steps from the bar. And there were two thirty-something women sitting at the other end of the bar, sipping wine and talking casually.

"Your dad here today?" I asked Liam.

"He'll be in later," he said.
"You're not here by yourself, are you?"
"No."
"Tony's here?"
"Yeah. He's in the back."
"Gotcha. I'm meeting my friend Sam. Do you remember him?"
"Yep. He's here's a lot."
"Oh. Well, if you see him, can you tell him I'm in the dining room?"
"Okay," Liam said, and went back to his schoolwork.

I grabbed a table and decided to answer some emails on my phone while I waited. After a few minutes, I heard a small, young voice call my name. I looked up and saw Liam pointing at me. Sam was at his side, and both were looking at me. Meanwhile, the two young women at the bar were eyeing Sam.

"Friends of yours?" I said, motioning to the women as Sam approached my table.

"What?" he said, turning around and scanning the bar. The girls giggled and smiled. "Oh." He shrugged and sat down in the chair opposite me without acknowledging them. Their smiles melted, and they turned their attention back to the bar, and their own business.

He was wearing nice clothes again, a light blue polo shirt tucked into black trousers and a belt. Looking him over, I wasn't sure I could get used to the new Sam, if that's what was standing before me. Sam 2.0. At least on the outside, he was a newer version of himself. Sam cleaned up well, as they say. I just wasn't sure if it was the outside that needed the most cleaning.

We hadn't seen each other in almost a week. Since he seemed to have everything under control at The Property, I told him I needed to take a few days to handle some lingering issues with Kevin's estate. When I was ready, Sam suggested we meet at Donovan's, so he could catch me up.

In those few days, I'd removed Kevin from our joint bank accounts, health insurance policies and website. I canceled his personal credit cards and social media accounts. I transferred our mortgage and his car into my name. I also signed off on the paperwork transferring LB Renovations to me, effectively changing the business status from joint partnership to sole proprietorship. I delivered that paperwork to Jake's office, and he'd ensured me he'd ship it off to the IRS the next day.

When we'd last met, the day he dropped the bomb about the term life insurance policy, Jake told me not to worry about it. He said he'd take care of it. So I didn't worry about it, but I did remind him to email Helen a copy of the policy.

He seemed confused by my request, as if he'd already done it, but when I mentioned that Helen hadn't received it yet, he hemmed and hawed and apologized and said he'd probably forgotten. It wasn't like Jake to forget small details, but I shrugged it off because I realized I wasn't the only one who'd lost Kevin. Jake and Kevin had been close. They'd known each other for as long as I'd known Kevin, so he had to be missing Kevin, too. Perhaps his grief was making him forgetful the same way it was making me feel lost and untethered.

I'd decided to not allow myself to feel any emotions while tackling my to-do list, lest my grief and sadness derail my progress. I would do as much as I could, as quickly as I could. Best to rip the band-aid off, I thought, get everything done, *then* cry. That way I could get it out of my system in one fell swoop and, eventually, move on.

When it was all said and done, when I'd crossed just about everything off the list, then allowed myself to shed just about every tear I think my eyes could produce, I emerged completely exhausted, in need of a full-day's rest.

And then I decided that, in light of the revelation about the double walker, I felt I needed one last day away from everything to come up with a game plan. Some distance was needed in order to figure out what to do with the information. Meeting Sam at Donovan's, I still didn't have a plan. But my intuition was telling me to let things play out—wait and see, and to keep working.

"You thirsty?" Sam said. "Let me get you a beer."

"Soda, please, Sam. Beer gives me a headache."

"Sure thing, Lil." Sam walked over to the bar and stood next to Liam, ignoring the two young women at the other end who were now stealing occasional glances at him. Just then, Tony emerged from a back room of the bar and greeted Sam.

Tony Russo had worked at Donovan's forever. Christ, it seemed like he was a hundred years old. He was Patrick's and Grace's first employee, and I remember thinking even as a teenager, sitting at the bar as he served me Shirley Temple after Shirley Temple, that he had to be almost eighty years old. He hadn't, of course; he'd been in his early forties. And now he was a spry seventy-four. It was a hard life that added years to his face—the drugs, the drinking, the two stints in county lockup.

Tony loved working at the bar just as much as the Donovans loved owning it. He took pride in his work, treated the place like his own. Which is why Patrick and Grace kept hiring him back after each of his go-arounds in the slammer. It was a loyalty thing; to the Irish and the Italians, loyalty is everything. So out of continued loyalty, and perhaps to honor his folks, Sean kept Tony on after he assumed ownership.

What I liked most about Tony is that he didn't feel the need to get in your business. I knew he knew what went down two years ago, but God love him he never passed judgement. Never asked questions, never thumbed his nose or looked down on me, kept his opinions about the matter to himself, and kept serving me like he would any other customer. I guess that was the felon in him; out of respect he let you have your privacy, because he knew better than anyone the demons in your head have a field day with your wrongdoings. No one needs humans to add insult to injury. Sam walked back to our table, a beer in one hand, soda in the other.

"Shirley Temple," Sam said, placing the glass in front of me. "Tony says compliments of the house."

I caught Tony's eye, and he winked and waved. I held up my glass in solute. Shirley Temples, my favorite. He remembered, the old bastard.

Sam took a long sip from his beer bottle and let out a big, "Ahhh!"

"So, what's with the clothes?" I asked.

"You like these?" Sam looked down at his shirt and adjusted the collar. "Not my usual, I know. I bought these awhile back when I entered the dating scene. Thought it would be nice to show up for dates in something other than an orange reflective vest and steel tips."

"How's that going? The whole dating thing?"

"Had a few flings awhile ago. Nothing serious. You know how hard it is to find someone at my age? I've got my faults, you know. But I'm a decent guy, right?"

"You're more than just a decent guy," I said.

Sam smiled and took a long swig of his beer.

"You seeing someone now?" I asked.

"Nah," he said, almost too quickly. "Oh, so I've got something for you." He reached into his breast pocket and pulled out three photographs. "Demo crew found these in one of the kitchen cabinets."

I spread the three photos out on the table and inspected them while I took a few sips of soda. The first one was a black and white photo of the front of the house, taken from the dirt driveway. There were a few blurry images of people wandering through the shot. To the left of the house, where the lake should've been, was a wide-open grassy area. In the lower right-hand corner of the photo, someone had written, *Becker Residence, 1911.*

The second photo, in color, was the exact same as the first, from the same vantage point. There were two cars in the driveway: a family car, and what looked like a luxury car. In the left-hand corner, sunlight shimmered on the surface of a dark lake. In the photo's lower right-hand corner, someone had written, *Becker Residence, 1965.*

Having finished his beer, Sam went up to the bar, where Tony popped the top on a second Bud Light and slid it to him. The whole transaction took less than ten seconds, real slick and fluid, like a scene in a play that had been rehearsed over and over—and over—again. It occurred to me in that moment that the scene before me had played out, in that exact fashion, time and again, perhaps week after week or night after night, even. The sight was a little gut-wrenching. Sam was struggling with booze, after all.

The two ladies from the bar were gone. They'd slipped out unnoticed.

Sam returned to the table and sat down, one quarter of his second beer already drained. I asked him to identify the two cars in the one photo.

"That one is a Chevy Impala," Sam said, pointing at the light-green colored car. "It was the family sedan of its day. And that baby," he said, pointing to a sleek, sexy-looking silver car, "is an Aston Martin. The Becker family had money."

The third photo was a sepia-colored group shot of about fifteen people lined up on the porch. In the lower right-hand corner, someone had written, *Becker Family, 1928*. I flipped the photo over and noticed someone had identified everyone on the porch with a first and last name, all written in pencil on the approximate spot where their head would be on the reverse. I studied the names and noticed some that I was already familiar with: Oskar, Frida, Anna, Oskar Jr., Walter, Karl. And one more name I definitely knew: Eric Becker.

"Notice anything?" Sam asked.

"Eric Becker."

"Weird, right?"

I flipped the photo over to look at Eric. He appeared to be about sixteen. Light brownish hair, tall and tremendously slender. Denim overalls. A neutral smile that betrayed nothing. He looked nothing like the Eric Becker I knew, and he looked nothing like Kevin O'Shea.

"Eric might've been a popular name at the time," I said, shrugging. "So maybe the Eric we know was named after one or more of his ancestors. Maybe named after him, even." I pointed to the unfamiliar-looking Eric Becker in the photo.

"You think?"

"Well, sure. I'm not the only Lilian in my family. And I know you're not the only Samuel in yours."

"Don't remind me."

"Did the demo crew find anything else in the kitchen?"

"A few weird odds and ends. Like newspapers from the 1940s. A pair of old baby shoes. Some wooden clothespins. Shit like that."

"Did the demo crew save the items? I'd like to give them to Eric. The photos, too. I think he'd want to have them."

"You think he'd want all that stuff?"

"I don't know, maybe."

"Well, he is the *official family historian*," Sam said, using air quotes. He rolled his eyes, then tipped his head back and downed the rest of his second beer.

My gut lurched again. *Sam is in love with you, Lilian. He loves you and drinks to try to forget that fact.*

The thought came to me quickly, a fully formed sentence that sounded like a voice in my head. I knew it to be true. My right temple began throbbing.

Christ, no. Not a headache. Not here. Not now.

"Is there anything else we need to talk about, business wise?" I said.

Sam pushed aside the empty bottle.

"Well, let's see. Demo will be done in about a day or two. Then I have the kitchen and bath guys lined up next. Do you remember Big Al? He and his crew are doing all the electrical. Hope you don't mind I made the executive decision. I remember you liked him. Such a great dude. And one hell of an electrician. The best, if you ask me. God I miss him. Haven't seen him in years."

Sam was rambling, and he was getting sentimental, and I knew then that he was intoxicated, and that it was time to go.

"That's great. It'll be good to see Big Al again. Hey, do you think we could get out of here?"

Sam raised his eyebrows. "Where do you want to go, Lil?"

"Home, Sam. I'd like to go home, if you don't mind. It's getting late and I'm tired and we both have busy days tomorrow ..."

"Right. Sorry. Didn't mean to, well, you know. Must be the beer talking. Sure, we can go."

Just then, as Sam and I were making our way towards the bar to leave, the pub door opened and a guy walked in and I thought, Shit. Now we *really* need to go.

The man stopped short when he saw the two of us. He wavered in place, uneasy on his feet.

"Sammy, my boy!" the man said.

It was Roy Patterson, the town drunk. He'd gotten fired from more construction crews (including my dad's) than I could remember, on account of his drinking. He wasn't a mean drunk, just the loud, obnoxious kind. And that kind of drunk is ... unpredictable. He had obviously walked into Donovan's already drunk, per usual, and probably wouldn't leave until Tony dragged his ass out onto the street.

Yep, time to go.

Roy's boisterous voice startled Liam, who whipped around in his bar stool, wide-eyed.

"Hey, kid," Roy said to Liam. Liam smiled faintly, mouthed a quiet "Hey," and returned to his schoolwork.

"Roy," Sam said, nodding at him.

"Haven't seen you in what? Few days?" Roy said. "What you been up to?" His eyes slid over to me, and his brows furrowed, as if trying to place me. "Lilian O'Shea? Is that you? Well, I'll be goddamned!"

A wave of vertigo passed through me, and I heard blood rushing in my ears. A throbbing headache wasn't far behind.

"Hey, Roy," I said. "We were just leaving."

"Where you been, pretty lady?" Roy shuffled up to me, close enough that I could smell his rancid breath. He reached out to touch my hair and I dodged his advances.

Sam took a step toward Roy.

"Calm down, Sammy," Roy said, raising his hands in a gesture of innocence. "Just looking to give my condolences to the pretty lady."

Out of the corner of my eye, I saw Tony motion to Liam from behind the bar. Liam gathered his books, slinked off his stool and disappeared into the kitchen.

"Sorry to hear about Kevin," Roy said to me, keeping his hands to himself this time but still in my face. I turned my face slightly towards Sam, evading the full brunt of Roy's breath.

"Thanks, Roy," I said.

"Seeing as you're single now," Roy said, grinning, "what do you say you and me, you know ..."

"Okay, Roy," Sam said. "That's enough."

"What?" Roy said. "Doesn't hurt to ask, right?"

Sam's nostrils flared, his fists clenched and he took a step forward as if to strike Roy. But then he backed down.

"I'm not warning you again," Sam said.

"You're right, Sam. You're right."

"Lil's husband just died. Have some respect, would you? For her and for yourself." Sam turned to me. "You ready?"

"Been ready," I said.

"Alright there, Roy," Tony said from behind the bar. "Pull up a stool. I'll get you fixed up."

"Aw, I'm sorry, Lil," Roy said, ignoring Tony. "I didn't mean anything by it. It's just a shame to see a hot piece of ass go to waste."

Sam was trying to do the right thing. Really, he was. Talking Roy down. Trying to ignore the insults. I had an easier time of it because my headache required all my attention and seemed to allow me to ignore Roy's crudeness. But Sam's a sensitive guy; his emotions can change on a dime. And change they did.

Suddenly, instinctively, Sam reeled back, and as he did Tony came out from behind the bar faster than any seventy-four-year-old had a right to. Swift as Tony was, though, it wasn't fast enough to stop Sam's fist from striking Roy square in the jaw. With a *crack*, Roy fell back against the bar.

Time stood still for a moment, all of us frozen in place. The bar, the dining area, the whole place fell into an eerie quiet, like a record scratch that stops everyone in their tracks. I imagined there were dozens of eyes on us, boring into my and Sam's backs, patrons wondering what had just disrupted their peaceful meals.

Then, all of a sudden, the record started up again and things hummed back to life. Roy looked up at Sam, rubbing his jaw.

"I warned you, Roy," Sam said. "I fucking warned you."

Tony looked around the dining area, seemingly scanning every corner for who might've noticed the fracas. He helped Roy to his feet and got him settled in a stool at the bar. Finally, he set his eyes on me and Sam. "Get the hell out of here, would you?"

"What about ...?" I asked Tony, pointing at Roy.

"I got this," Tony said.

Sam opened the door for me and ushered me out. As he did, I turned to Tony and said, "I'm so sorry. Thank you for the Shirley Temple. I owe you one."

Tony winked. "I like you, Lilian. Always have."

And then, as I made the decision to leave Sam's truck at Donovan's and drive his drunk ass home, with him ranting and raving in the passenger seat and my head now throbbing, I thought to myself:

The client who was a dead ringer for my deceased husband, with a secret I needed to discover.

A business partner with a drinking problem, who was secretly in love with me.

The project binding the three of us, that I was secretly hoping wasn't a mistake.

And a quickly-developing ability to know all this shit without knowing *how* I knew, that sometimes gave me debilitating headaches.

For fuck's sake, Lilian. What the hell have you gotten yourself into?

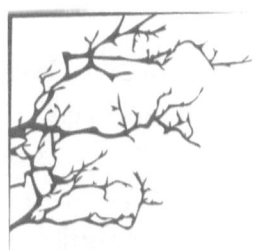

CHAPTER THIRTEEN

IT WAS NINE A.M. A few days after the incident at Donovan's. I pulled into the dirt driveway of The Property, windows down. Hammering and buzzing and sawing filled the air. Two men sat hunched over a portable workbench, looking at blueprints. Two others carried a cast iron bathtub across the front yard to a forty-yard roll off dumpster, now overflowing with other remnants of an old house.

I walked the three floors of the house, introducing myself to the new faces, and saying hello to the familiar faces I'd worked with before. As I walked down the staircase from the second floor, I spotted Eric standing in the vestibule, his hands in the pockets, staring off into some distance beyond the parlor.

"Lilian," he said as I approached him. "There you are. Do you have a moment?"

Two men emerged from the kitchen and walked past us, through the vestibule and out the front door, each carrying one end of a freestanding cupboard.

"Of course," I said.

"Aunt Em wants to make sure you've received the two checks she mailed you."

"I did. Please thank her."

"Excellent. I will."

He said nothing further, and we stood there in awkward silence for a few seconds, looking at each other.

"That was all," Eric finally said, smirking.

"Oh, okay," I said, laughing nervously. "Well, in that case, I have something for you." I held up the paper bag I had been holding.

"A present?"

"Something like that."

I motioned for us to go outside and over to my car. For a little less noise and a little more privacy, I'd explained. Once there, I opened the bag and laid the items on the hood.

"Some of my workers found these items in a kitchen cabinet," I said. "I thought you'd like to have them."

Eric looked over the items. "I'll give the three photos to Aunt Em. Everything else can be discarded. No use for them, really."

"My crew also found piles of old newspapers. Any reason to keep them?"

He thought a moment, said my crew could throw them out, then turned his attention back to the three photos. He smiled, as if remembering long-ago memories.

"Is that your great-grandfather, Oskar Becker?" I said, pointing to him. Eric nodded. Suddenly an image flashed in front of me: an older gentleman in a black suit, floating face down in the lake. It startled me, how quickly the vision emerged, before just as quickly vanishing.

"Lilian?"

I looked up from the photo, still in a daze. Eric was eyeing me curiously and I said, "He's not...um, he's not what I imagined."

"Really?" Eric said, looking at me with a curious smile. "What were you imagining?"

"That he'd be taller, maybe? More stout? I think society imagines successful, ambitious men should strike more of an imposing figure." The man in the photo was on the short side, trim, and dwarfed by the person identified as Eric Becker.

"My great-grandfather immigrated to this country from Germany with nothing but a dream of becoming a bread baker," he said. "Little did he know that the Becker Bakery company he founded with his two brothers would become a huge success. With skill, luck, and courage, my great-grandfather created an empire. And this," —he motioned to the house, the lake, and the property as a whole— "Is part of our family legacy."

"I'm sorry, Eric. I meant no disrespect."

"No offense taken. It's the truth."

I smiled, relieved.

"What he lacked in size, he more than made up for in his reputation," Eric said. "He was an absolute tyrant. He was notoriously hard on everyone in his life. His wife, his kids, the rest of the family, his employees, even the builders of this house ..."

"Why?"

"His size? Maybe it made him feel like he had even more to prove. Or maybe he was a product of his environment. His parents were mean, so he grew up to be mean. Perhaps it was societal pressure. He thought that to achieve the level of success he did, being a tyrant was expected of him."

The top of my scalp tingled, as if a thought was about to be downloaded.

Suddenly Sam's pickup sped up the dirt driveway, the engine revving. Eric and I turned as he skidded to a stop behind my car. Sam hopped out and walked up to us, greeting me and giving Eric a fleeting glance and a head nod. I put the items back into the bag and handed it to Eric. I was cognizant of Sam's eyes on me.

Eric tenderly took the bag from me, tilted his head and with a smile said, "Thank you, Lilian."

I blushed, lowered my head and managed to squeak out a quick, "You're welcome."

Sam cleared his throat. I looked up at him.

"Sorry to interrupt," he said to me. "But can I borrow you a minute?"

"Sure, Sam."

Sam gently took me by the elbow and led me off to the side, out of earshot of Eric, who continued standing next to my car, hands pocketed and smiling at me.

"Bye, Eric," I called to him. "I'll see you later."

Eric waved. "Until then, Lilian."

I turned my attention back to Sam. "Where's the fire, Sam?"

"Sorry, Lil. I had to talk to you."

"What is it?"

"I wanted to apologize about the other night. At Donovan's. It was a bad idea, going there. I shouldn't've suggested it and I'm sorry."

"It's okay, Sam ..."

"It's not."

I sighed and admitted to myself that it really wasn't. Sam had made a lot of bad decisions that night.

"Too many memories for me there. You know that. I can't ... there are some things I'm not ready to face yet. I will. I mean, I have to. But not yet."

"Yeah, I know."

"Not to mention the fact that you were drunk. You were already drunk when you got there."

"I was not," Sam said, and I gave him a look. "Okay. I might've had one or two before meeting you."

"Is your drinking going to be a problem? I can't have you going off the rails again. There was a lot more at stake last time, but still ..."

"It's not going to be a problem. I promise." He put both hands on his heart and, with his eyes, implored me to forgive him. On the surface, I forgave him. But somewhere deep down inside, I felt like I couldn't buy it.

When Sam made no attempt to get to work and continued to stand there staring at me, I said, "Something else urgent on your mind?"

"There's something else. We've got a bit of an issue."

Just then Miguel, Big Al's journeyman electrician, burst out the front door and came pounding down the porch steps in a panic.

"What is it?" I said, taking a fleeting glance as Miguel made his way to his car.

"Miguel!" Sam called out. "Wait a sec! One minuto. Uh, por favor!"

Miguel nodded and said something under his breath. He took his hat off and nervously played with it while pacing before his car.

"Miguel quit," Sam said.

"What? When?"

"He called me about twenty minutes ago, ready to walk off the job. I told him to stay put and not leave until I got here."

I stole a glance at Miguel and then at Eric, who was watching the scene unfold.

"We don't have time to replace him," I said. "We've got to talk him into staying."

"Why do you think I'm here?"

"Okay, Sam. Okay. Let's deal with this. Miguel!" I called to him.

Miguel stopped pacing and looked up at me.

"La casa. Ahora!" I said.

He shook his head violently.

"Cinco minutos, por favor," I said to him.

Miguel paced for a few more seconds. Then, in an act of submission, forced his hat back on his head and shuffled into the house behind us.

The three of us gathered in the parlor, which at this point was just a storage space for construction materials—old things to be carted out and new things to be installed.

"Qué pasó?" I said to Miguel. "What happened?"

Miguel stared at the floor and said nothing.

"Did you have a fight with someone?" Sam tried.

"No," he said meekly.

Just then a worker passing through the vestibule saw the three of us standing in the parlor and loudly called to us. Miguel gave a start, looked over his shoulder, then in every direction around him as if watching out for something. He looked genuinely spooked.

"Do you not like the work?" I said. "El trabajo?"

"No es el trabajo. Me gusta."

"Well, if you're getting along with everyone, and you like the work, then I'm at a loss."

Miguel lowered his head again,

Sam leaned over and whispered in my ear, "I just remembered he kept saying something about 'el lago' on the phone."

"El lago?" I said, louder than I anticipated.

Miguel's head snapped up, his eyes wide.

"The lake? As in that lake?" I said, pointing outside. I turned and looked out the bay window. Eric stood at the lake's edge, hands in his pockets, his back to the house. I lowered my hand and watched him for a minute. He turned his head to the right, as if to look over his shoulder. Then he slowly faced forward again, overlooking the expanse of the lake. In that moment if felt to me like he knew I was talking about the lake, knew I was watching him, and that he wanted me to know it. I turned back to Miguel.

"Are you afraid of water?" I said.

"Don't know how to swim?" Sam said.

As Sam and I peppered him with questions, Miguel became noticeably more agitated, shaking his head and saying no after each question.

Suddenly an image of Oskar Becker floating in the lake flashed in my mind.

"There's something in the lake," I said under my breath. In that moment, it made no sense, but that exact phrase was implanted into my brain, and in that instant I knew it to be true, even if it didn't make sense to me at the time.

There's something in the lake.

Miguel heard me because he stopped saying, "No, no, no" and started saying, "Sí, sí, sí." He gesticulated wildly, both hands towards the lake.

"Did you say there's something in the lake?" Sam said. Miguel was firing off in Spanglish as Sam and I spoke amongst ourselves for a few seconds. "What the hell are you talking about, Lil?"

"Give me a minute, Sam."

"Senora! La casa, el lago ... es no bueno!" Miguel interrupted.

"What's no good?" Sam said. "What's going on?"

"Sam?" I said, grabbing his arm. "A minute. Please."

"Miguel, escuchame," I said, motioning for him to calm down. "Listen to me."

"Hay espiritus!" he added. "Este lugar esta maldito!"

"Entiendo," I said. "I understand. You think there are spirits and a curse. And that there's something in the lake."

"Sí, Senora! Sí!"

"Nothing will hurt you, Miguel. La casa, el lago ... es seguro."

"No es seguro," Miguel said. "Es malo. Es ... es *malvado*." He emphasized the last word: Evil. He believed something evil was lurking in the house, or in the lake, or both.

"Hay otras, Senora," Miguel said. "Otras que lo sienten."

There are others who feel it.

"How many others?" I asked.

"Tres."

"Do they want to quit, too?"

"Sí."

"Christ, I can't afford to lose four of you," I said.

"*Four* guys want to quit?" Sam said, and I nodded. He paused a moment, thinking. Then he blurted out, "We'll pay you more. All of you. If you'll stay."

Miguel looked at me, then at Sam, then back at me.

I nodded in approval, then implored Miguel one last time in Spanish. "Trabajo, por favor. Nada te hara dano. Lo prometo."

I made a promise to Miguel that I wasn't sure I could keep. I said no harm would come to any of our crew members. But I didn't know yet what, if anything, we were dealing with. Ghosts in the house? Something in the lake? A curse? If it was true, did they have anything to do with the double walker? I needed help figuring it all out. So promise Miguel, I did.

And as Miguel walked away and back to work, I cursed myself for making that promise.

"Good job back there, Lil," Sam said, once Miguel was safely out of earshot. "I didn't know you knew all that Spanish."

"Eh, picked it up here and there over the years. You're the one that saved the day by offering them more money."

"Hey, money talks," Sam said, shrugging. "So what were the two of you talking about?"

I told Sam the truth, but I was careful with it. I didn't need him freaking out over something I couldn't substantiate yet. Not that he would believe any of it. But I couldn't take that chance, in case he did take it to heart. His drinking was bad enough.

"Oh, just some silly superstition. No big deal."

"Miguel said something about the house being bad? My Spanish isn't as good as yours, but I understood that part. What's he mean, the house is bad ..."

"He thinks the house is haunted."

Sam laughed. "Haunted? Like, ghosts and stuff?"

"Yep."

"That's crazy. There's no such thing as ghosts."

"He believes in them."

"Well, don't you worry, Lil. I'll protect us. I'll keep my eye on the *ghosts*." Sam chuckled and rolled his eyes.

"Keep them in line, Sam," I said, playing along. "So, you gonna be here for awhile?"

"Yeah."

"Good. I've got some paperwork to do. And I'm going to pay Frank Jones a visit, see if I can scrounge up any more history on this place. You can hold down the fort, right?"

"What do you think I've *been* doing?" he said.

"Yeah, I know. Thanks."

Sam made his way upstairs to check on the progress being made in the bathrooms, and I walked out to my car. Eric was still staring out at the lake, deep in thought. I called out to him, saying goodbye as I got in and started the engine. He turned to me, waved, and gave me the sexiest, most suggestive of smiles. Somewhere deep within, I quivered at the very thought of him, of being with him. I sat with the car idling as we eyed each other from across the driveway.

Who are you? I thought to myself.

How do you look like Kevin?

Why don't I want to trust you?

But why do I still want you in spite of it?

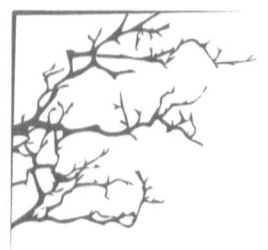

CHAPTER FOURTEEN

THE PENNSGROVE HISTORICAL Society building is located, appropriately enough, inside a historic, late 19th-century house on Main Street, downtown Pennsgrove. Main Street itself is lined with similar such old buildings, which were once homes, and were converted into doctor's and dentist's and lawyer's offices in the 20th century. The first and second floors of the historical society are filled with exhibits and historical artifacts, intermingled with 19th century Victorian-era furniture, all to sell the feeling that you're walking back in time when you step through the front door.

The front door has an old-fashioned bell attached to the top that chimes every time the door opens and closes. It rattled when I opened the door and made my way into what was once the foyer, but had since been converted in a reception area.

Frank Jones, the historical society president, sat at a desk towards the back right corner of the reception area, staring at a computer screen. When he heard the chime, he looked up and smiled.

Frank and I went back a couple years—back to the time when Kevin and I were thirty-somethings, several years into running our business together, and we decided (I decided, actually) to remodel our first—and last—older home. We'd met Frank on several occasions after that, on behalf of clients whose homes we were renovating, when we needed blueprints or information.

Because he was a talker, I felt like I knew him pretty well. It's like every time we met he filled me in on a new decade's worth of his life. So I knew, for example, despite only having encountered him sporadically over fifteen-plus years, that he'd fought in Vietnam, been married to his wife Nancy for fifty plus years, had raised six kids and buried two, had fifteen grandkids, held only three jobs upon release from the army before retiring, and that his love of history had led, during retirement, to him becoming the historical society president, a position he'd held for as long as I knew him.

The fact that he'd gone to school with Emma Becker put him in the eighty-year-old range. It also meant he might know a lot about the Becker family.

"Well I'll be a monkey's uncle," Frank said, looking at me over his glasses. "Lilian O'Shea!"

"Hi, Frank."

He stood and placed his glasses on the desk and walked over to me. "Been a long time, Lil. How's my favorite home renovator?"

"I'm good, Frank."

"No, you're not. Your husband just died."

The other thing I knew about Frank was that he could be, well, frank. It was disconcerting if you were meeting him for the first time. He could make you feel uncomfortable with his personal, prying questions, and offend you with his blunt, seemingly insensitive comments and inquiries. The first time Kevin and I met him, in fact, we'd stood in almost the same spot inside the historical society building, introduced ourselves as newlyweds starting our own renovation business, and told him we might be involved in old home projects in the future, so, of course, we might be asking for his help from time to time.

I'll never forget Frank's response. "Well, I guess you two will be wanting to make babies now, huh? That's what most people do after getting hitched, me and my wife included. Don't set your sights on having six like us, though. Too hard to balance work and life. One or two ought to do ya."

I thought the comment was hysterical; Kevin thought it was rude and presumptuous, which it was, but that was why it was hysterical. But it was also oddly sweet, and had a dollop of sound, endearing advice.

As we left the historical society that day, Frank had said, "All the other renovators in town do shit work. We need a good one around here. So I'm really rooting for you kids."

Love it or loathe it, that was Frank's way of welcoming you to the neighborhood. And that was Frank Jones in a nutshell: equal parts sweet and sour. Once you got used to it, you were used to it.

"I am truly sorry to hear about Kevin," he was saying to me now. "I read about it in the paper."

"Thanks, Frank."

Frank smiled softly and nodded. "You know, Lilian, when you're my age, the obituaries are the first section of the newspaper you read. Sometimes they're the only part you read. You get so damn depressed you can't keep going. That's how I felt the day I read about Kevin."

I cleared my throat and blinked back a few tears.

"Hey, do you remember the Hiller property?" Frank said, giving me time to compose myself. "That Georgian house on the edge of town? Such a rare gem, that one."

I remembered the Hiller property. It had been built in 1742 by a wealthy Philadelphia merchant named Joseph Hiller as a summer home for his family. The house looked like it had leapt off the pages of a British architectural building manual, with its symmetrical arrangement of windows and doors, all-stone exterior, and formal, classical interior details. It was intact but shabby and needed mostly cosmetic touches inside and out. It had been the first and only Georgian-style home Kevin and I had renovated. In fact, it was the only old home Kevin had relented on after I'd practically begged him to take the job.

The oldest homes, the truly historic ones, like the Hiller house and even The Property, were rarities in my portfolio. Most of the homes Kevin and I had remodeled over the years were newer Cape Cods or Colonials.

"A young family lived there at the time when you renovated it, if I remember," Frank said. "They had no idea what they were getting themselves into. A place like that?" He whistled and shook his head. "That family still live there?"

"I couldn't say, Frank. We do the job and then we move on."

"I suppose so. So, what can I do for you?"

"My associate came in about two weeks ago. Sam Hunter?"

"I remember the fella. Mentioned you two were working on the old Becker place. Took a blueprint from me."

"Right. That's why I'm here, actually."

"Something else you need?"

"Information on the Becker family."

"Uh-huh. I see. You sure about that?" He was silent for moment, and it felt like he was inspecting my face for signs that I was ready to accept the information. "Because your partner wasn't ready."

"What do you mean?"

"What I mean is, I tried to offer Sam the same information I'm about to offer you, but, well ... he didn't seem interested."

"Oh, he didn't tell me that."

"Just wanted the blueprint so he could be on his way. A bit impatient, that one. And moody to boot."

"Aw, he's an alright guy, Frank."

"He'd better be, if he's going to be working on the Becker place."

"Now you're just scaring me."

Frank walked around to the other side of the desk and sat down. He donned his glasses and motioned for me to sit in the chair opposite him.

"You know, Lilian," said Frank, "one of my favorite sayings comes from Theodore Roosevelt. He said, 'The more you know about your past, the better prepared you are for the future.'"

I sat down and put my bag on the floor next to me, contemplating this statement.

"You're going to need the information I'm going to tell you," Frank continued. "I feel duty-bound to let you know what you might be getting yourself into."

"Tell me everything you know," I said, suddenly apprehensive about the project. Even though I knew quitting wasn't an option; we were already too far down the rabbit hole.

"Do you need me to go back to the beginning, when the Beckers first got here?"

"I don't think so. I know Oskar Becker, Sr. emigrated from Germany and built the house in 1900. I know that he was ... mean. Tough on people. Wasn't very well liked."

"The man was an asshole."

I laughed. "Alright then, the man was an asshole."

"Not too many people were upset by his death, aside from his wife, brothers, and a few other family members. Most of his workers were happy to see him go."

"That's harsh, Frank."

"Just stating a fact."

"Let's not forget he built a very successful business that employed nearly this whole town."

"Don't get me wrong, Lilian. He was well-respected, but an asshole all the same. Now what else do you know about him?"

"Um, well, I know he shot himself, and was found by his wife the next day, floating in the lake."

Frank shook his head. "The man was a jerk, but still, it's a shame how he met his maker."

"Read about that in some online archive. Sounds like a cover-up to me, though. His obituary said he died of melancholia. I really had to dig to find the suicide part."

"Not exactly a cover up. But not an open admission, either. Oskar was having financial difficulties near the end. The Great Depression decimated the business. The Depression destroyed a lot of lives, as you know. Including Oskar's. Apparently he just couldn't handle the stress of it. And as you can imagine, suicide wasn't really discussed back then."

"I figured as much. That his cause of death might've left a stain on the family legacy so they kind of skirted around it."

"That they did. Went with the classic 'melancholia' cause of death instead."

"He left behind a wife and three children, one of which was Emma's father, right?"

"Yes. Oskar, Jr."

"I was told you know Emma?"

"Emma and I went to school together. She was three grades ahead of me, but we were friendly. Our families knew each other, hung in the same social circles, so we saw each other often enough. We lost touch, hell I lost touch with everyone, when I shipped off to Vietnam in '68. Came back four years later and everything had changed."

"How so?"

"My brother had eloped and moved out west. My girlfriend secretly married someone else while I was gone. And Becker Bakery, the company that at one time had literally owned this town, had ceased all operations."

"Ceased all operations? As in, defunct?"

"As in completely bankrupt. In ruins. Sold to some food brand conglomerate for pennies on the dollar and disbanded."

"So that was the early '70s?"

"There abouts."

For some reason I hadn't put two and two together that the company wasn't in business anymore. I hadn't bothered to Google the actual Becker Bakery name to see if there was a company website. I just assumed it was still operating, just under a different business model, like wholesale only or online only, since they didn't seem to have any more retail locations in town. Growing up, Becker Bakery was a name I sometimes heard my parents talk about, and I remember eating their bread growing up, so I took it for granted they were still around.

"So I got back in touch with Emma after Vietnam," Frank was saying as I was coming out of my memory fog. "I'd always been sweet on her. Boy, the legs on her ..." He whistled and shook his head. "But she didn't want anything to do with me, or any other man, apparently."

"Who took over the business when Oskar died?" I asked.

"The middle brother, Karl. He was a co-founder along with Oskar. Karl ran it until he died."

"When was that?"

"Karl died in 1938, five years after Oskar."

"How did Karl die?"

"He fell through the ice while skating on the lake. Died from hypothermia."

I took a moment to reflect on this coincidence, that both brothers' deaths involved the lake. I supposed much weirder things happened to families every day, but the Becker family was starting to prove itself anything but ordinary.

"Wow, that's...odd," I said.

"Just wait. It gets better," Frank said, raising his eyebrows. "So now two brothers are dead, and the youngest brother, Walter, takes over. He's already in his late sixties at this point, not really excited by the notion of being in control, but does it out of familial obligation. Walter ran the company for a little while, managed to remain profitable through World War II."

"That's quite an accomplishment."

"People say even though Walter didn't want the job, he was the best at it."

"What happened to him?"

Frank exhaled slowly. "That's a sad story. To tell it, I first have to tell you about Gabrielle."

"Who's Gabrielle?"

"Walter's granddaughter. The absolute apple of his eye. He made no bones that she was his favorite grandchild. She accidentally drowned on the property."

"Oh, no. That's awful. Like, in the bathtub?"

"No. She drowned in the lake."

I hadn't seen that one coming, and the shock of it sent me to the edge of my seat. "She drowned in the lake," I said, leaning in close as if I hadn't heard him properly. But I'd heard him just fine.

"While swimming with her older brother and cousins. She was ten-years-old."

"You're telling me three Becker family members died in or near the lake?"

"That's what I'm telling you, Lilian."

I mean, even one death-by-lake is too many, but multiple? What was going on? Sam said our flooring guy Bob was mesmerized by the lake, couldn't take his eyes from it... Sam himself had his own trance-like experience while standing in front of it...Miguel was freaked out over the lake and nearly quit... And as Sam and I were convincing Miguel to not quit, Eric had stood by the lake, his stance strong and authoritative, as if lording over it...

Frank continued talking, seemingly not noticing, or perhaps not caring, that he didn't have my full attention. I was still stuck in my own head.

"Walter resigned the day after Gabrielle died, citing age and health reasons. But people closest to him knew the truth, that the spark of life left him when Gabby died. The business existed for about thirty more years after that. Thirty unremarkable years, really. Blah blah blah you know the rest."

Eric hadn't told me any of that history. Especially not the family deaths tied to the lake. All he had chosen to share was the bit about Oskar emigrating from Germany and starting a bakery, and how it'd been a huge success. The end.

In all fairness, it was none of my business. I was just there to renovate his family's house. He didn't need to tell me much of anything. But he didn't exactly feel the need to tell me any more than he had, either.

But Frank did.

We'd arrived at the crux of the conversation, which provided the perfect opportunity for me to ask what I really wanted to know, why I wanted to meet with Frank in the first place.

"You told Sam the property is a hellhole."

Frank laughed. "I did call it a hellhole, didn't I?"

I nodded. "Hellhole because the place is falling apart?"

"Places that are falling apart—I call them shitholes. This place is a hellhole. And I'd tell you to stay away, but it's too late for that."

"Jesus, Frank. What are you trying to say?"

He leaned forward and looked me dead in the eye. "The place is cursed."

"Cursed," I said as neutrally as possible.

"The house, the lake, the property ... cursed. It started with the family, because of all the tragedy and death and misfortune."

"Do you believe that?"

"You've been renovating there for a few weeks now. You tell me."

I exhaled loudly and thought for a moment. Things *were* starting to get a little weird...

"Can you honestly tell me you haven't seen or heard—or felt—anything strange?" Frank said, seemingly determined to get an answer out of me.

"Maybe? I don't know. Maybe it feels like something's not quite right. But cursed?"

Frank raised his eyebrows and shrugged. "Becker family curse, Lilian. It's been a local rumor for decades."

"Have you had any strange experiences there?"

"Nope. But that's only because I won't go within a hundred yards of that place. Never have, never will. Call me superstitious, but...not worth the risk."

Eric's comment about Frank spinning tall tales popped into my brain, followed by Sam's insistence that Frank was a harmless old man. I could see both arguments—Eric trying to protect his family legacy from any more damage, and Sam just wanting to call a duck a duck.

I glanced at my watch. Time to go, as I still had a few things to accomplish on my to-do list. I stood, gathered my bag and said, "You've definitely given me a lot to think about."

He stood, walked around the desk and we made our way to the front door. "The more you know about the past, the more prepared you'll be for the future," he said, winking. Then, looking pensive he said, "Be careful, Lilian. There's a darkness surrounding the Becker place. And the Beckers themselves."

I extended my hand. "Thanks for your time, Frank."

We shook hands and Frank said, "I'm going to need that blueprint back when you're done with it. It's the only copy of the original we've got."

"We're done with it. Sam or I will get it back to you."

"You don't need it anymore?"

"Eric Becker had the original blueprints from 1900, if you can believe that."

Frank furrowed his brow. "I don't believe that, actually."

"Why?"

"Because Eric Becker's been dead for fifty-two years!"

"What? He's not dead, Frank. He's—"

"Been dead since 1968."

"We must be talking about two different Eric Beckers. I'm talking about Emma's nephew. About my age. Blonde hair, blue eyes ..."

Frank was shaking his head. "Emma Becker doesn't have any nephews, let alone one named Eric."

"I just saw him an hour ago!"

"Well, I'm telling you that if Emma Becker has a nephew, I've never met him."

"So then who are you talking about?"

"Oskar Jr. had a son named Eric, born in 1912. Lived a bit of a rough life. Died of cirrhosis of the liver in 1968."

"That makes sense," I said. "I saw an old family photo recently. Dated 1928. There was a tall, lanky kid in the photo with what looked like blondish hair wearing overalls, identified as Eric Becker. Based on the dates you're telling me, that would've made Eric sixteen in the photo."

"Yep, that's him. That's Eric Becker." Then for emphasis, Frank said, "The one and only Eric Becker."

That's when I felt the first twinge, my left temple this time—a warning sign that a tsunami of a headache was coming. I didn't have much time.

"Then who have I been communicating with for weeks now?"

"Lilian, there is no other Eric."

Frank and I stood there staring at each other, each resolute that we were right. I had no more time or energy to discuss the matter further. I had to go.

"Thanks again, Frank."

"No hard feelings, Lilian." He held up his hand. "Stop in again soon."

I hurried away from the historical society, full of more questions than when I'd arrived.

CHAPTER FIFTEEN

I ARRIVED AT THE PROPERTY the next day to find Sam huddled in the corner of the kitchen with the kitchen and bath installers. Luckily for us ,their company did HVAC, electrical and plumbing too, so they were our one-stop-shop, of sorts.

The kitchen wasn't large, which was typical for a turn-of-the-century Victorian home. Kitchens back then didn't get as much attention as other rooms in the home, and comfort wasn't a factor in their design. Kitchens were merely workshops, a place to perform the basic function of cooking in order to keep the family fed. So they didn't need to be large; they needed to be compact. This was so the lady of the house, or the cook, need only take a few steps in any direction to grab anything needed. Convenience and time-saving were the biggest factors that influenced kitchen design in early 20th-century America.

Sam and I had decided to remove a non-load-bearing wall in order to expand the kitchen, make it more spacious, and to create the open concept so many people seemed to want in their homes. Removal of the wall also allowed easier access to the dining room, and the two rooms would blend seamlessly together.

Our crew was going to leave the kitchen for last. They'd already started work on the bathrooms on the second and third floors, and planned to work on the plumbing and electrical throughout the rest of the house as they went. Timeframe: six weeks?

As I arrived, seven workers, including Sam, were just wrapping up going over timeframes and building materials.

Sam greeted me when I walked into the kitchen. "We're still on the third floor bathroom, and the bathroom at the end of the hall on the second."

"The guys know which wall tile and flooring goes in which bathroom?"

"We're about a week in. They oughta know."

"Fixtures and paint colors?"

"Yeah, Lil. We got it."

"What about the new hot water heater for the basement? We'll need to work on that sooner rather than later, as the bathrooms get installed and we turn the water back on."

"We'll install that at some point. We'll probably work on the new HVAC unit at the same time, while we're down there. We're not overly concerned about that since it's spring, and the house seems to be at a constant temperature."

"Sounds good, Sam."

"So how'd it go with Frank? Learn anything interesting?"

"We discussed the history of the Becker family and the business, mostly."

"Sounds boring." Sam took a sip of something from a thermos that had been sitting on the counter. I wanted to assume it was coffee but...yeah. I decided to let it go.

"I also learned," I went on, "that three Becker family members died in or near the lake."

Sam nearly choked on what was in his mouth but managed to swallow. "What?" He cleared his throat. "Well, that's interesting ..."

"Yeah, something about a family curse." I wanted Sam to know what Frank and I had talked about, without lending it much credence. He was already dismissive of Miguel's opinion about the house being evil, so I didn't want to add fuel to the fire. And with Sam obviously drinking again, I knew he would be more prone to emotional outbursts.

"Family curse," Sam said calmly, nodding his head.

"But you know," I added, "It's like Eric said. Frank is probably just spinning tall tales."

Sam eyed me curiously. "Speaking of Eric, did he come up at all during your chat?"

Shit. How was I going to be nonplussed about this one?

"Oh, well...yeah. Apparently Eric Becker doesn't exist."

Sam slowly placed the thermos back on the counter. "I don't understand."

"The Eric Becker that we know doesn't exist. There was only one Eric Becker in the whole history of the Becker's, the one we saw in that photo from 1928, and he died in 1968 of cirrhosis of the liver."

"How is that possible?"

I shrugged as Sam kept talking. "I mean, we've seen him, several times. In the flesh. And he introduced himself as Eric Becker. How can he not exist?"

"I don't know, Sam. Frank claims Emma doesn't have a nephew named Eric. He says there are no other Eric Beckers."

Sam's emotions went from confusion to now anger. He raised his voice. "How did Frank explain the fact that we've seen him?"

"He didn't," I said calmly. "He just said for us to be careful. That the house has dark energy, or something like that. I think he might've been kidding."

"Oh, great. Just fucking great. Dark energy? What the hell does that mean? Is Eric a goddamn ghost or something? Are we seeing ghosts now, Lil? Is he, like, one of the ghosts that Miguel is so scared of?"

Sam was pacing the floor now, running his hand through his hair. I hadn't seen him this agitated in a long time, and I'm sure the contents of that thermos were agitating him further.

"Aw, c'mon, Sam. I'm sure Frank was just messing with me." But Sam didn't seem to be listening.

"First Miguel and now Frank with the ghost shit." He stopped pacing and looked at me. "I'm not crazy, Lil. And neither are you. We're not seeing ghosts. All that stuff is bullshit. Eric Becker is as real as you and me!"

"I know," I said, regretting now the need to confess any of it to Sam. Why hadn't I just said that Frank and I had talked about boring family history stuff, and left it at that? "Frank didn't say anything about the house being haunted."

"No, but he thinks there's a family curse. Which is even more ridiculous."

Was it?

"Frank did say he tried to tell you—warn you—about the house. That you shut him down."

"Yeah, I shut him down. Resident ghosts...dark energy...a family curse? C'mon. None of it is our business, anyway. We're here to do a job." He leaned against the kitchen counter and took a few deep breaths. He was starting to calm down. Maybe we could have a rational conversation about it, after all.

"All this could affect our job, so maybe we ought to at least hear Frank out."

Sam blinked. "Are you saying you believe all this supernatural nonsense?"

"I mean, you did have that experience by the lake that you couldn't explain. And you've been saying all along that something wasn't right about Eric."

"Yeah, OK. I don't know what happened at the lake. But Eric? He's just a little strange, is all. Maybe he was dropped on his head as a kid or something. I don't think he's Casper the Friendly Ghost."

"So you don't think it's weird that our historian, who knows everything about this town and everyone in it, doesn't even believe he exists?"

"I don't know, Lil. Maybe Frank has dementia or something?"

I ignored that comment because I didn't believe that Sam believed that. "And you don't think it's odd that not one, but three Beckers died in close proximity to the lake? I mean, one of them was a ten-year-old girl!"

"It's tragic. Really. But evidence of a family curse?" Sam looked at me almost disapprovingly. "Since when did you start believing all this supernatural, superstitious stuff?"

Oh, I don't know. When I started getting Montana-sized headaches every time some truth was revealed to me out of thin air, with no obvious explanation? When Stella repeated, verbatim, my husband's dying words when she wasn't even there to hear them? When I met a man who so eerily resembled him to seem impossible?

"I'm not saying I believe any of it," I said. "I'm just repeating the words and knowledge of an eccentric old man. He might have dementia. His memory might be clear as a bell. Maybe he's just superstitious. Who knows."

Sam pushed off the counter, his mood seemingly lifted though I could sense his ongoing irritation. "Well, then. Nothing to worry about. Right?"

Just then Eric walked into the kitchen, stopping when he saw Sam and I. His timing was perfect, as usual.

"Am I interrupting?" he asked. "I'd like to speak with Lilian, if I may."

"Nah, we're done," Sam said. He walked up close to Eric and extended his hand. "Good to see you again, Eric." It sounded insincere and contrived, like he was trying to convince himself that Eric was indeed real.

"Likewise, Sam," Eric said, nodding his head and accepting Sam's hand. Sam put his other hand on Eric's shoulder and gave it a light squeeze. The two men stared at each other for a few seconds, shaking hands and smiling. As he left, Sam turned to me and said, "I'll be on the third floor if you need me."

Eric paused a moment, perhaps to give us a moment to finish any necessary goodbyes. Sensing none, he motioned for me to follow him. "There's something I'd like to show you," he said.

"Is everything okay? Something wrong with the house?"

"No, nothing like that."

We walked upstairs to the second floor landing, where we made an immediate left into the first of three bedrooms. Since no work was being done to this room yet, I hadn't been in here since the project started, or perhaps I would've noticed the change. The room had been outfitted with a twin bed with a simple metal headboard, a small side table with a lamp, and a square floor rug in front of the bed.

"What's this?" I asked.

"It's for you."

"Thank you, but I don't intend to spend the night here while construction's going on."

"Well, you never know," Eric said. "I've noticed that you stay late sometimes doing paperwork, once everyone has gone home for the day. So now, if it gets too late, you'll have a room of your own if you want to rest. Or do decide to stay over."

"How do you know that I stay late sometimes?"

He hesitated. "We've bumped into each other once or twice. Remember?"

I wracked my brain and fuzzily started to recall a time the week before, or maybe it was the week before that, when I'd said goodbye to the crew as they were leaving and it was just me standing outside on the porch alone and Eric had suddenly appeared when it was about six o'clock and ... wait. When was that again? If I was saying goodbye to the demo crew, it had to be about two to three weeks ago. But if it was the kitchen and bath guys, that was just last week.

I was suddenly having a brain freeze: all my days were blending together. But I sort of remembered that Eric had appeared from around the side of the house, and there was no other car in the driveway other than mine, so I'd assumed that he'd walked. And I think we started talking right away about something we were so focused on (the old pictures we'd found of the house? How Aunt Emma was doing?) that we never circled back around to how Eric had gotten to the house in the first place.

And actually, now that I think about it, I don't ever recall having seen Eric drive. He just always seemed to appear, usually when I was already in the house, so it made sense that I didn't see how he'd gotten there.

Which crew was I saying goodbye to on the porch that day? And when the hell was it?

"Lilian?" Eric said.

I looked up from the red rug on the floor and saw my dead husband standing in front of me. "Yes, Kevin?"

Eric paused and gave me an empathetic smile.

"I'm...I'm sorry," I said, realizing my error. "It's been a long day. Yes, I remember bumping into you a few times." My brain needed a moment to recover, which Eric seemed willing to give me as we stood in silence for a few more seconds.

Then suddenly I felt like my brain was officially done cycling through all these images and flashes of memory, sharpening its focus once more on the conversation at hand.

"I walk the house sometimes after everyone's left for the day," I said. "To make sure everything's okay. Then usually I'll do some paperwork at the kitchen counter."

"Of course."

"I hope you didn't go to too much trouble setting this up."

"No trouble at all," Eric said. "All things Aunt Em already had on hand."

"Please thank her for me. Or I will, when I speak to her next."

"She's very fond of you, you know. She feels like you're part of the family."

"Oh, that's very sweet. Your aunt is a special lady," I said. "Um, so, speaking of your family ..." I said. I wanted to take this opportunity to clear up a few misconceptions. Perhaps I could relay the information back to Frank and settle the score with him. Eric sat on one end of the bed and motioned for me to sit on the other.

"You know the three pictures we found?" I said, sitting on the bed.

"Aunt Em was so thrilled. She's displaying them in her room at the nursing home."

I smiled in acknowledgement. "One was a family portrait, dated 1928. One of the people on the porch was named Eric Becker."

"Ah, yes. Great-uncle Eric. Bit of a black sheep."

"Who was he?"

"He was the illegitimate son of Oskar Jr. and his mistress, Geraldine. Oskar Jr. was Aunt Em's father. He had Eric very young, many years before he met and married Aunt Em's mother, Mary. Geraldine was a wild one, the town tramp, but Oskar kept insisting they were in love, right up to the very moment she dropped a newborn Eric on the porch outside and made off with all of Oskar Jr.'s money."

"That's awful. I bet Oskar was devastated."

"Some say he never recovered from it. Loved and hated her until the day he died."

"What happened to her?"

"God only knows. Given what she'd done to Oskar, no one in the family tried to find her. She was never heard from again. Oskar did his best raising Eric by himself. By the time Mary came into the picture Eric was already in his late twenties, and Oskar Jr. was in his late forties."

"Was Eric a black sheep just because he was illegitimate?"

"Well, bastard children were frowned upon in that day and age, and sometimes treated cruelly by family. So, yes. But also because he was a troublemaker from the get-go, despite being surrounded by a loving family that accepted and raised him. They say he had his mother's devious ways in his blood, not to mention a lot of alcohol. Never learned to quit the bottle, in fact, and died quite young of cirrhosis."

"Were you named after him?"

"I was," Eric said, and laughed, probably realizing how ironic it sounded to be named after the troublemaking black sheep of the family.

"Why would your parents do that?"

"Well," Eric said, scooting closer to me on the bed. I looked down and noticed that I too had shifted positions and was sitting closer to Eric. The space between us was maybe two hands lengths. "Aunt Em said the family felt like they failed Eric. So they vowed to try harder with the next Eric."

"I guess that makes sense. And you turned out fine so I'd say your parents did a good job raising you."

We were now only one hands length apart, our knees nearly touching. I was playing with a strand of my hair and Eric was smiling so big and wide my own cheeks hurt. I caught a whiff of his scent and in that moment never realized before how good he smelled—like a mixture of soap, musk and woodsy tree essence. Kind of the way Kevin smelled. And the only thing preventing me from wanting to kiss Eric right then was the fact that he looked just like Kevin. Because if he looked like Kevin, and smelled like Kevin, well, I was too afraid to find out if he kissed like Kevin, too.

I subtly eased back onto my side of the bed. Eric kept smiling and made no similar move to adjust his position.

"I was sent to boarding school in Germany when I was five," Eric said after a beat. "The same school that my great-grandfather Oskar went to. I didn't set foot back on American soil until I was eighteen, and by then my parents were dead. So my parents never really raised me."

"Oh my God, Eric. I had no idea. I'm so sorry." Instinctively I reached my hand out and touched his hand and we looked at each other, and I felt connected to him. I knew his pain and he knew mine, and we shared our separate losses together.

Just then I heard a voice echoing out in the hallway.

"Lil? Hey, Lil?"

The voice grew louder, accompanied by approaching footsteps.

"Lil? There's something I gotta show you! Where are—"

I looked up. Sam was standing in the doorway, his eyes wide, looking frozen mid-step.

"What's going on?" he said, now sounding angry.

I retreated my hand and shot up from the bed. "Oh, hey Sam."

"Everything okay in here?" he said, looking between me and Eric, who continued sitting on the bed.

"Yeah, Sam. Everything's fine."

There was a brief pause when none of us spoke, and Eric finally stood up and said, "Well, I should go. Lilian, it was a pleasure talking to you, as always." Then he walked to the door and nodded at Sam. "You're doing a great job with the house, Sam. It's coming along nicely. Aunt Em and I are very happy with the work you're doing."

With that, he slowly walked downstairs.

Sam watched him descend the stairs, then turned his attention back to the bedroom. He looked around at the new furnishings but made no comment about them. "Yeah, so, you got a minute?" he said. "Something I, uh, something I need your opinion on."

As I followed Sam upstairs to the third-floor bathroom and the cracked porcelain tub neither of us had noticed before, and as he asked me if I wanted to change design ideas now that we needed a new tub anyway, I thought to myself:

Don't you dare, Lilian. Don't you dare fall for Eric Becker.

CHAPTER SIXTEEN

A FEW MORNINGS LATER, I awoke at 3:44 a.m. from a dream that The Property had been lost to fire. The house was engulfed in flames, obscured by thick plumes of smoke. Eric stood on the porch smiling, his hand raised in greeting, seemingly unaware of the imminent danger. There were other family members standing around him: Oskar Sr. and Oskar Jr. and the other Eric Becker and all the faces I recognized from the family photo. Aunt Em was there, too. Even though we'd never met and I didn't know what she looked like, I knew it was her. She beckoned to me, waved for me to join them on the porch as it burned and splintered and crackled under the heat of the flames.

I approached the house from the dirt driveway where I stood, compelled to join them, wanting to meet the Beckers at long last, having read and heard so much about them. I wanted to hug them, shake their hands, ask them if all the stories were true.

The house was ablaze and it was beautiful, like a painting, a canvas I wanted to walk into. I didn't hear the roar of flames, couldn't smell the asphyxiating smoke, couldn't feel the intense heat on my skin. All I heard was silence, and all I felt was perfection.

Perhaps that was the lure. All my senses had been muted so that I could approach them, so that I wouldn't feel or taste or hear or smell what would certainly be my death—so I wouldn't be scared of it. Because I knew, just then, that's what I was meant to do: join the Beckers in hell and die for my sins, just as some of them had died for theirs.

They all welcomed me, smiling, as I stepped onto the porch, and looked at each other and nodded. They seemed relieved that I was there, as if I completed some picture. I turned to Aunt Em, more curious than scared, and I said, "Where do we go now?"

They outstretched their arms in unison and pointed toward the lake. I turned and saw that the lake, too, was on fire, white sheets of mist rising from the low-lying flames.

"With your sacrifice all is forgiven there," Aunt Em said to me, still pointing at the lake.

"When I go, please tell Kevin I'm sorry," I said to her, and she nodded. Eric took my hand and asked if I was ready. I said I was.

"Please tell Kevin I'm sorry," I repeated, this time to Eric. He smiled but said nothing, so I said again, more forcefully, "Please tell Kevin I'm sorry."

And as he led me off the porch, his hand in mine, a burst of black smoke blinded me and I jerked awake. Tears ran down my face as I came to, and the words "Please tell Kevin I'm sorry" tumbled out of my mouth.

I rolled over, buried my face in a pillow and succumbed to the grief.

"Please tell Kevin I'm sorry," I sobbed to the empty room.

I knew it meant nothing, the dream, but in my moment of weakness, several minutes after the sobbing had stopped, I composed a text and hit *Send* before I had a chance to rethink it, and without even knowing what time it was.

Sorry to wake you ...

Sam's reply came barely a minute later: *I'm awake. Can't sleep. You okay?*

Yes. How's The Property?

House is fine. Why?

Just a nightmare. Tell you later.

Sorry. Everything fine. Don't worry. I got you.

I know you do, Sam.
Go back to sleep.
Zzzzz ☺

THE DREAM STAYED WITH me all day, an uneasiness gnawing at me that I couldn't shake. Yes, I'd made a mistake, but a sin? I'm not religious so I didn't necessarily believe in sins, per se. But the dream seemed to suggest that I needed to repent for my mistake or I would burn in hell. Did hell even exist? I wasn't sure I believed in that, either. I told myself that the dream meant nothing, just stress, but still the unshakable feeling persisted.

The uneasiness continued as I drove to the Historical Society later that day to see Frank. I'd been looking forward to killing two birds, returning the blueprint copy and telling him that yes, Eric Becker did exist.

Helen sat at the desk in the foyer when I entered, her hands massaging her temples, her eyes closed. When she heard the doorbell chime, her head snapped up and she gave me a weak smile.

"Lilian, honey." She wiped her eyes and nose on a tissue and rose to greet me. She sniffled a few times and cleared her throat. "So nice to see you again."

My head started tingling, and I knew something was very wrong. "You too, Helen. You, uh, you're volunteering today?"

"Unexpectedly, yes," she said, and her lips pursed and she looked like she was fighting back tears. She cleared her throat again and composed herself. "What have you got there?"

"A copy of the blueprints from the Becker estate. Frank loaned them to me." I looked around for signs that Frank was there.

Helen blinked at me grimly. "Lilian, honey. Have a seat, would you please?"

We both sat and she looked at me and sighed. She pulled a tissue from the box sitting on the desk as her face crumpled into a red mask of grief.

"Frank, um ... Frank passed away two days ago," she said.

"What? He's ... he's dead?"

Helen dabbed at her eyes. "Heart attack. He just ... apparently he just... well, it was very sudden."

"Oh, my God. Oh, Helen. I'm so sorry. I know you were close ..."

And as Helen kept talking, the tingling at the top of my skull grew more intense, and I felt a twinge in my right temple.

"He was at home," Helen said. "His wife was with him when it happened." She blew her nose and reached for another tissue. "His wife and doctors said they couldn't understand it. He was the picture of health."

"That is...strange. Is there going to be a funeral? Sam and I would like to pay our respects."

Helen showed me his online obituary, which indicated that Frank Jones had died of natural causes on the morning of May 5, 2020. He was to be cremated, his ashes interred during a private ceremony at Woodlawn Cemetery on May 8th. Flowers and gifts of condolences were welcome.

"Cremated ..." I said. The twinge in my right temple turned to a throb and I felt like that detail, his cremation, was somehow important. "Helen, are you the Jones' estate attorney?"

"I am," she said, dabbing her eyes and looking at me curiously. "Why?"

"This is probably none of my business, but was there anything in writing expressing Frank's wishes for final arrangements?"

"You're right, Lilian. That is none of your business."

"Please, I think it might be important."

Helen hemmed and hawed for a minute or so, and finally relented with a sigh. "Both Frank and his wife, Claudine, have final wishes. He wanted to be buried in Woodlawn Cemetery next to his parents, and Claudine will be next to Frank. The Jones' already had the burial plots paid for."

"Buried," I said. "He wanted to be buried."

"Well, yes, his ashes will be buried in the plot."

"The obit says his ashes will be *interred*. Doesn't that mean something different?"

"Interment is a catch-all phrase that the funeral industry uses to indicate any final, permanent resting place."

"But do his final wishes go into detail as to whether his *body* will be buried, or his *remains* will be buried?"

"I ... I don't know, Lilian. Claudine said that Frank told her he wanted to be cremated. So she's going to honor his dying words."

My back stiffened at that revelation. "Dying words?"

"Yes, apparently as he lay there ..." She fought back tears. "... as he lay there, he said he wanted to be cremated."

I thought for a moment while Helen continued to dab her eyes. I couldn't shake the feeling that there was something more to this.

"Lilian, honey," Helen said after a beat. "Why does it matter? Frank is ... gone."

"I'll tell you why it matters, Helen. Because the exact same thing happened with Kevin. We have burial plots that his parents bought for us. Our final arrangements, as you know, stipulate that we're supposed to have public ceremonies, with our bodies buried in those plots. Our *bodies*. We didn't indicate that we wanted to be cremated."

"Yes, I remember you and Kevin were very specific."

"So then how come, as Kevin lay dying in our driveway, was he suddenly so adamant about being cremated?"

Helen blinked. "He ... he what? He said that?"

"Dying words, Helen. Just like Frank."

"You never told me that."

"I went against his verbal dying wishes and stuck to what we originally agreed to in writing."

"Oh, honey. I don't know what to say ..."

"There's nothing to say," I said. "It was the decision I made. But do me a favor: look again at Frank's request for final arrangements. See if there's something you missed."

"Why?"

"Because if it was clear and specific that his body was to be cremated, why would he waste his dying breaths telling his wife something she already knew?"

Helen stared at me a minute, puzzled and dazed. "I'll review it and let you know," she said finally. Then, "Maybe it's just a coincidence ... Kevin and Frank ..."

"If it had been just Kevin, maybe. But Frank, too? Passing away only weeks apart, and both requesting to be cremated?"

Helen let out a long breath.

"Listen, can you keep this between us, please?" I implored. "It could wind up being nothing, but I don't want this getting out."

"Okay. Sure, Lilian."

I had a pile of paperwork yet to tackle and a headache that was needing my attention, so I nodded and thanked Helen for her time. She walked me to the door, taking a few deep breaths.

"So ... how's the Becker renovation going?" she asked, dabbing some lingering tears from her eyes. "The ladies here—and myself, of course—are very anxious to know."

"About as good as can be expected. It's an old house that's been neglected for some time, so it's going to take a lot of work."

"And such a big house, too," Helen added. "But so beautiful. I've been inside several times. Back when the Beckers used to host holiday parties." She gave me a weak smile and I could tell she was trying her best to gather her thoughts and pull herself together.

"I didn't realize they ever opened the estate to the public."

"Oh, that had to be at least thirty years ago now. Back before the family became so ... elusive. And they only did it for a couple years, by private invite only."

"Well, once it's all renovated maybe you'll get a chance to see it again."

"I highly doubt that. Emma's really the only one left, and, well, she's pretty much a recluse."

I didn't know if Helen knew the current state of Emma's health, or that she wasn't living there anymore, or that the house was empty. And it wasn't my business to pass any of that information on. So I left those facts unspoken, as well as my thought that Emma wasn't the most elusive Becker in the bunch. That award went to Eric.

But I did want to take the opportunity to bring him up. Frank had been convinced he didn't exist. And Helen, surprisingly, hadn't mentioned him when I told her I was tackling the project. She knew everyone in Pennsgrove, so surely she knew him, too? And if she knew he was the caretaker of the estate now, she would've mentioned that. I was hoping she wouldn't deny his existence too, because that could officially mean Sam and I were nuts, or seeing a ghost, or both.

"Emma's not the only Becker left," I said. "There's Eric, her nephew."

"Ah, yes. Eric. How could I forget that handsome devil?'"

"He's the one I've been dealing with, regarding the renovation."

"Reaaaally," she said, as if that was the most interesting piece of information she'd heard all day.

"Do you know him? Have you met?"

"We met once, about three months ago. At the Borough Hall meeting regarding the community day that's happening in July. I believe ..." She furrowed her brow and looked up at the ceiling a moment. "I believe Kevin was at that meeting."

"He was."

Helen waited for me to explain further and when I didn't, she continued.

"Well, anyway. Eric was there but didn't participate, just listened intently to the rest of the townsfolk. I approached him afterwards to introduce myself since I'd never seen him before. But when he said he was Eric Becker I nearly fell over!"

Because he looked just like Kevin O'Shea? I thought, while actually saying, "Because he wasn't what you were expecting?"

"Not at all!" Helen said. "He doesn't look anything like the other Beckers. He looks like he was adopted! The rest of them are all fair-haired, for the most part. And light-colored eyes. But Eric! That black hair and those dark eyes ...!"

Wait. What did she just say?

"Black hair. Right," I said. "I haven't, um, I haven't met any of the other Beckers, so I have no one to compare him to."

"Well, believe me when I tell you he looks like the black sheep of the family. Literally."

What was happening? How could the same person look like two different people? I tried to contain my confusion, to compose myself.

"You said that..." I started, then lost my train of thought. My mind was swimming with questions and possibilities. "Um, sorry. You said that was the first time you'd met Eric?"

"First time we met. Hard to believe, isn't it? I mean, I know *everyone* in this town. How did it take so long to meet him? The Beckers are elusive, but still..."

"Right," I said, drawing out the word in order to give myself time to think of more questions. "But you knew he existed?"

"I'd heard rumors he existed, but honestly I didn't believe it until we met."

"Did you talk long?"

"Only a few minutes. I got the sense he had just gotten into town. He hadn't been home long, something about living elsewhere for a long time. The details were fuzzy. He didn't elaborate."

It was entirely plausible that Eric hadn't lived in Pennsgrove for some time, and possibly the reason why Frank had never heard of him, or met him. (And let's face it: if Helen had never met him, it stood to reason that Frank hadn't either.) Maybe Eric had moved back home when Emma got sick. Who knew? Anything was possible. What I wondered most, though, was if Kevin had met Eric that night.

Kevin and I had heard about the community day event and thought of setting up a booth. Kevin had gone to the meeting to get information, hobnob a little, network. He was on the fence about it, for some reason, and I couldn't remember why. So we put it on the back burner and never came to a decision. It was one of many things left unsaid—and undecided—when Kevin died.

"... I joked the next day to our archivist that if only I was thirty years younger ..." Helen was saying when I pulled myself away from that moment in time and refocused on our conversation.

I laughed at Helens' joke and thanked her again for her time. As I was leaving the historical society and walking the two blocks to my car, I said to myself: Frank's death, however tragic, was weird timing. His insistence on being cremated, however coincidental to Kevin's request, was a fluke. And the dream? Just a dream. It means nothing. Absolutely nothing at all. The house is not going to burn down, and I will not have to suffer in the fiery pits of hell for my one instance of indiscretion.

If only I believed that. I tried my best to convince myself all that was true. But I was having a hard time of it, because I was starting to not believe in coincidences. I was starting to believe in double walkers and other supernatural phenomenon, and I was starting to believe that something was very rotten in Denmark.

And as I got into my car and turned over the engine I said, perhaps to the Universe more than myself, "More questions, more mysteries, and another fucking headache."

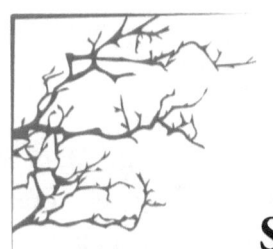

CHAPTER SEVENTEEN

JAKE WAS SITTING IN his car, scribbling in a spiral notebook when I arrived at The Property. I parked next to him in the driveway and we both got out of our cars.

"Hello, Lilian," he said. "Good to see you."

"Hey, Jake. Wasn't expecting to see you here."

He held up a thick manila envelope. "I had some final paperwork for you I thought I'd drop off. Figured you'd probably be here."

"You got the final paperwork back already?"

"A sole proprietorship is the simplest type of business structure that exists, so there wasn't as much paperwork as you'd think. Plus, it has been six weeks."

I listened to the sound of electric drills and buzzsaws and hammers as Jake's words sank in. It'd been six weeks already since Kevin died. I swear it felt like yesterday. And all the things that had happened in that period of time, too: the Property project falling in my lap, reconnecting with Sam, my strange visions and intuitions, Frank's death...

I must have been zoning out to the cacophony of construction noise, because when I looked up, I saw Jake's mouth moving but all I heard was the echoing sounds of power tools. Finally, my brain connected, and Jake's voice came into focus.

"Lilian?" he was saying. "Is everything alright?"

After a pause I said, "Sure, Jake. Just wondering where the time went."

Jake smiled and motioned to the house. "That's where your time went."

"Guess you're right. Hey, you want a tour?"

"That's the other reason I'm here, actually." When I gave him a funny look he said, "I've always been fascinated by this house. Ever since I was a kid." He looked over at the house, taking it all in. His eyes briefly scanned over to the lake, then settled back on me.

"Huh. I never knew that. This is the house of my dreams, yet I never knew it existed until Kevin and I were married."

"I know you love Queen Anne houses. Your dad did, too. Me, though?" Jake shrugged. "I have no idea where my fascination with old houses comes from."

"Maybe you were an architect or a builder in a past life," I said, half-jokingly, but also somewhat seriously because, well, I suddenly believed in all that shit now.

Jake made a face. "Okaaay."

"You know, maybe you failed as an architect or builder or had unfinished business as an architect or builder in a previous life, so you were reborn in this lifetime in order to fix the karma from that life."

"But I'm not an architect or a builder now. I'm a financial accountant."

"Doesn't matter. Could just mean you were involved with old structures in some capacity in a past life, which bled over into a love of old houses in this life."

"Well, I don't know about any of that. What I do know is that I've been fascinated with this house since we were kids and I've never seen the inside of it."

I laughed. "Well, that's a hint if I've ever heard one. C'mon." I lead Jake across the driveway and up onto the porch.

We walked through the entire house, excluding the basement because, well, there's nothing sexy about a dusty basement. Jake's mouth hung open the entire time, his head on a swivel, as if he was touring the Sistine Chapel. He thanked me for the tour and I thanked him for the paperwork and as I walked him to his car I said, "Hey Jake, can I ask you something?"

"Of course."

"When did you say Kevin came to see you about the term life insurance policy?"

He exhaled loudly and looked up at the sky, as if the answer was written among the clouds. "I want to say early February."

"Do you remember the exact date?"

"I don't, because he didn't have an appointment. He just showed up at my office. I do remember that."

"Oh, I hadn't realized that. Did you tell me that?"

"I didn't think to mention it. Sorry." I waved off his comment.

"That's odd, right?" I said. "The fact that he showed up without an appointment, wanting a life insurance policy out of the blue?"

"It was definitely out of character."

"Not to mention unprofessional and presumptuous of him. Expecting you to drop everything you were doing..."

Jake shrugged. "Well, hey. It was Kevin. I would've done anything for him. And you, of course."

"Thanks, Jake. I appreciate that."

"So...Are you still trying to figure out if Kevin knew about...you know...?"

"Yeah. I can't shake the feeling that he knew something bad was going to happen."

As I was talking, Jake's face changed, like he suddenly recalled something.

"What?" I said. "What is it?"

"I remember now. Kevin and I met the Monday after Groundhog Day. We made idle chit-chat about it when he first got there. Kevin said he was glad Punxsutawney Phil had seen his shadow over the weekend because that meant an early Spring, which is good for your business. I said Groundhog Day never usually falls on a Saturday, and I joked that even animals have to work weekends sometimes."

I chuckled. "Groundhog Day is always February 2nd ."

"Which was a Saturday this year. So I met with Kevin on Monday, February 4th."

Monday February 4th was the day after the Borough Hall meeting. The meeting Eric had attended.

Now I had to figure out what happened in the days or weeks leading up to Groundhog Day that would spook Kevin into paying Jake an impromptu visit. I couldn't think of anything else going on in our lives at that time, so I had to start with the Borough Hall meeting. Did one event cause the other? Did something happen at the Borough Hall meeting that caused Kevin to seek Jake's help?

"Lilian?" I heard Jake say. I looked up from the driveway and he was frowning.

"Sorry, Jake. What did you say?"

"I said does that help?"

"I don't know yet."

When Jake sensed I didn't want to elaborate he said, "Okay, well. I should be going. Thanks for the tour. You need anything else, you call me." He got in his car, turned the engine, and rolled down the window. "By the way, you're okay that I filed the death claim with the life insurance company, right?"

"Yeah, Jake. I told you that on the phone the other day."

"Just double checking. I'm concerned there's going to be a months-long delay in the payout, or God forbid a denial of the claim, so I wanted to get started sooner rather than later."

A life insurance company can delay, and sometimes outright deny a beneficiary payout, especially during what is known as the two-year contestability period. That's the two years right after a life insurance policy is bought, and death within those two years can automatically open the door for investigation due to suspicion of fraud.

I understood the principle, and I understood Jake's concerns. Hell, even I was suspicious of the fact that Kevin got a life insurance policy months before his death. And the last thing I needed on my plate was a fraud investigation.

"Don't worry, Lilian. I'll get our money....I mean, I'll make sure you get your money."

Jake smiled awkwardly and diverted his eyes. He maneuvered his car around the other vehicles and pulled away with a wave goodbye.

"Bye, Jake," I whispered to myself.

I pulled out my cell phone to search my calendar. I went back to mid-January and started swiping through each day, stopping when I reached Saturday, February 2nd. Groundhog Day. The Borough Hall meeting was on the calendar: Sunday, February 3rd. Monday, February 4th was blank.

Just then Sam came walking down the porch steps, followed by six or seven guys all leaving for the day. They said their goodbyes to each other, and to me, and I waved and watched them all disperse and drive away.

"There you are," Sam said. "Was wondering where you got to."

"LB Renovations is officially mine," I said, holding up the manila envelope.

"That's great, Lil."

"Sure it is."

"Don't sound so thrilled. So, uh, you got a minute? Got some things to run past you."

"Sure, Sam. What's up?"

"You hear about Frank?"

"I spoke with Helen yesterday at the historical society. She told me. I couldn't believe it."

"I was shocked when I saw it in the paper."

"The funeral's tomorrow. We should go."

"So sad," Sam said. "I liked Frank. I don't care what your boy Eric said about him."

"He's not my 'boy.'"

"He's got a thing for you, Lil. Don't think I haven't noticed."

"He does not."

"If you say so. Anyway, we should send flowers or something."

"I'll have an arrangement sent to the church," I said. "Anything else?"

"While you're at it, you might want to have an arrangement sent to St. Luke's Hospital."

"Why?"

"Ben fell down the first-floor stairs today."

"Jesus, Sam! Is he alright?"

"Just a broken ankle. He'll be alright."

"How did it happen?"

"Says he was pushed. There were two other guys with him, but they both swear they didn't touch him. Ben says he felt a hard push on his back. So who knows? They were probably horsing around and Ben tripped over his own feet. Nothing to worry about."

"Easy for you to say. Now I'll have a work comp claim to worry about." I sighed and rubbed my shoe in the dirt. "Why did I want to keep this company again?"

"Hey, if you don't want the responsibility, I'll take it off your hands," Sam said. "Buy it from you or something."

"You got the money for that?"

"Well, no. I'm struggling, but I'm, you know, doing okay."

"I know you are, Sam."

"If you wanted to sell, I'd find a way to buy it from you."

"You'd seriously want to own a company again?"

"Sure, why not? It would give me something to do. A new lease on life, as they say. Plus it would keep me in shape." He smiled and patted his stomach. Then he paused, and I could tell there was something else on his mind.

"What?" I asked.

Sam looked at the ground. "Nothing."

"What it is?"

"Well, it's just that ... another option is, we could, you know, run it together ..."

"We *are* running it together."

He exhaled and ran a hand through his hair. "You're right, we are," he mumbled.

My sudden discomfort caused me to avoid his eyes and instead look up at the house. There was a figure standing in one of the windows on the third floor. Was that a face? A man, in a black suit? Or was it one of our workers? I squinted to make sure I wasn't seeing things and continued to stare at the window, waiting for a flicker of movement. I closed my eyes and reopened them and the figure in the window was gone.

My cell phone rang. I pulled it from my back pocket. The caller I.D. said *Unknown* and I knew it was Emma. First, I'd take her call, then I'd search the house for whatever it was I'd seen in the third-floor window.

"I have to take this call," I said.

"Fine. I'll see you later," he said gruffly. He got in his pickup and drove away, leaving a swirl of dust in his wake.

"Hello?" I said. I started walking towards the house to escape the plume of dirt circling around my head.

"Lilian, dear? It's Emma."

"Hi, Emma."

"Oh, my. You sound so tired, dear."

"Yeah, well."

"Is everything alright?"

"I'm fine. Just tired, like you said."

"Where are you?"

"At the house. Everyone has left for the day and I'm here to check on things, like I usually do."

"That's just wonderful."

I walked through the front door and stood in the vestibule, listening. Absolute stillness and quiet. Early-evening sunlight illumined the first floor, shining through the rooms' large windows. I peered to my right and saw the soft glow of a night light emanating from the kitchen. There was still enough natural light for me to do my walk-through, but I decided a flashlight was in order in case some areas of the house were too dark—including the third floor, where I thought I'd seen the figure in the window.

"Why don't you go upstairs and take a nap?" Emma said. "That's why Eric set up that bedroom for you."

"Oh, no. I'll be alright. I'm just going to do a few minutes of paperwork while I'm here and then I'm going to go home."

"You could use that little desk Eric put in the bedroom for you. It's the perfect place for paperwork."

"What desk?" I said, grabbing a flashlight from the kitchen counter. "I thought there was only a bed and nightstand."

"Oh, my. I hope I haven't ruined the surprise. Go have a look, would you, dear?"

I climbed the steps and made the immediate left into the bedroom. There was a little desk and chair tucked into the opposite corner from the bed. A small lamp sat on top of the desk. I flipped the switch for the overhead light and got nothing.

I walked over to the lamp, pulled the cord and soft, white light encased the corner of the room. The room had power, so the bulbs in the overhead light must've been burned out. If I worked up here at night, it'd have to be in partial darkness.

"That was nice of you, Emma. Thank you."

"Completely Eric's idea."

"I'll be sure to thank him when I see him." I stifled a yawn and sat on the bed. It was more comfortable than I remembered, and the bedspread softer. I'd sit for a moment, finish my conversation with Emma, then search the third floor.

"I must be going," Emma said. "Oh, wait. Lilian?"

"Yes, Emma?"

"I want you to know that I'm very fond of you. Please remember that."

"I'm fond of you, too," I said, confused by her sudden emotion.

We said our goodbyes and I finally let the yawn out. I stared out the room into the darkness of the second-floor landing. The third floor was waiting for me, but so was this bed. This warm, soft, inviting bed. I let my bag slide to the floor and put my cell phone on the nightstand. Then I slowly slipped out of my shoes and put my head on the fluffy feather pillow.

The third floor, I said to myself. I'd seen a man in the third-floor window. I swear I had. I needed to search. But I just needed to lay here for a few minutes first. Not to sleep, just to rest. Just to clear my head. To convince myself Eric was real but my feelings for him were not. To tell myself I adored Sam and nothing more. To lie to myself that Kevin's decision to purchase a life insurance policy three months before his death was a complete coincidence.

To ... to ...

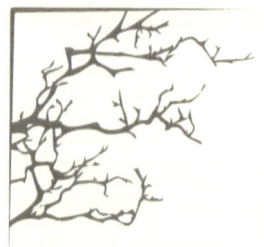

CHAPTER EIGHTEEN

... TO WAKE UP TWELVE hours later to the sound of drilling and hammering and sawing and loud voices echoing up from below. And to realize that I was still at The Property, and I'd just had the most blissful and most sound sleep I'd had in months.

I sat up and looked around the room. The desk lamp was still on. Suddenly, Sam appeared in the doorway.

"Hey, sleepy head," he said, and I jumped. "Oh, sorry."

"Is one of those coffees for me?" I asked, motioning to the two cardboard cups he was holding.

He handed me a coffee. "You sleep here all night?"

"I guess I did."

"Were you, uh, by yourself?"

"Of course I was by myself," I said. "What time is it?"

"Six."

"In the morning, I hope."

"Yeah, Lil. In the morning."

I stood and stretched and took a big swig of black coffee. Then I put the cup down on the nightstand to put my shoes on. "Love that everyone's getting an early start," I said.

"Thought you would," Sam said, looking out in the hallway before continuing. He lowered his voice. "Listen, Lil. I gotta tell you something ..."

He looked nervous and it made me nervous. His hand that held the coffee was trembling slightly. I could feel his emotions were all over the place.

"What's going on?" I asked.

"Well, it's just that ... most days I feel fine, you know? But other days I don't feel like myself. Physically, I'm good. But mentally?"

My scalp started to tingle. Some thought was working its way down into my third eye— something I needed to know, something I needed to be wary of, something I needed to fear.

"What are you trying to say?" I said.

"Lately I've been having these weird thoughts that aren't mine, and I get angry really easily which isn't like me, and the dreams ..."

Sam was rambling, and that could only mean he was nervous, or nursing a buzz, or both. He couldn't possibly be drinking this early.

"Someone spike your coffee, Sam?"

He gave me a look. "I'm being serious."

"Sorry. What weird thoughts?"

"Well, what if ... what if Miguel was right?"

"About there being spirits in the house?" I said. "Are you saying you believe the house is haunted? After literally just telling me the other day you don't believe in any supernatural stuff?"

"Maybe that's what I'm saying. Because I...I started seeing and hearing things recently. All of a sudden. Flashes of light, dark shadows, random voices and noises. One time I swear I saw a short man in a black suit walking up the stairs to the third floor."

My body started tingling all over and suddenly got very hot, like I was breaking out in a cold sweat. "What?" I said.

"I think I saw a ghost." He pointed behind him out into the hallway. "Walked right up those steps, right in front of me!" He paused. Then, sensing what I might say next he went on, "And I'm sober when these things happen, Lil. I don't drink on the job. You know that."

"I believe you, Sam. I ... I do." Now I was starting to freak out. Had Sam and I both seen the ghost of patriarch Oskar Becker? "Are there other workers here when these things happen?"

"I'm always alone." Sam took a swig of coffee and started slowly pacing the room. "I'm usually the first person here every day. I open up the house. Do a walk-through, like you do at night. Get things set up. You know, my normal routine." He paused and took another sip of coffee. His hand appeared to tremble more than before.

"And, you know," he said, continuing to pace, "if it happened once or twice I could say it was my imagination, or I was tired or something. But something is happening almost every damn day now. It doesn't make sense, Lil. I mean, what's wrong with me?"

"I don't think there's anything—"

"No, seriously!" Sam said, interrupting me. "I feel fine when I'm not here. But the minute I walk inside this ... this *place*"—he looked around the room with his hands skyward—"I feel ... different. Not myself. Like someone else is inside my body." He stopped abruptly and faced me, his eyes wide. "And oh, holy shit, the dreams, Lil! The dreams I've been having..."

Sam and I had possibly seen the same ghost. Were we having the same dream, too?

"Tell me about the dreams, Sam."

"This house burns down, right? Nothing sparks it. It just, I don't know, spontaneously combusts or something. After we'd just finished renovating it. That's the first dream."

Shit. Same ghost, same dream.

"Then I dream that you and I go back to inspect the damage and there's nothing left. There's just a big black scorch mark where the house should've been. It's like the house was never even there. The weirdest part is that the dream felt so real, like we were really here!"

I must've zoned out again, been lulled into a waking void like I had that time with Jake in the driveway, and all the other times before, because suddenly I looked up and Sam's mouth was moving but all I heard was hammering and buzzing and sawing. I could see Sam's lips saying my name repeatedly. My ears finally connected to his voice, and I was stirred awake and could hear him speaking.

"Lil?" he said. "Lil, are you listening?"

"Sorry, Sam. I'm listening."

Sam paused, his face a mask of concern. "What's wrong?"

"Nothing. I'm good. Go on."

He paused a few more seconds before continuing. "So then I dream that we go back to the house to make sure we weren't seeing things, that the house was still gone, and Kevin's there."

At the mention of Kevin, my hand jerked as I was taking a quick shot of coffee and caused a surge of coffee to flood my mouth. A few drops dribbled down my chin and I wiped them with the back of my sleeve.

"What was Kevin doing there?" I asked.

Sam scrunched his face. "It was a dream. How the hell should I know?"

"Okay, Sam. Okay," I said, gently giving his left arm a squeeze with my free hand.

"Sorry," he said, glancing behind him as if to make sure no one heard his outburst. He lowered his voice. "Kevin was standing by the lake. We approached him, and he said he'd been waiting for us."

"Are you sure it was Kevin, and not, maybe, Eric?"

"It wasn't Eric, trust me. It was Kevin's voice."

"How did he sound?"

"I don't know, Lil. Like himself. Kevin sounded like Kevin."

"I mean, was he happy to see us? Glad? Angry...?"

"He seemed ... neutral. Not happy or sad."

"So then what?"

"I woke up." He took a large sip of coffee, his hand still trembling.

"Oh," I said, hoping he'd received a little more information before waking.

"What's happening? The shadows, the voices, the apparition, the dreams ... am I losing my marbles?"

"Kevin has a message for us," I said out loud, without really realizing it, and without answering Sam's question. I'd been speaking to myself and not to Sam, but the words just came out. "Kevin was trying to communicate with you."

And just like that, the tingling on the top of my head stopped. I'd received my message: my intuition had delivered it to me, so my third eye could stop working on overdrive. I sat back down on the bed, as if sitting would allow me to absorb the large piece of information. Plus, despite twelve hours of uninterrupted sleep, I suddenly felt drained.

Sam drank the rest of his coffee, put the empty cup on the nightstand and sat down next to me.

"What the hell are you talking about, Lil? Kevin's ... Kevin's gone."

"His spirit, his soul, I mean. I think he has a message for you. He was communicating with you through your dreams. Or maybe you involuntarily astral projected here in your sleep."

Sam looked at me incredulously. "What?"

"Listen, Sam. You're the one who said the dreams felt real, like you were actually here, right?"

"The most vivid dreams I think I've ever had."

"So maybe your spirit and his spirit 'met' somewhere in order to communicate."

"You're saying I had like, uh, like an out-of-body experience type of thing?"

"Sort of, yes. That's one way to describe it."

Sam sighed heavily and ran his hand through his hair. "Christ, I don't know, Lil. It all sounds so out there."

"I know it all sounds far-fetched, but look—you must think there's something to it or else you wouldn't be so freaked out by all your experiences."

"I guess so," Sam said, looking defeated. "So, what was Kevin trying to tell me?"

That Kevin had unfinished business? Unfinished business because he was still upset at me and Sam and his soul couldn't rest until we both knew it? Unfinished business because he wanted to do the opposite: apologize to me and/or Sam, make peace with the past so that he could move on, cross over? Maybe he wanted to issue the same warning to Sam that he'd issued to me: beware the double walker. Or maybe Stella was right with her simple explanation: his soul's not at rest because of the tragic way in which he died.

Since Sam woke up before Kevin had a chance to speak, perhaps we'd never know.

"I don't know the message Kevin has for you," I said. "But I know the person who can tell me."

"Your boy, Eric?" Sam said, rolling his eyes. "Come to mention it, I don't know about all this woo-woo stuff you're talking about, but I do know it started when Eric entered the picture."

"Sam, not now." I stood, grabbed my bag from the floor and my cell phone from the nightstand. I walked over to the desk and switched off the lamp.

"Where you going?" Sam said, rising from the bed as if to follow me. "I want to show you the third-floor bathroom. It's all done. You want to see it?"

"Maybe later, okay? I have to go see someone first."

"Eric?"

"No, not Eric."

Sam was silent for a moment, watching me gather my things. Finally, he said, "What's your deal with him, anyway? What's going on?"

"Nothing's going on."

"I don't like the way he looks at you," Sam said, his voice firm. "You need to ... he needs to ... he needs to disappear!" His voice bellowed, causing me to flinch.

Just then Tyler walked by the bedroom. Sam's outburst made him pause in the doorway.

"Everything okay, boss?" he said to Sam, looking between the both of us.

Sam's chest was puffed out and his face was red and his hands, balled into fists, were visibly shaking. He wasn't looking at me, but through me. It was like his body was standing in front of me, but his mind was somewhere else. And with his mind somewhere else, there was no way he'd be able to answer Tyler.

"Yeah, Tyler," I answered for Sam. "Everything's fine."

He hesitated, silently looking at each of us. Then he nodded and continued downstairs.

"Sam?" I said, positioning myself directly in front of him. I said his name again, louder and more forceful. "Sam!"

"He needs to die, Lil," he whispered, his eyes still trained on me. "Eric Becker needs to die."

I shook Sam's arms, which caused him to snap to. He flinched, shook his head, and suddenly I knew Sam was back.

He blinked, looking confused. "What?"

"Why did you say that?"

"Say what, Lil? What did I say?"

"You said Eric Becker needs to die."

"What? I don't know why I said that. It's just kind of ... came out. I don't really remember saying it. You know I didn't mean it ..." He sighed heavily. His face slid into a frown and my heart skipped.

"Listen, Sam. I have to go. Are you going to be okay?"

"I'll be fine."

"I bet the third-floor bathroom looks amazing. I'll look at it later today, promise."

And as I left Sam and walked out of the house, texting Stella as I went, I thought to myself: who had I been kidding? Wanting redemption for Sam and a clean slate for myself. Maybe this project was too big, too stressful for the both of us. Maybe working together was causing more pain than it was solving. Dredging up the past, creating more bad karma, doing more harm than good.

This project I wanted for us? I was starting to think it could destroy us both.

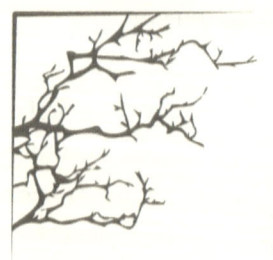

CHAPTER NINETEEN

WHAT I HAD IN MY KITCHEN wouldn't cut it—there was nothing organic, gluten-free, cage-free, or all-natural in my pantry that Stella would touch. So I drove home, showered, tidied up the house, then ran to the grocery store for supplies.

"Thanks for coming over, Stella," I said, greeting her at the door. "I know it can't be easy, arranging childcare on such short notice."

Stella looked stunning for ten a.m. on a Thursday. Her long auburn hair was braided loosely down her back, her face was fresh and bright, and her jeans and peasant blouse perfectly accentuated her figure. Stella Matthews looked like she'd just stepped out of a magazine cover.

"Anything for a friend, Lilian! You know that! Thank you so much for the invitation. Plus, I'm a sucker for breakfast foods."

We sat at the kitchen island and made small talk over my attempt at a healthy meal: omelets with free-range eggs, organic, raw cheddar cheese, naturally gluten-free oatmeal, pesticide-free berries, and sustainably sourced coffee.

I cleared the table and sat back down, increasingly aware that Stella had been watching me the whole time. She folded her hands together on the table and tilted her head.

"How are you, Lilian? I'm sensing you're in spiritual distress."

"You can tell that just by looking at me?"

She crinkled her face and nodded. "Yes, honey. Your aura is contracted, and you have a huge rip in it, near your heart chakra."

"Great. What does all that mean?"

"It tells me that you're stressed out, overwhelmed, maybe wanting to be left alone."

I nodded, thinking that it took neither a rocket scientist nor a clairvoyant to figure that out. You only had to have known me for a few weeks.

"And the rip near my heart chakra?" I said.

"First of all, do you understand what chakras are?"

"Yes, sort of. I've been Googling a lot lately. Because of my headaches. And I may have gone down a rabbit hole or two."

"Headaches?"

"I've been getting them ever since Kevin died. At first I thought it was just stress or lack of sleep, but these felt different than an average tension headache. And they seem to come on when it feels like my intuition is trying to tell me something. If that makes sense."

"Of course it does, Lilian," Stella said.

"I remember getting a doozy of a migraine that day at your house. When you gave me the message from Kevin about the double walker."

"What do you think that message meant?"

"I don't know yet. I just know that anytime someone says something or tells me something, and it feels important or meaningful, I get a headache. It's like my brain is telling me to pay attention because a message is coming, and the only way it knows how to do that is through pain. My scalp tingles, my head throbs, and then I get this thought that enters my head, and sometimes I verbalize that thought involuntarily. It literally comes out of nowhere."

Stella silently took a sip of coffee, grinning at me from ear to ear.

"What's that look for?" I said.

She ignored me. "Keep going, Lilian. Tell me more."

I sighed and kept going.

"At first the headaches would last for hours, and I'd feel hungover for a day or two afterwards. Then, as I started putting two and two together, realizing that the headaches were happening at certain times, it started to develop to the point that as soon as the message is received, so to speak, the headache stops. And whatever the thought is that I received, I know it to be true. Like, deep in my bones. No question. I don't know how or why I know, I just ... do."

Stella was still grinning, and now shifted excitedly in her chair, even doing little happy claps. "That is called claircognizance," she said. "A psychic power. And it's a very wonderful gift to have."

"It feels like a curse," I mumbled into my coffee cup.

"The headaches may make it feel like a curse, but you should see it as a blessing. Your brain is getting a download from your intuition, your higher self, perhaps even your spirit guides. Not everyone can or has the ability to do this. And it's a sign of a spiritual awakening!"

"I read about spiritual awakenings, among other things: receiving signs from the universe, seeing synchronicities, getting information via visions and dreams ..."

"Yes, Lilian! That's all part of the process: recognizing that the universe speaks to us, gives us signs, and that we have to be open to receiving those messages. We do that by shutting off our brains and listening to our hearts. And we can only do *that* when our energy centers, our chakras, are unblocked. Which apparently you're familiar with?"

"I did some research on chakras," I admitted. "So why does my heart chakra have a hole in it?"

"The hole indicates unhealed trauma. I'm sensing that's grief for Kevin. And the dark spot in your aura near the heart—"

"Wait? There's a dark spot, too?"

"Yes, Lilian. There's a thick smudge, like scar tissue. That's an indicator that you're carrying past trauma, some unhealed hurt. A burden, perhaps. Or judging by the thickness of it, several burdens. Does that resonate with you?"

I sighed. "Yeah, it does."

Stella pulled her braid from behind her back so it was resting over her left shoulder. I got a faint whiff of lavender. "I can help you heal that, when you're ready," she said.

"Actually, I could use your help with that warning you passed on to me from Kevin."

It felt ridiculous at first to talk about Kevin in the present tense, as if he was alive. It felt even more ridiculous to act like he was alive only in spirit form, like I couldn't see him but I could still communicate with him. Yet this kind of thing was second nature to Stella, whose spirituality allowed her to feel as if anything in the world were possible. And I felt that, no matter what I said to her, she wouldn't bat an eye. She wouldn't judge and she would automatically believe me.

I had to get into the same mindset. I had to be open and receptive to whatever was going on in my life, including: ghosts, dreams, psychic gifts and doppelgangers.

Doppelganger.

A chill went through me as I thought of the word.

I decided I needed a third cup of coffee, and a more comfortable place to sit, in order to have that conversation with Stella. I offered her a second cup, which she politely declined. Something about coffee giving her adrenal exhaustion.

I motioned for us to adjourn to the living room.

"Beware the double walker, I think he told me?" Stella said as we made our way to the living room. She sat down on the couch and tucked her legs underneath her.

I placed my cup on the coffee table and sat next to her. "Right. A double walker is a doppelganger?"

"Yes. Doppelganger is a German word. Doppel meaning double, and ganger meaning walker."

"Doesn't it mean 'evil twin'?"

"The term doppelganger technically means a biologically unrelated lookalike of a living person."

"So if a doppelganger is simply someone who resembles someone else, why do we think of them as evil?"

"Well, the concept of the doppelganger goes back pretty far, to ancient Egyptian mythology. They called them 'spirit doubles' and didn't think of them as evil. But other cultures did, like the Greeks, the Scandinavians, the Normans ... Regardless, most older cultures portrayed doppelgangers as paranormal phenomena like ghosts and spirits, rather than the true definition of a doppelganger, which is just a real person. It was the Germans who helped popularize the doppelganger concept itself within the last two hundred years, introducing it into our pop culture. Once pop culture got a hold of it, the true German definition of it was swept aside and the paranormal concept of doppelgangers took off—ghostly doubles, alter egos, and evil twins."

"Guess that's because 'evil twin' sells better than 'biologically unrelated lookalike,'" I said, with a chuckle.

I thought about Eric, about his striking physical resemblance to Kevin. He didn't sound like Kevin, though, or walk like Kevin, or talk like Kevin. Eric didn't have his mannerisms, or share his taste in clothing. But he looked like him, almost down to the freckles on his face. In my eyes, that was enough to fit the bill of a doppelganger.

So that would mean Eric was simply the true and traditional concept of a doppelganger: a biologically unrelated lookalike of Kevin. Which, given their non-physical differences, made sense. Plus, Sam and I had touched him enough to know he was solid, not some spirit.

But I couldn't ignore the fact that I'd gotten The Property project and met Eric soon after my husband's death. That I was getting signs that something wasn't quite right with him. That Sam and I were having disturbing dreams about The Property. That one of my workers believed The Property was haunted and another had been inexplicably hurt on the job. That Frank had died soon after telling me about the history of The Property ...

That was the common denominator, wasn't it? The Property. All the bad luck and negative signs had started happening once I accepted the job and met Eric. Perhaps Eric wasn't the true and traditional concept of a doppelganger, but rather something paranormal: an evil twin, or a harbinger of doom.

"By simple definition, a doppelganger is one human being that resembles another human being," I said.

"Right ..." Stella said, drawing out the word in two syllables. As if to say, *We've been over this already.*

"So do both human beings have to be alive for that definition to apply?"

"Well, no. They both just have to be, you know, human. It's a pretty straight-forward yet strict definition."

"And the more popular paranormal concept?"

"A lot more flexible," Stella said, smiling. "There's the ghostly double of a living person, like a spirit that haunts its living counterpart. There's the evil twin or alter ego concept, which could mean a demon or some sort of monster inhabiting a human body. There's the shapeshifter or spirit that takes the form of a person after killing them ..."

I shifted on the couch as a chill went through me. A twinge in my right temple told me we were hitting the bullseye with the paranormal doppelganger.

"Listen, Stella. I need your expertise. But there are things I need to tell you first. I know you're all about love and light, so evil twins and harbingers of doom aren't exactly your thing but—"

"Oh, honey," Stella interrupted, leaning forward and giving me a look that bordered on wicked. "Trust me when I tell you I have experience with the dark side."

I shrank back slightly, surprised yet resolute. "Good, you'll need to tap into that. Because I think I found him, Stella. I think I found the double walker."

She grabbed my hands gently in both of hers, her bracelets jangling. "Tell me everything."

So I told her everything. Starting from the beginning with Kevin's death plea and getting The Property project and everything I knew about its history. I told her about Emma and Eric and how I felt something wasn't quite right with him, even as I felt inexplicably drawn to him. I told her about Frank's death, about Sam's and my dreams, and I even filled her in on the history of my marriage to Kevin and my complicated history with Sam. I mean, I told her *everything*.

When I was done, Stella sighed and sat back and closed her eyes. She was silent for a few minutes and I could tell she was tapping into something, sensing a vibe, seeing the future, perhaps.

Finally, she spoke, her eyes still closed. "Renovating The Property is your destiny. You were fated for this. My spirit guides are telling me you must continue." She opened her eyes and looked at me with a weary smile.

I knew this to be true. All of this was predestined. Kevin's death. Renovating The Property. Reuniting with Sam. Meeting Eric...

Sure, I had free will. I could walk away. But even if I tried, I didn't think I could.

I wanted Sam to be successful again, to get a new lease on life, to be financially stable so he could continue caring for Carly and Becca. I owed him this.

And I owed it to myself. I needed a new lease on life, too. So, if I had to, I would step through the gates of hell.

And in doing so, I would honor what was destined for me.

Stella nodded. In that moment, I felt she knew what I'd been thinking. She sympathized with what I'd gone through so far, and, I sensed she knew what was yet to come.

"There is something powerful sleeping within you, Lilian," she said. "An awareness that you didn't have before. Abilities that are developing. I know you can feel it awakening inside you. Embrace it."

"I can feel it," I said. "And I know exactly what I need to do next."

Stella brought her hands together and grinned. "If that's the case, let's get started."

CHAPTER TWENTY

THE PROPERTY WAS IN chaos.

It had been raining for three days straight. A Nor'easter had swirled up the coast and stubbornly parked itself over New Jersey and southeastern Pennsylvania, bringing with it damaging winds and four inches of rain. Nor'easters were not unusual, and neither were hurricanes, earthquakes, tornadoes, landslides, or blizzards. But when you're doing home renovation, such weather—any type of weather, really—can set you back days.

And actually, I was counting my blessings that, four weeks into working on The Property, we'd yet to experience even a drop of rain.

Now, on day three of the storm, I pulled into the mud-slicked dirt driveway to find two workers standing next to the lake, nearly in fisticuffs.

I pulled as close to the house as I could and geared up to face the downpour, as well as the two grown men yelling, each threatening the other with a hammer and a screw driver. I yanked the hood up on my raincoat and jumped out of the car. The men stopped when they saw me approaching, lowering their hands as if to hide their weapons.

I yelled to be heard over the pouring rain. "Miguel! Where were you yesterday? You didn't show up for work!"

"Hola, Senora O'Shea," Miguel said sheepishly.

I turned to the other worker, a tile installer. "Paul, shouldn't you be upstairs putting marble in my bathroom?"

Paul's one eye was closed, rain dripping off his head. "Hey, Lil."

"Well?" I said. "What's going on?"

Miguel started speaking his Spanglish, shaking his hammer at Paul, and Paul gave Miguel a death stare, looking like he was about ready to give him a gut-full of screwdriver. They talked over one another, voices raised, and all I could make out was that Miguel was accusing Paul of stealing some of his tools, and Paul was accusing Miguel of hitting on his sister.

I stepped between the two of them, my arms raised at their chests. "Are you coming back to work or not, Miguel? I could use you."

"No, Senora," Miguel said, then he pointed at the lake. "No me gusta el lago."

"You'll be working inside, Miguel. No lago inside the house. Comprende?"

"Si, pero tengo miedo. El lago esta maldito ..."

Paul laughed and wiped the rain off his scalp. "What a joke. The lake isn't cursed, you superstitious fuck!"

"Whoa, whoa!" I said. "That's enough, Paul!"

I turned back to Miguel. "If you're not coming to work, I'm going to have to ask you to leave. Got it?"

"Si, senora. Entiendo."

"I'll sort the tool thing out with Paul. If there's something that belongs to you, I'll make sure you get it back."

"Gracias," Miguel said, glaring at Paul one last time before getting into his truck, hammer in hand.

"Now can we go inside, please?" I said to Paul.

We both ran into the house. Paul took the stairs, two at a time, to the second-floor bathroom that was waiting for an octagon and dot marble tile floor. I stood in the vestibule for a minute and shrugged out of my coat, allowing it, and myself, to drip on the drop cloth protecting the hard wood flooring.

That's when I heard the incessant sound of dripping water, less than a waterfall but more than a trickle. It came from my right, the pitter patter sound of water hitting a bare floor. I ran into the kitchen and saw three streams of water coming down from the ceiling, directly underneath where the bathroom was located on the second floor. There was a half inch of water under my feet. Two men hurried about, placing empty buckets under the leaks and emptying full ones into the sink.

One of the workers, Tom, saw me out of the corner of his eye. "Oh, hey, Lilian," he said, which caused the other man at the sink to twist around. His eyes grew wide when he saw me, and he quickly turned back.

"Hey, fellas." A second bucket was nearly full, so I grabbed it and dumped it into the sink, nearly colliding with the worker, a young man in his twenties I didn't recognize. I replaced the bucket back under the leak. "What's the status of the main water shutoff valve?"

"It's off," Tom said.

"Where's the shop vac?"

"Over there." He motioned with his head to the corner of the kitchen, where a shop vac sat waiting for an occasion such as this.

"This literally happened, like, a few minutes ago," the other worker said, avoiding eye contact. He seemed nervous, like it was his first day on the job. "Thank goodness we were nearby."

"You want me to set up the vac?" I asked, feeling helpless just standing there watching the two of them hustle to keep ahead of the water.

"Nah, we got this," Tom said. "Besides, this is nothing. They got it worse upstairs."

"What?" I said, and I turned away from them and started back for the vestibule before either of them could say anything further.

Standing at the bottom of the stairs, I yelled up to Sam. I heard voices as I jogged up the steps and down the hall to the first bathroom on that floor. Bob stood in the doorway assisting Paul, who was on his hands and knees laying down squares of tile. Paul's head was still slick with rain, but he seemed to have recovered from his argument with Miguel. I didn't feel the need to tell his boss, Bob, about the incident.

Bob smiled when he saw me. "Lil! Long time, no see! How the hell are ya?"

I'd always liked Bob. He had a smile for everyone, all the time. Never seemed to be in a bad mood, never let anything get to him.

"Hey, Bob. Yeah, it's been awhile. I'm good. How you been?"

"Never better, Lil. All your floors so far are looking great, huh?"

"Top quality work from you and Paul, as always." Paul smiled at my compliment and kept working.

"This time next year it'll just be Paul running my business," Bob said. "Or Paul and someone else. I'm retiring, you know."

"I heard. I'm happy for you, Bob. You've earned it."

"Thanks, Lil." He motioned down the hall to the other bathroom, where two other voices were growing louder. "I'd love to continue to shoot the shit with you but, uh, I think you got bigger fish to fry."

"Sounds like it. We'll catch up real soon, Bob."

"You got it, Lil."

I approached the second bathroom and came to an immediate halt in the doorway. Sam stood before the overflowing toilet, plunging it with an auger. He and Tyler, a plumbing apprentice, were nearly ankle-deep in water.

"Sam?" I said.

"Not now, Lil," he said, not looking up at me as he cranked he auger.

"Has the toilet's shutoff valve been turned off?" I asked.

When Sam didn't respond, Tyler looked at me and said, "Just did it."

"Was the water supply to the house shut off at the main?" I asked.

"It was off when I first got here this morning," Sam said, sounding agitated.

I looked at Tyler for clarification, who shrugged. "Somehow it got turned back on," he said. "I just came up from the basement from shutting it back off."

"How did that happen?" I asked.

Sam stopped cranking the auger and looked at me, his face red. "I don't fucking *know* how that happened, Lil."

The water seemed to have stopped overflowing from the bowl, but the bowl itself was still full, almost to the rim.

"Is there a clog?" I asked. "How could there be a clog? You just installed the toilet yesterday."

"There must be a blockage somewhere in the pipe leading to the main drain line," Tyler said, watching Sam as he kept twisting the auger handle.

"Well, no one's been using it, so it ain't blocked with toilet paper," Sam said. "Unless someone stuffed a whole roll down there for shits and giggles."

Suddenly there was a loud whoosh, and a loud sucking noise. The toilet seemed to vibrate as the water in the bowl was forcibly vacuumed down the drain. Sam pulled the auger out of the toilet. "Flush," he said to Tyler.

Tyler flushed and the bowl filled up again nearly to the rim. Clearly there was still a clog somewhere.

"Goddamn it!" Sam fished the auger back down into the toilet.

"Sam, did you see Miguel?" I asked.

Sam started cranking again, without looking at me. "Yeah, Lil. I saw him."

"Did you say anything to him? About missing work?"

"I kind of had my hands full."

"He and Paul were nearly having a fist fight in the driveway."

"Sounds like a personal problem."

"It could end up being *our* problem."

"Yeah? Well, right now it ain't my problem." Sam motioned with his head to the full toilet. "Right now, *this* is my problem."

"So you don't care that two employees almost had a physical altercation on client property?" I said, perhaps too harshly.

Sam stopped cranking, looked at me and said, "No, I don't. Just like you don't care that the third-floor bathroom is done."

Tyler backed himself against the wall and stared at the floor.

"What?" I said.

"You heard me, Lil."

"Of course I care the third-floor bathroom is done."

"You haven't even fucking looked at it! Have you?"

"That's not fair. I haven't had time. I—"

"Oh, that's right," Sam interjected. "You're too busy spending time with your boyfriend, Eric."

"He's *not* my *boyfriend*. The only time I see Eric is on this jobsite. And I haven't seen him in days."

"You sure about that? You're here every night, after we all leave. And you've been sleeping here almost every night for who knows how long. Seems to me you see him more than you're letting on."

"He's not here then, Sam. It's just me. Not that it's any of your business. I don't grill you about your personal life."

"Feel free. I'd tell you the truth: that there's nothing to tell. I'm here all day and by myself at night. I'm not dating anyone, and there are only three people in this world I truly give a shit about: Carly, Becca and—" He stopped short, eyes growing wide. He went back to cranking the augur. "And anyway, I've seen the way you look at each other and the flirty smiles and the way your face blushes when he's around." He gave the augur a few more angry cranks, then stopped. "Oh, and I saw him give you a pair of earrings."

Shit.

That had happened a few days before. It was midday and, when I arrived, The Property was buzzing with activity inside and out. Sam was talking to one of the workers near the lake and we waved to each other as I parked my car. Eric came out from the house to greet me and handed me a small, old, somewhat dusty black velvet box. Inside was a pair of heirloom diamond earrings that were Emma's great-grandmothers. She'd wanted me to have them as a gift, for all that I was doing for her and Eric, but also because she said she was dying and didn't have anyone else to give them to. I was grateful of course, but initially refused them. Eric insisted I keep them to make Emma happy, so I relented and put the box in my car so I wouldn't misplace or damage them while onsite.

Sam must've seen the exchange and assumed they were a gift from Eric.

"Listen, Sam. Eric and I have a professional working relationship, nothing more. Those earrings were a gift from Emma."

"Sure, Lil. If you say so."

In the nearly thirty years I'd known Sam, he'd never, not once, raised his voice to me. Or appeared outwardly jealous. Not even when he was drunk or a little bit tipsy, and certainly not when he was sober. So this anger? His need to hurt my feelings? This was something else. Maybe Frank had been on to something. Maybe The Property *was* a hellhole. A personal hellhole that brought out the worst in people.

But I had to be sure there wasn't something else at play.

"Have you been drinking?" I asked.

Sam pulled the auger out from the toilet a second time and threw it on the tile floor, where it landed with a splash. "Are you fucking kidding me? Are you seriously asking me that right now?"

"Tyler," I said, "I think you should go."

"Yeah, Tyler," Sam said. "Beat it, would you?"

Tyler scampered past me without a word, and I heard him race down the steps.

"Yes or no, Sam," I said. "I need to know."

"Give me some fucking credit, would you? I'm not that person anymore!"

We stood looking at each other, and although his eyes were full of anger, I knew in that moment he was telling the truth. But my eyes must've been conveying something other than trust, because he felt the need to hurt me, again and again.

"You don't believe me, do you?" he said.

"Of course I do."

"No, you don't. You think I'm some drunken loser who can't keep a job and will never outlive his past."

"Fuck you, Sam. You don't know what I think."

As I turned to walk back down the hallway, Sam yelled after me, "That's it, Lil. Do what you do best. Run away when shit gets tough!"

I sped down the hallway, past the first bathroom, where Bob and Paul stood, eyeing me with concern.

"Lil, are you—" Bob started to say, and I cut him off.

"Everything's fine, fellas."

I made it to the bottom of the steps and saw Eric standing in the vestibule.

"Lilian?"

"Hi, Eric," I said, walking past him.

"Do you have a minute?"

I had just made it to the front door. I spun around and said, "I don't, actually."

"There's water ..." he said, pointing towards the kitchen.

"Yes, Eric. There's water everywhere. I'm sorry about that. A little plumbing issue. Nothing to worry about. Really. Sam's got everything under control." I grabbed my coat off the vestibule floor, zipped myself in and yanked the hood over my head.

Then I turned and walked out the front door into the relentless rain, got in my car and sped home.

CHAPTER TWENTY-ONE

THE THROBBING STARTED as I was driving home, and this time I think it was from my anger, my anxiety, my stress levels, and my elevated blood pressure. No intuitive message this time; just a good old-fashioned tension headache.

I got home, popped two Advil and chased them with water. It was a little after five and I should've been thinking about dinner but I'd lost my appetite as of late. So I kept drinking water instead.

I paced the kitchen floor and tried the yogic breathing exercise Stella had taught me to keep stress and anxiety and possible panic attacks at bay. Equal counts in and out through the nose. Inhale one two three four, exhale one two three four. Keep your focus on your breath, she'd told me. This should bring your breath and your body into balance.

I was only in round one of breathing—and still angry as hell—when the doorbell rang. My breathing was shallow and I felt like I couldn't get enough air into my lungs. I stomped to the door and flung it open and there he stood: Sam, all six feet of him, taking up the entire doorway and dripping wet and looking sexy as hell for it.

His face was red and he was breathing as heavy as I was and he walked in without being invited. That's when I smelled it on him: not just the faint whiff of booze, but fear, desperation, and hunger, too. There was a heat in his eyes, a primal look of desire, a passionate urgency. He searched my eyes and they must've conveyed *yes* because he rushed forward and I felt him on me—his lips on my mouth, his hands pressed to my jaw.

"I'm sorry," he said between kisses, "for everything I said."

"I know you are," I whispered. "I am too."

He kissed my neck and we tugged at each other's clothing. We gravitated toward the living room and I lay down on the couch and Sam pulled off his shirt. He kneeled on the couch and loomed over me, long enough to take in my naked body head to toe. I ached for him in that moment, to experience every inch of him, to feel his powerful shoulders and to taste the fullness of his lips and to hear his labored breathing in my ear.

He put his weight on me and I felt our hips align and with one hard thrust I took him in. And then there we were, two wounded souls longing for each other, trying to move on from the past, and failing spectacularly.

There would be no staying at The Property that night. No eight hours of blissfully restful sleep. No paperwork being done by the light of a single lamp. There would only be stillness there, and silence, and shadows keeping watch.

CHAPTER TWENTY-TWO

DURING OUR BREAKFAST date, I told Stella that I knew exactly what I needed to do next. And that thing was to *not* have sex with Sam.

Not that I regretted it, exactly. Because I didn't. It happened and there was nothing I could do about it. The past is the past, even if that act in the past was so fresh I could still smell it on me. Be done with the past, I say, and move on from it.

There was no shame, either. Sex with Sam felt as good as I remembered, and we were, technically, both single. I felt foolish, maybe. Perhaps I'd been too impetuous, too quick to give in to my urges. But I didn't feel shameful.

What I did feel, though, was guilt. My husband had recently died and already I had slept with another man. I kept the guilt at bay by telling myself it hadn't been just any man. It'd been Sam. It wasn't a stranger I picked up at a bar or some dude I met on a hookup app. Plus, it'd been only once, and it had been Sam.

That's how I justified it back then, too. Only once, and with Sam. Kevin had said he wished it had been a stranger, multiple strangers even, and many times, versus one time with Sam. Because then he'd feel secure that no emotions were involved. But the emotions were already there before I'd slept with Sam the first time, they were there after I cheated on Kevin, and I was now realizing that my feelings of adoration for Sam had never gone away. They'd been buried for two years, but never really forgotten.

I justified sleeping with Sam by saying it wouldn't happen again. Which is exactly the same thing I told myself the first time, too.

I'd beaten myself up enough two years ago with guilt and shame and regret and decided that, this time around, guilt was enough. No shame or regret, thank-you-very-much. Just guilt. So I made room for the guilt beside the loss and the grief I felt for Kevin, and then realized that, once again, I was dealing with distressing emotions in triplicate. No matter how hard I tried, my punishments came in threes.

There'd been no couples therapy, or trips to church for confession, when Kevin found out about Sam. Kevin's was a family that toughed stuff out, as was mine. Problems were kept in the family without outside interference. You dealt with things yourself, or you didn't. Either way, no outsiders allowed.

There had been a fight that night, when I sat Kevin down and told him. I told him immediately after it happened, but Kevin hadn't taken that into consideration, just like he hadn't given any credence to my stranger analogy. There'd been lots of crying too, and eventually I fled the house to be with Sam. Counterintuitive, I know, but Sam was my best friend and closest confidant other than Kevin, so it made sense to me at the time.

Kevin had yelled after me as I was running out the front door: "Run away when shit gets tough!" And I remember having a flashback to that moment when Sam was yelling the same thing to me as I ran down the steps at The Property. I'd been pissed at Kevin at the time for saying it, and pissed at Sam when he accused me of the same thing. But looking back now I wonder if the two of them knew me better than I knew myself. Maybe I *had* been running away.

Even recently, after Kevin died, had I been running? I mean, had I even *cried* after Kevin died? There were one or two really good cries, but that was it. Had I kept myself so busy and so distracted with work, with Sam, with Kevin's estate, that I hadn't allowed myself to stop, stand still for a minute, and actually feel something?

Something other than desire, that is?

Grief and loss, sure. But shouldn't I also be feeling anger, sadness, helplessness, pity, vulnerability? Where had *they* been? Had I packed them away in a suitcase and hung it around my neck to be carried with me everywhere, unseen and unrecognized, even by myself? How long had I been schlepping that shit around? I don't remember feeling any of those things since my dad died.

Two years ago, when Dad died. That's when I remember feeling those things.

My dad had three rules to live by: work hard, play hard, and don't cheat on your spouse. So, when he found out I'd broken one of those cardinal rules, it crushed him. He'd never looked at me the same after that. That's how much it mattered to him. And he never looked at Sam the same after that, either.

My dad had been like a father to Sam, whose biological father was an absentee alcoholic. His parents divorced when he was fourteen and, like most kids, Sam started acting out and fell in with the wrong crowd, got in trouble at school and with the law. Petty offenses—driving without a license, low-level assault, and underage drinking. He never did jail time, but paid hefty fines that neither of his parents could really afford. After that Sam became the ne'er-do-well kid from the wrong side of the tracks with no future, no prospects, and no hope of redemption.

But my dad saw a diamond in the rough. He saw potential. He took a chance on Sam when he was sixteen, gave the troublemaking teenager a shot when everyone else had written him off. He took Sam under his wing and taught him everything he knew about construction, giving him a way to burn off all the angst and anger he felt about his father and the divorce. It gave Sam a new lease on life, offering him a brighter future than he would've had.

When the affair became public and my dad found out, it was a double whammy: his little girl, and the man he considered a son, had committed a cardinal sin. He was disappointed in me, but he was truly angry at Sam. Let him know it, too. Told Sam that he had lost his respect and broken his trust. And that broke Sam. Devastated him to know that he'd let down the man he trusted and respected and loved more than his own father. And he'd never get the chance to earn back that trust or respect.

As for me? Well, I thought it was enough that I felt the embarrassment of shaming the family, the guilt of disappointing those I loved most, and the regret of nearly ruining my marriage. Again—negative emotions in triplicate.

So when my dad suffered a fatal heart attack a week after finding out what Sam and I had done, I added blame to the emotional arsenal I inflicted on myself. By then rumors had spread and opinions had been made. After only a week, I was the pariah, Kevin was the victim, and Sam the drunken monster who'd screwed the boss' daughter. The saving grace was that at least it stayed (mostly) within the confines of my dad's company.

Some of my dad's employees tried to take the blame off me by saying he'd been partaking too much in two of his own cardinal rules—working and playing hard—to be concerned with the other one that I'd broken, and that's what killed him. But I took the blame, nonetheless. I was old enough to know better, and at the time, I told myself I had literally broken his heart.

I stepped in to help my uncle for a few weeks after my dad died and until Sam took over, while simultaneously running LB Renovations with Kevin. I know now that that was my way of running, because if I was crazy stupid busy, then there'd be no time for guilt, shame, regret and blame. And when Sam was made the new co-owner of the business alongside my uncle, and I had extra time on my hands to actually deal with my bullshit emotions? Well, I decided to not deal with them. Instead, I bought the largest suitcase I could find, stuffed all those feelings in there, locked it up and threw away the key.

Perhaps if I hadn't been so busy running, if I'd stood still long enough, if I'd not been so preoccupied with dragging my suitcase around, I could've seen what was happening to Sam.

Sam was the best candidate for co-owner, and my uncle loved him, but his reputation preceded him. He walked into his new office full of piss and vinegar, the same piss and vinegar that would further tarnish his character. He was effective, but feared (what if he shows up to work drunk?). He was fair, but judged unfairly (he's been the boss' pet for years!). And he was hardworking, but disrespected (did he work this hard on the boss' daughter?).

Sam was fully aware of the double standard that he represented. It burned some of the employees who thought Sam hadn't earned his position. Sure, he'd paid his dues as far as seniority was concerned, put in the actual time. But actions matter, too. So when the rumor mill got going about the affair and his drinking, his time in the trenches suddenly didn't mean shit.

The judgement made him paranoid, and the paranoia made him drink even more. Not noticeably at first, but within a few months he became his own self-fulfilling prophecy. All along, some people feared he'd show up at jobsites drunk, which he did. And suddenly his drinking became a problem. He missed meetings. Acted irrationally around clients. Treated subordinates harshly. Lost or misplaced paperwork.

Worst of all, I feared my dad's name would be dragged through the mud, because of his decision to make Sam co-owner and his replacement all those years before. But my dad's reputation preceded him too, so his character remained intact, and respect for the dead ruled the day.

I tried to step in again to help the business, against Kevin's wishes, to diffuse the situation, to try to save Sam and his reputation. I told him to take a break for a few weeks, maybe go on vacation with Debbie and the kids, that I'd handle things until he came back. Again, that was my vain attempt to stay as busy as possible so I wouldn't have to think about that suitcase full of emotions.

But it was no use, and by then it was too late. When Sam showed up to work one day, six months into being co-owner, his office had been cleaned out. His personal belongings had been put into two cardboard boxes, and he was personally escorted to the door by my uncle and the head of Human Resources.

Sam went on a three-day bender, spending most of his time at Donovan's—and not with Debbie. He arrived home early one morning, hungover and staggering through the house, to find her and the kids gone. Soon after I was gone, too. As painful as it was, I walked away from Sam in order to repair my marriage.

And I maintain, to this day, that Sam really was a great boss and a wonderful man. He just couldn't get out of his own way.

Maybe that was my problem, too. I couldn't get out of my own way. Maybe I'd been running for years without ever realizing it. Without dealing with the emotions that kept me running. The affair with Sam, my dad's death, Kevin's death ... all those unprocessed emotions.

Maybe it was about time I unpacked that suitcase.

So no, the thing I told Stella I needed to do next had nothing to do with Sam. And it wasn't dealing with my own personal demons, although that was now on my list. But there was no time for hidden demons just yet.

First, I had to confront the demon within in my view.

A doppelganger named Eric Becker.

CHAPTER TWENTY-THREE

I WAS ON MY WAY TO The Property. It was a Sunday evening and I knew no one would be there for another twelve hours, at most. I'd decided to call the in-laws during the twenty-five minute drive, to kill two birds with one stone. I dialed the number and put them on speaker as I drove.

My mother-in-law, Dorothy, answered.

"Lilian, honey. It's so good to hear from you." I heard her whisper, "Robert, it's Lilian" to my father-in-law, who said "Hello." In my head, I imagined them sitting in front of the television, her sipping tea and him reading the newspaper.

"Hi, Dot. I'm sorry I haven't called in a while. Things have been, well ..."

"We completely understand. You probably have your hands full."

My in-laws had sold their funeral home business and retired to Florida in 2016, when my father-in-law turned seventy. Kevin and I had flown down there several times in the ensuing years to visit, usually only for a few days at a time because of the business. Kevin's funeral was the first time the in-laws had left Florida, and never in a million years did any of us think it would be to say goodbye to their son.

They'd stayed with me for a week, in one of our spare bedrooms. My older sister Kathy flew in from Denver for the funeral, and stayed for a few days in our other spare bedroom. My in-laws cooked and cleaned for all of us while they were here, and were very hospitable hosts during the wake I held at the house.

I'd always had a good relationship with the in-laws; I was the daughter they never had, just as Kevin was the son my parents never had. They never knew of the affair; at least that's what Kevin told me, and I believed him. Perhaps he felt the need to protect them, save them from unnecessary worry. Perhaps he was protecting the both of us from Round Two of shame and embarrassment. Maybe he thought one parent dropping dead from shock was enough. Perhaps a combination of all three. But whatever. I was grateful my in-laws didn't know, and even more grateful for how easy it was to keep it from them, since being down in Florida meant they didn't have any contact with our social circle. And neither of them were on social media.

My sister knew. I told her the day after it happened. I texted her the simple phrase, "I cheated on Kevin," and her simple response was, "Does dad know?" Not, "Have you told Kevin?" or "Are you okay?" or "Need to talk?" I think even Kathy knew the news had the potential to kill our father.

"Is there anything you need, Lilian?" my mother-in-law said. "Robert and I are here for you. Do you need us to come back up, stay with you for a while?"

"No, I'm fine, really. I just, um ... I really miss him." My voice cracked and tears filled my eyes and suddenly I felt so fucking sad. I felt a large, jagged hole in my heart where Kevin had been. The grief that washed over me was immediate and all-encompassing, like a large bubble quickly falling from the sky out of nowhere and trapping me inside. And that's the funny thing about it: sometimes grief comes without warning, so quickly and unprompted, that it leaves you helplessly locked inside its grasp. And then it takes longer to leave than it did to arrive, slowly and achingly leaving a long trail of unbearable pain in its wake.

I blew my nose one-handed while I drove, and took a series of deep breaths to try and compose myself. Dorothy prattled on a bit, which I was thankful for, as it allowed me to gather my thoughts. What I mostly wanted to know about was cremation. I figured Dorothy's undergrad degree in mortuary science and Master's degree in Thanatology could answer my questions on death and, more specifically, the medical, spiritual, religious, and social and cultural aspects of cremation.

Dorothy said that cremations were more accessible and acceptable now, mostly due to their lower cost, but also as a reflection of changing times and our understanding of the environmental impact of burials. Religion plays a part, too, in the decision to bury versus cremate. The United States is still a predominately Christian nation, and Christians still, for the most part, reject cremation. And that's based on the biblical belief that the bodies of those who have died will one day resurrect and be reunited with their souls, just like Jesus. But if a body has been destroyed by fire, then the body can't resurrect.

"And if a body has been destroyed by fire," I remember whispering, "It also means it can't be taken over or possessed by another soul."

In that moment, as I was mindlessly driving and focusing on Dorothy, I momentarily blanked out. My vision went blurry and my ears shut off. With my senses gone, Kevin's request came into focus.

Cremate me.

And then, suddenly, after Kevin's request faded a message appeared inside my brain, so quickly and unexpectedly that I inhaled in shock. My head started throbbing, and I knew my claircognizance was in full tilt—my brain was receiving an instantaneous download from my subconscious. The message was important, I could feel it, I could sense it. And it came into my conscious mind with such force it almost felt too big for my brain to handle, like there wasn't enough room inside me to hold it, so I had to set it free. I had to say it aloud, I needed to say it aloud, if only to unburden my mind of the weight.

"Kevin knew everything."

The headache began to subside. I felt like the message, the whole truth of it, had been lying dormant in my subconscious the entire time, waiting for my open ear. Stella had given me a glimpse by saying Kevin knew about the double walker, and I sensed he knew he was going to die, but I hadn't been able to piece it all together until just then.

Kevin had known he was going to die, and he knew he needed to be cremated; maybe he didn't know how he was going to die, or when or why, but he knew it would be soon. So he got a life insurance policy, ensuring I'd be taken care of.

And perhaps Kevin knew that, after he died, I'd be reunited with Sam, either professionally or romantically, or both. Which is why he visited Sam in his dreams, to say hello, or to wish him well, or to voice his displeasure, or to say goodbye.

In that moment, while attempting to drive my car and talk to my in-laws, I knew all this to be true. I don't know how I knew, and I had no evidence, I just felt it so very deeply in my gut. Kevin knew.

He knew everything.

As I let my mind wander, I forgot I was on the phone. It was a wonder I was still driving my car in a straight line. I snapped to and my vision sharpened once more, and I heard my mother-in-law's voice.

I thanked Dorothy and Robert and promised to stay in touch, just as I was pulling into the driveway of The Property. As expected, no one was there, and that's exactly what I wanted. I wanted—needed, somehow—The Property all to myself. It had become my sanctuary of sorts, a place I could hide from everything and everyone. There was a silence there I didn't know I needed, away from barking dogs and squealing cars and loud lawnmowers.

There was fresh air and cool breezes I didn't know existed, that somehow got trapped in between the long rows of boxes that was my housing development, but was free to roam in the open spaces of The Property. And there was a cooling calmness that wrapped itself around me like a blanket, inviting me inside to help me focus my thoughts, to help me calm the stresses of the day, to help me sleep.

And my thoughts focused now on Kevin.

Kevin was not a religious person, so his request to be cremated had no religious implications. It had everything to do with some future event, or events, that he'd somehow known about.

By extension, I had to assume the same must be true with Frank. Why the last-minute request to be cremated, when he knew full well he had a casket and a grave waiting for his body? Had he too received some precognitive message about his own death? Or had someone, or something, told him he was going to die?

I was emotionally and physically wrecked. I would unpack my emotional suitcase. Honest to God I would. But first I needed to sleep. And there was only one place I could do that.

I got out of the car just as the sun was disappearing behind the horizon. As I climbed the porch steps, the sun's rays cast a brilliant red-orange glow on the surface of the lake, so much so it looked like the water was ablaze.

I went upstairs without pause, without searching for a flashlight, without even caring about the state of the house. I knew Sam had taken care of the leaks and the flooding. All I cared about was crawling into that comfortable bed and escaping into oblivion.

But when I entered the bedroom, Eric was already there, lying on his right side, facing me, fast asleep. The lamp on the desk was switched on, illuminating his blonde hair and fluttering eyelids. He looked still. He looked peaceful.

He looked like Kevin.

I removed my shoes and tiptoed towards him. How badly I wanted it to be Kevin, for him to hold me one last time, to speak one last time, to get the closure we were denied. And as I got closer, I doubted what I was seeing—it *was* Eric, wasn't it? If so, then how did he look more like Kevin than ever before? The freckle on his left cheek, the small scar above his right eye. Kevin's left cheek and Kevin's right eye. Had I noticed them on Eric before? Was I dreaming?

I tried to restrain myself, but I couldn't resist. I had to touch him. As I reached my hand out, his eyes opened ever so slowly, and he smiled at me.

"Lilian," he said calmly.

"Kevin," I said.

Then he opened the covers and invited me in.

CHAPTER TWENTY-FOUR

I WAS AT THE PROPERTY, upstairs in the bedroom I'd called home for the past two weeks or so, doing paperwork at the desk by lamp light. It was a little after 8 p.m., and the house was peaceful and dark. The sun had just about set, and moonlight was starting to fill the room from the two windows devoid of curtains or shades.

Every now and again I stole glances behind me at the bed, wondering if I had really crawled into bed with Eric the night before, or if I had been dreaming about Kevin. I woke up that morning by myself, with no sign that I'd had company—no articles of clothing left behind, no scent on the pillow. I remember crawling into bed and nothing more: the moment I laid down, my world went black, and I simply woke to the light of a new day.

I tried focusing on the paperwork in front of me, but there was something else on my mind: the conversation I'd had with Sam earlier in the day. I'd called him to get a status report of the house, but he was more interested in rehashing what had happened between us at my house. He started off by saying he felt like I'd been dodging him—not answering his calls or texts and avoiding the house during the day in order to avoid seeing him—perhaps because of some guilt or shame about it. He said that although he had things handled at The Property, he needed me around more. He was starting to feel like we were no longer a team renovating the house; I was slipping away from him not just physically, but emotionally too, and it was making him feel insecure.

In response, I said I'd put some distance between us, because I was upset that he'd become judgmental and angry and jealous and mean. I said I thought the stress of the job and the anxiety over needing the money to care for his family was starting to get to him; he was turning to the bottle, instead of me or, better yet, professional help, in order to cope. I feared that his drinking would destroy his life, again, and I couldn't stand by and watch him do that. And I couldn't allow him to jeopardize this job.

I did admit, though, that Sam was doing a great job as foreman. Yes, there had been an injury and a spooked ex-employee, but none of that was Sam's fault. And there had been a toilet blockage, and a subsequent leak, but that wasn't his fault either. He'd handled that pretty well, and from what I could tell by talking to the other trades, they all liked him. Many times I arrived at The Property to find Sam and some random employee shooting the shit, busting each other's balls, talking about what they'd do if they won the Mega Millions or the Powerball. It didn't seem fake or forced; it appeared to be genuine mutual respect everyone had for one another.

So he agreed to try to control his emotions and I agreed to be around more, and nothing more was said about what had happened on my living room couch. But I knew that wasn't the end of it, not by a long shot. Because emotions left unsaid, events left undiscussed, always have a way of coming back around. And because what happened between us two years ago had happened again, pandora's box had now been reopened. There would be many more intimate nights with Sam, I was sure of it. Our own curiosities and, perhaps, destiny itself, was waiting to see how it would all work out.

I did eventually get my status report, but by the time we had that discussion, I was pretty sure we were both psychologically wrecked. Sam started rambling and I couldn't focus. What I gathered was that all three bathrooms were done, the source of the toilet blockage was found and fixed, and the kitchen was about ready for new wiring and plumbing. All the historic replacement windows, made of old-growth pine reclaimed from the local salvage yard, had arrived and were being stored in the downstairs parlor; did I want to take a look at those? So in about a week we'd have historically accurate and efficient windows, and another two weeks or so after that, Sam had said, we'd have a beautiful new kitchen.

I was rehashing the conversation with Sam as I sorted through a stack of bills. I was just starting to dig into the previous week's payroll when a sudden chill went up the back of my neck.

It was warm for mid-May, in the high seventies. The house wasn't air conditioned yet, but I was comfortable wearing long sleeves. No reason for me to be cold. I shrugged it off and kept typing on my laptop. Suddenly I heard a noise, a soft *thump* from the third-floor bedroom directly above me. It sounded like someone had bounced a ball, or dropped a book on the floor. I stopped mid keystroke and listened. There was no one else in the house, nor was there any plumbing that ran through the middle of the ceiling, and I'd been in enough houses over the years to know the typical creaks and cracks of a house settling.

This didn't sound like a house settling.

I went back to typing and soon heard it again, a little louder this time, directly above me. I sat and listened for a minute and decided I needed to investigate. I took the small flashlight that sat on the desk and made my way to the doorway, shining the light down the stairs into the vestibule. Nothing down there but the soft glow of the nightlight emanating from the kitchen. I shone the flashlight straight ahead, down the second-floor hallway where there were two more bedrooms and a bathroom. All was silent and still in that direction. When I didn't hear the thump a third time, I thought I could shrug it off as stress or fatigue or an overactive imagination. But there was no ignoring my instincts.

I walked around the banister, stood at the bottom of the stairs leading to the third floor, and shone the flashlight up.

"Hello? Calling any and all boogeymen."

I laughed at myself and started up the stairs. The original hardwood oak creaked under my feet with every step, bringing to mind all the clients over the years who'd asked me to "fix" their squeaky natural wood floors and stairs. I'd done it, of course, with the explanation that noise doesn't mean there's anything wrong with the wood, and with the caveat that fixes are really just band aids. With time and age, other squeaks would unavoidably pop up, whack-a-mole style.

So while a lot of homeowners went out of their way to quiet a noisy floor or staircase, I'd learned to love them. The clicking and clacking of hardwood was a sign of wear and tear for sure, but to me, it was also a sign of a well-lived-in and well-loved home. Why would you want to get rid of that?

I did a sweep of the third floor, pausing in the middle of the bedroom where I thought the noise had originated. I stomped on the floor twice, the second time louder than the first, imagining what that echo and vibration would be like to the person occupying the bedroom below. Without a second person to help with the experiment, I could only guess.

I saw nothing out of place, and so made my way back to the second floor and walked down the hallway to inspect the other two bedrooms and the bathroom. Nothing there, either. Then I decided, what the hell, I might as well walk the whole house, since I hadn't when I first got there.

I went down to the first floor and into the parlor. All the new windows were stacked up on the floor and leaning against the wall, waiting for install. Maybe one of them had slid off its pile or slipped away from the wall? Maybe that was the source of the two thumps? On inspection, it looked like everything was in place.

I crossed through the vestibule again and into the kitchen. I leaned the front of my body against one stretch of counter, my forehead resting on an upper cabinet. There I stood for a few minutes, my back to the doorway as I questioned my sanity.

Suddenly that chill went up the back of my neck again—an urgent feeling I wasn't alone. I turned my head to the side and startled when I saw Eric out of the corner of my eye. I spun around, my hand pressed to my chest as if to lower the hammering of my heart.

"Eric! You scared me!"

"Lilian, I'm sorry." He was wearing jeans and a short-sleeved collared shirt and appeared to be freshly shaven, from what I could see by the dim light of the nightlight.

"How long have you been here? In the house, I mean?"

"I just arrived."

"I didn't hear you come in." When he didn't say anything further, I said, "I heard noises earlier, two thumps. Coming from the third floor. Is that anything you might have heard before?"

Eric thought a moment. "I don't think it's anything to worry about."

"It's just a little scary when you're by yourself."

He took a few steps closer. "Are you alright? You look like you've seen a ghost."

His choice of words, and the way he said it, felt intentional.

"I might have," I said.

I continued leaning against the counter as Eric came closer. He stopped just in front of me, within arm's length.

"I remember being scared of this house as a child." He glanced around the kitchen, then settled his eyes back on me. "Especially at night. So many nooks and crannies, and dark corners for monsters to hide."

"No excuse for me, though. I'm a grown woman who knows better."

Eric cocked his head slightly and smiled. "We can easily forgive a child who is afraid of the dark. The real tragedy of life is when adults are afraid of the light."

I laughed nervously, unsure exactly what he was referring to. I wondered if he knew how truly terrifying the house could be, for anyone, of any age, if you were alone or vulnerable or superstitious. Maybe that's what he meant. And I wondered if he was hinting at a bigger picture that I had yet to see, some "light" he thought was being hidden: a beam of untold truth.

Yes, children can be forgiven, he seemed to be saying. They are just children, after all, and don't know any better. But adults—we *do* know better. We ought to be bold, we ought to be fearless, we ought to have nothing to hide.

That's what I sensed Eric was trying to convey, anyway.

"There's nothing to fear," Eric was saying when I refocused. "It's just a house."

"I'm not scared of the house. If I was, I wouldn't be staying here every—"

I stopped myself because there was a small piece of me that didn't trust him. For whatever reason, there was something I couldn't put my finger on. And I stopped myself because I'd temporarily forgotten about my nocturnal visit with him the night before, and was suddenly reminded—reminded that it had happened at all, that it hadn't just been a dream. It was like when Eric and I had supposedly met on the porch weeks before, as everyone was leaving for the day. I had only fuzzy memories of both moments, as if they'd been blurred in my mind—not erased completely, but rather lazily smudged over with an unseen fist.

"You're welcome to stay over as often as you wish," Eric said. "That's why the bedroom was set up for you."

"Were you ... were you here last night? Did you stay the night, I mean?"

Eric paused and smiled. "You asked me to vacate while construction was ongoing. Remember?"

But I saw you last night! In my bed! You invited me to join you! Or was that a dream? A dream about you, or maybe it was a dream about Kevin? Which is it? My mind was screaming but I couldn't find the courage to open my mouth.

"Right," I said, feeling more confused than ever.

"What it is, Lilian? What's troubling you?"

"It's nothing. I'll be fine."

He took a step closer and gently stroked my arm. We were both silent a moment, and it was about that time I felt it. An intense desire to be as close to Eric as possible, to be inside that bubble of warmth that seemed to surround him. It was like he'd suddenly put a spell on me. I shuffled forward and fixated on his face, his perfect nose and perfect lips and empathetic eyes. The nose and lips and eyes that looked just like Kevin's.

"Such sad eyes you have," Eric said, inching closer to me.

I instinctively inched closer to him, close enough to see the freckle on his left cheek and the small scar above his right eye.

"You know, I understand what it means to lose loved ones," he said softly. "My parents died when I was very young."

"I ... I had no idea," I said. "I'm so sorry."

"Car accident. They both died instantly."

"A car accident ..." I repeated.

"I was at boarding school in Germany at the time. I wasn't allowed to come home for their funerals."

"How very sad."

"And that lake ..." He motioned with his arm. "We lost so many family members to that lake."

"You did?" I said, still feeling like I was in a trance, and like I was hearing this news for the first time.

Come on, Lilian. You knew that. What's wrong with you? Snap out of it!

"It's the Becker curse, Lilian. Dying in that lake."

"Uh huh," I said, transfixed on Eric's moving lips.

"I wanted to acknowledge our family and their bitterness and their greed and their jealousy and their hatred. How it affected their lives and their relationships and how, in the end, it killed them all. I wanted to talk about how almost every single one of them was afraid of the light ..."

"Afraid of the light," I said.

"Yes, Lilian. Aren't we all afraid of the light, at some point in our lives? Scared of the truth and what it might do to us, should we reveal it?"

"Yes," I said, nodding, still feeling entranced, unable to move.

"That's right. So you see, it's okay to talk about your past. It's okay to talk about him. About Kevin."

When I heard Kevin's name, I shook my head, feeling tears drip down my cheeks. "He's gone. He's gone and he's never coming back." I was sobbing now, shoulders hunched, face in hands.

Eric gently pulled my hands away from my face. "You are a beautiful, strong, independent woman." He pushed a strand of hair out of my face. "You can face this."

In that moment, in the dim light of the kitchen, I felt the urge to kiss him. It wasn't the unbridled passion or animalistic hunger I'd had with Sam. This was something entirely different. This was a need to be held, to be heard, to be close to a man who understood. That's what Eric was giving me, so I allowed it to happen. I allowed him to kiss me.

It was tender and sweet and gentle. I felt my knees buckle and I know it sounds cliché but I think I swooned. Eric must've felt me slipping away, because he grasped my hips to hold me up, to keep me in place, his lips never leaving mine.

I remember worrying about getting close to Eric, about any intimacy that might happen, because I thought it was bad enough he looked like Kevin. I didn't want to know if he kissed like him, too.

The good news was that he didn't kiss anything like Kevin.

The bad news: it was better.

CHAPTER TWENTY-FIVE

I'D MISSED THE OPPORTUNITY to grill Eric. Test him. Find out if he'd met Kevin. I could've extracted information from him; instead, I made googly eyes and fell into a trance and then fell into his arms.

But at least I'd remembered what he'd said about his family. About his parents dying when he was a boy. How greedy his whole family was—the need for more money and more power. And how the greed had killed them all. And he'd even acknowledged the evil nature of the lake, how it had taken so many of his family members.

I mentally replayed the conversation, such as it was, as I sped along highway 276 toward the Historical Society to see Helen. I knew this was a day she volunteered, and I had more questions for her—about the Becker family, and about the borough council meeting where she first met Eric.

"How are you, dear?" Helen asked as we got situated, her behind the desk and me in the chair in front of it. "How's the renovation going?"

"That's why I'm here, actually. I have questions about the Becker family."

"Sounds like you're doing more research than renovation," she said slyly, and I smiled. Then her face changed. "Does this have anything to do with Kevin's and Frank's cremation requests?"

"It does. I'm piecing things together."

"Well, here's another piece for you. I reviewed Frank's final requests and verified with Claudine. They did not originally want to be cremated. Their bodies were to be buried. Claudine has no idea why Frank would make such a request."

My pulse had quickened during the ride to the Historical Society, in anticipation of what else I might out. Now, with Helen getting straight to the heart of the matter, and being so oddly calm about it, made my heart skip a few beats.

I took several deep breaths and exhaled slowly, attempting to regulate my heartbeat and give my brain time to think.

"Are you OK, Lilian?"

"I'm OK."

"What does it all mean? What are you piecing together?"

"I don't know, Helen. But I'm hoping you can help me."

"What I don't know I can certainly research for you."

"Do you know where the Beckers are buried?"

"They're all in Woodlawn Cemetery," she said. "Same as your parents, same as Kevin, same as my husband. Same as just about every deceased person in Pennsgrove And now Frank, too."

"I didn't realize the Becker family was at Woodlawn ... I've never seen any of the their plots."

"No plots. They have two columbariums. There's a whole columbarium section clustered in the very back corner of the cemetery."

"So none of the Beckers were buried?"

"I'm pretty sure all the Beckers were cremated. All the way back to the patriarch, Oskar Sr."

I made a face of disbelief and Helen said, "I know. Interesting, right? Frank told me that. And actually ..." She put her reading glasses on that had been sitting on the desk and started typing on the computer. She rambled as she typed: "We have access to Woodlawn's archives and all the internments dating back to the very beginning, and I kind of remember now Frank telling there were two Beckers who were buried ... let me see if I can find their plots ..."

She spoke aloud as her eyes scanned the screen. "Okay, so we have Oskar, Sr., his wife, and their three children. The other two brothers, Karl and Walter, and their wives and kids ... I think there might be a bunch of grandkids, too ..." She trailed off as she scanned the rest of the list of the Becker internments. "There must be at least fifty Beckers on this list. Now let me see ..." She scanned the list again. "So there was an Eric Becker that was originally buried." She looked up from the computer screen, peering at me over the top of her glasses.

"Eric was the bastard child of Oscar, Jr.," I said. "Bit of a black sheep, according to the other Eric Becker."

"Died 1968, aged 56, of liver disease."

"Yep, that's him."

Helen scanned the screen again. "He was originally buried, exhumed six months later, cremated, then reinterred in the family columbarium."

"That's odd. Why not originally cremated? Why six months later?"

"My records aren't going to tell me that," Helen said, laughing.

"Oh, I know. Just thinking out loud. Who was the other Becker that was buried?"

Helen glanced at the screen again. "Oscar Becker, Sr."

"What?"

"Originally buried in one of the oldest sections of the cemetery when he died in 1933. He was exhumed in 1968, three days after Eric Becker was exhumed. Oskar was exhumed, cremated, then reinterred in the family columbarium, just like Eric."

I stared off in space for a moment, digesting everything Helen had said. There could be an easy explanation for all the cremations, but I couldn't think of one. In fact, the conversation with my mother-in-law reminded me of all the reasons why all the Beckers shouldn't've been cremated. They had the money, so the cost of burial shouldn't've been a problem. They were of European descent, and Europeans are, like Americans, by and large Catholics, and the Catholics don't cremate their dead. Finally, cremation didn't start gaining popularity in America until the 1980s, and the Beckers were cremating probably as far back as the 1940s?

"One more thing, Helen," I said. "If you don't mind. Have you seen Eric Becker since meeting him for the first time in February at the borough council meeting?"

Helen scrunched her face. "I haven't, actually. Which is odd, considering he's apparently back in town, at least for now, while the mansion is being renovated."

She may have seen a version of him, I thought, but not the version she met in February.

"I got the impression that he'd been living elsewhere for awhile," she continued, "but he dodged my questions about that. No surprise there—I think being elusive runs in the Becker DNA."

"Anything else you remember about the meeting?"

"Let's see. I spoke to Kevin briefly." Helen gave me a sad look. "He was so excited about Community Day ... I remember Eric left shortly after the meeting was adjourned. You know, why he even showed up to the meeting is beyond me. He didn't ask any questions, he left as soon as soon as it was over, and he didn't talk—"

Helen stopped mid-sentence, causing me to sit up.

"What is it, Helen?"

"I saw Kevin and Eric together in the parking lot, when I was walking to my car. I had forgotten about that. I couldn't see Eric's face because he had his back to me with his hood pulled up. But I remembered Eric's coat. Kevin was doing most of the talking, and he seemed agitated."

"Could you hear what they were saying?"

Helen shook her head. "Kevin noticed me watching them as I walked by. He stopped talking and gave me a quick wave. Now that I think about it some more, Kevin looked nervous, scared almost. Eric never turned around or waved or anything. He just stood there facing Kevin the whole time. So strange."

Helen sat there for a minute, silent, looking equal parts frustrated that she hadn't given much importance to the event, and confused as to what it meant.

I stood to leave and thanked Helen for her time, trying for a hasty exit.

"Wait! What's going on, Lilian?" she asked, following me to the door. "Should I be worried?"

I knew there'd be more questions where that came from, none of which I was prepared to give her. Mostly because I didn't want to be responsible for any rumors that might spread via the town gossip, but also because I knew I was afraid of the possible answers.

I knew we should all be afraid.

CHAPTER TWENTY-SIX

IT WAS EARLY AFTERNOON and warm. The sky was clouding over as I drove to Woodlawn Cemetery, and a soft drizzle started as I arrived.

I drove the winding, narrow lanes to the furthest back corner of the cemetery. The road dead-ended and I found myself facing three large columbariums, side by side by side, with a sidewalk that stretched the entire length in front of them. Two stone benches were positioned equidistant between the three columbariums, facing them.

There was an old woman standing at the columbarium furthest to the right, leaning heavily on a cane. She was about twenty feet away, with her back to me. There was an umbrella in her other hand, which she used to shield herself from the rain. I didn't know which columbarium was the Beckers' without approaching, so I shut off the engine and sat in my car for a minute, deciding what to do. Should I wait for her to leave? Hope that the Beckers were in one of the other two and take my chance?

The old woman decided for me.

She turned around, using her cane for assistance, and slowly made her way to the bench, each step looking like a struggle. She saw my car and then looked at me and smiled wearily. With the shaky hand that held the umbrella, she motioned me forward, as if inviting me to the bench. It took great effort for her just to sit, and it was painful to watch.

I got out of the car and paused at the hood.

"Don't just stand there and watch," the woman said, her voice hoarse. She let out a short wheeze of a cough. "Come over and say hello."

I knew that voice. I recognized that cough.

"Emma?" I said, easing down onto the bench next to her. She was short and thin and looked every one of her eighty years. Each inhaled breath was long and deep, and each exhale sounded like an ounce of energy she'd never get back. Her eyes were blue and sad and they told me she was tired of living.

"You must be Lilian," she said. "I recognized your voice probably just as much as you recognized mine."

She turned her attention back to the columbarium in front of us. It was a large standalone marble structure on a limestone slab base. The structure was six niches high and eight niches across, each with a flat niche cover with a name engraved on it. The monument could accommodate forty-eight urns, forty-eight cremated human beings; every niche cover had a name engraved on it. Some of the names I recognized, most I didn't.

The other two columbariums to my left were identical, and as I turned my head to look at them, Emma said, "More Beckers. But the ones I care most about are here." She pointed to the one in front of us.

I stood, walked the ten feet to the columbarium and scanned the names.

"Your father." I ran my finger across his name, Oskar Becker, Jr., then pointed to the adjacent niche. "And your mother, Mary."

"Eric has told you about our family?" she asked.

"A little. Here and there." I scanned the names again, looking for ones that were familiar. "Thomas Becker, your brother and Eric's father. And Vivian, your sister-in-law and Eric's mother."

"Did Eric tell you what happened to his parents?"

"He said they both died in a car accident."

"Eric was an orphan at fourteen." She paused to catch her breath. "I became his guardian. I made him stay in Germany to finish his schooling. That's when we started to go wrong."

"You mean your relationship?"

"Eric was eighteen when he came home to me, to the house. Without the structure of private school, he was restless and bored." She shifted on the bench. The drizzle stopped and Emma attempted to close the umbrella. Sensing her struggle, I took the umbrella from her, closed it and placed it on the bench between us. She coughed once, cleared her throat and continued.

"I got him a job at the bakery, doing odds and ends. But he hated it, and he hated me. So I told him I'd pay for college, but he didn't want to do that either."

"What *did* he want?"

"He wanted out of that house, and away from me."

Emma went on to tell me, in slow, painful fits and starts, that Eric had packed a suitcase and a couple of duffel bags and drove off in his car a month after coming home from boarding school. He didn't want to go to college, he'd told his aunt. He wanted to experience life. And so he did.

He mailed Emma postcards from the road, and more formal letters once he'd settled somewhere. She sent him money wherever he went, even though he claimed to be self-sufficient enough to not need it. But he accepted it all the same.

He'd stay somewhere for a year or two, have a girlfriend or two, an odd job or two, then come home for a stretch, and live with whatever family members were occupying the house at the time. Emma was the constant fixture in the house, and during his return visits Eric would help her fix it up: new light fixtures, fresh paint, updated kitchen counters. These were all skills he claimed to have picked up on the road. Then he'd be gone again—a new job, new friends, a new girlfriend, a new life somewhere else.

He lived this itinerant life, his vagabond existence, Emma called it, for twenty-five years. San Francisco, Portland, Salt Lake City. Dallas, New Orleans, Oklahoma City. The wilds of Maine and the chaos of New York City. Tijuana and Toronto, too. He lived everywhere and nowhere, was known by everyone, yet to his family he remained a ghost. A specter that floated in and out of their lives, who came and went as he pleased—untouchable, unknowable, invisible.

It made sense to me why Frank had a hard time believing Eric was real. Because to the people of our town, he wasn't. He'd spent his entire adult life living somewhere other than Pennsgrove, so to them he simply didn't exist. Out of sight, out of mind.

Eric came home for good, though, four months before in January, when Emma was diagnosed with cancer. Over the course of that bone-chilling month, Eric moved Emma into a nursing home where she'd start receiving treatment. He sold off most of the items in the house or put it into storage, and set about figuring out what to do with the house. Emma and Eric still didn't agree on what to do with it, whether to stay or sell. The only thing they could agree on was that the house was in serious need of repair. And that's when I came into the picture.

"What a Godsend you are," Emma said. "I don't know where we'd be if you hadn't said yes to renovating the house."

Did you give me much choice? I thought.

"So what's it going to be?" I asked. "Stay or sell?"

Emma's eyes grew wide and showed a spark of life. "We have no choice. We must sell the house."

"Oh, so Eric finally convinced you."

Her face was somber again. "I've always wanted to sell the house. He's the one who—well, he wants ownership." She coughed gently into a thin, frail hand.

"I thought it was the other way around. Eric told me he wanted to sell. He said you want to die in the house."

"Oh, Lilian," she said, placing a cold hand atop mine. "Why would I want to die in a house that has already seen so much death?"

"I don't understand. Why would Eric lie to me?"

Emma took her hand back, lowered her head and sighed. "Eric has plans for the house," she said.

"Like rental units, or a B&B...?"

"Hmmm...perhaps." Her eyes narrowed as she looked up at me, every crease on her face a warning. "But the house would never allow it. The house doesn't like strangers."

That's when the headache started, quickly escalating from a twinge to a throb in less than a minute. I paused for a moment, listening to the old woman's slow, labored breathing, waiting for my pain to ease. I shifted to the edge of the bench, suddenly impatient for answers.

"What does that mean?" I said.

There was a distant rumble of thunder. The sky had darkened again, and the clouds looked full, ready to burst.

"I think you should go now," Emma said.

"Wait. What aren't you telling me? Why would Eric lie to me?" I tried the question again. A few drops of rain fell.

"Please go. I've said too much."

I scanned the area and found no vehicles other than my own. "How will you get home? I can't just leave you here."

She ignored my statement and stared straight ahead at the columbarium, at a hundred years' worth of ashes of her ancestors. "You're like a child to me, Lilian. Like the daughter I never had." She looked at me with a sense of urgency. "Now go." She coughed into her hand and strained at the effort.

Emma was done talking. She had been drained to the point of exhaustion. I would get no answers from a dying woman that day.

But I would get an answer, just not from her.

I climbed into my car and made my way down the winding alleys of Woodlawn Cemetery. As I did, I tried listening to what the headache was trying to tell me.

What message do you have for me today?

By the time I arrived home, and after having listened only to the silent sound of my own intuition, my headache was gone.

I got my answer.

Emma had nothing to do with any of this. She was innocent. This was all Eric. Whatever he had planned, this was his game. And I was an unwilling pawn.

CHAPTER TWENTY-SEVEN

I SHOWED UP MID-AFTERNOON on a Tuesday, expecting to see people and progress. The first red flag was the silence: a pin-dropping, almost bone-chilling, quiet. Various first and second floor windows were open, curtains billowing about the open spaces.

When did we get window treatments?

I walked up onto the porch, cautiously opened the front door and tip-toed into the vestibule, almost expecting to be bum-rushed by a barrage of construction workers who'd had me punk'd. But there was no one. No one hiding in the closets, cowering in corners, or pressed up against walls.

"Hello?" I called out to the empty spaces all around me, and I think I heard my voice echo back to me.

No noise whatsoever, but signs of life. In the kitchen, a table saw's blades slowly spun to a stop, as if the operator had just shut it off and left the room. In one exterior wall of the parlor, a yawning hole waited for a replacement window. A new chandelier lay on the floor in the dining room, wiring and lamp shades and suspension chains all splayed as if just unpacked from the box.

And then finally, a noise—running water.

From one of the bathrooms on the second floor, it sounded like. I walked to the top of the second-floor landing and again said, "Hello?" to the emptiness. Nothing but the sound of water.

I narrowed the source to the bathroom with the clogged toilet; as I stepped into the room, I noticed the sink tap was on, and a steady flow of water circled down the drain.

I turned off the water, then heard another noise: Sam's voice, calling me. Soft and echoing yet muffled, coming from the third floor. I took the stairs to the third floor, walked through both bedrooms and the bathroom and found them empty.

No Sam.

Without investigating further, I returned to the second floor, then down the steps to the vestibule, where Eric patiently waited for me. Something about him frightened me: the fact that he'd showed up while I was in the house? His devilish smile and the squint in his eye? The way he'd held out his hand, as if expecting me to take it and follow?

"I have something to show you," he said.

"Where is everyone?" I asked.

He didn't answer or shrug or change his facial expression even the slightest. He just motioned to his hand and silently bade me to take it. He led me outside onto the edge of the porch, where he released my hand and turned his head in the direction of the lake. I followed his gaze and shrieked in horror. I cried and started shaking.

There were bodies floating in the lake: about two dozen, bloodied and bloated and brackish from the scummy water. The bodies of Big Al and Miguel and Tyler and Bob Watson and everyone else who had worked on the house. And then I saw him.

Sam. Dead, floating on his back, his eyes skyward.

And I ran to him, through the grass and to the edge of the shore where I lunged myself into the lake, clothes and shoes and all. I waded through the corpses until I reached his. I grabbed his cold body and pulled it to me, shoving him against my chest and sobbing. When I looked down at him, at his vacant stare, his eyes suddenly shifted and he looked at me. His moss-covered arms grabbed me, pawed at my back, trying to pull me below the surface. I panicked, thrashed and flailed and attempted to shove him away. But it was no use; I felt Sam dragging me under. As I took one final breath, I saw Eric standing on the porch, watching me.

I woke to the sound of my cell phone ringing loudly in my ear.

The caller I.D. said *Sam Cell*. It took me a minute to realize I was indeed awake, that I wasn't having a dream within a dream.

I answered. "Sam?"

You were just dead, and now you're alive.

"Where are you?" he said, loud and out of breath. I could hear hurried voices and a flurry of activity in the background.

I sat up and smoothed down my hair as if Sam could see through the phone. "I'm at home. What's the matter?"

"I've been calling and texting..."

"I'm sorry. I fell asleep."

"We have a problem. Can you get to the house?"

"When?"

"Right now," he said sternly.

"What's happening?"

"It's Bob. He's...gone. He died, Lil."

The shock sent me to the edge of the bed. "What?"

"He had a stroke."

"What do you mean he had a stroke?"

Sam's demeanor went from somber to angry. "For fuck's sake! He had a stroke! What else is there to say?"

"Okay, Sam. Okay. What happened?"

I put Sam on speaker phone and threw my shoes on as he spoke.

"One minute he was laying carpet in the upstairs bedrooms, the next minute he's in the fetal position. Now can you get here or not?"

"Who's there with you?"

"Police. Ambulance. Our entire crew. It's a shit show!"

"Listen, Sam. First I need you to calm down, take a few breaths. Then I need you to get our crew out of there. Send them home. They're done for the day. Got it?"

Sam took a large inhale of breath and let it out slowly. "Got it."

"Do you think the police and ambulance are almost done?"

"Ambulance literally just pulled out of the driveway with Bob's body. Cops are wrapping up some interviews with eye-witnesses."

"I'll be there in thirty minutes. Think the cops will be gone by then?"

"Yeah, I think so."

"Good. When I get there, Sam, you better be gone, too."

Emma had been right. The house didn't want people. It didn't like strangers.

And, if allowed, The Property would continue to chase them off, scare them away, injure or kill them if necessary.

There was only one person who could help me with what I needed to do next.

CHAPTER TWENTY-EIGHT

I WALKED NEXT DOOR and frantically rang the doorbell, once, twice, three times. The front door opened with a whoosh and when Stella saw me her smile melted into gloom. We stood there staring at each other for a moment, she stiff and me shaking, and I could tell Stella was reading my thoughts, assessing what I might need.

"Where do you need to take me, Lilian?" she finally said.

"The house I'm renovating."

She ushered me into the foyer.

"I'm sorry, Stella. I didn't know where else to go." Then the tears came, and I covered my mouth to hide the intense sobbing that wanted to come out. I didn't want to alarm her family, or make them think their wife and mother was friends with a crazy woman. But, given her line of business, I'm sure Stella's family had seen their fair share of otherworldly people, places, and things.

She put both hands on either side of my face. "Lilian, you are always welcome here, you know that. I'm here to help. Now, you wait right here. I'll be back in a jiffy."

As she left me alone in the foyer and made her way into the kitchen, I heard her yell out, "Joe and the kiddos? Mommy's got to go out for a bit! Be good while I'm gone!"

After a minute she joined me back in the foyer, a big bag slung over her shoulder.

"What's all that?" I motioned to the bag, wiping my eyes on the back of my shirt.

Stella's eyes narrowed, and she smirked and said, "Supplies."

Once we were a few minutes into our half-hour journey, I said, "Are you familiar with the Becker estate? That's the house I'm renovating."

She sighed. "Had I known that, I might have dissuaded you. I've heard stories ..."

"Have you heard of the Becker curse?"

"Oh, sure. And I believe it. But curse or no curse, you also have to believe that there was a lot of bad luck in the family over the years, too. Plain and simple bad luck—a lot of it of their own doing."

"I agree. But the place is cursed, Stella. I didn't believe it at first. But I do now. I believe in all of it." I went on to tell her about all the negative things and bad luck that had been happening to my crew, and to Sam and I. I told her about my dreams and Sam's paranormal encounters. About my visions and Sam's change in behavior. I told her about Frank and Miguel and Ben and Bob.

And I told Stella about Eric. About how I nearly fell for the doppelganger of my deceased husband whose house I was hired to renovate. A doppelganger I was starting to think was responsible for his death. Eric Becker—the double walker, the demon in my view.

"Oh, Lilian. I'm so sorry you're going through all this." She placed a hand on mine as it held the steering wheel. "It's that damned lake, you know. It's a portal."

"Portal to hell, maybe."

"Yes, that's it exactly, Lilian. It's a portal to hell. It's a lake of fire."

"Like the Nirvana song?" I quipped, trying to calm my nerves. I had no idea what we were about to face, so any attempt at levity to calm my nerves? Yeah, I was all over that like a cheap suit, however fleeting the moment would be.

Stella laughed. "I'm familiar with Nirvana and Kurt Cobain and my goodness what a damaged soul he was ..." she trailed off for a minute, then refocused. "But ... I'm not familiar with that song."

"It basically says good people go to heaven when they die, where the angels fly, and the bad folks go to the lake of fire and fry." I quoted the song as close to verbatim as I could.

"That's an accurate description."

"What does it mean? What are we dealing with here?"

"The concept of a lake of fire goes as far back as the Egyptians, who believed in an underworld filled with fiery lakes and rivers, populated with fire demons, where the wicked would go when they died."

"Hell, in other words?"

"Yes, exactly. The ancient Egyptians are oftentimes credited with the invention of hell. Most modern-day people, Christians especially, are familiar with the concept of hell because of the Book of Revelation. It references a 'second death,' or death of the soul, spiritual death, after your body's biological death. Sin and wickedness mean eternal pain for your soul, with no hope for redemption or salvation."

"Complete with fire and brimstone and all the trimmings," I said, just as we pulled into the driveway of The Property.

We were the only ones there. Luckily, Sam had heeded my warning. My instructions to him had been simple and explicit: don't be there when I get there. Everyone, including you, Sam, needs to be gone. I didn't want anyone to know what we were going to do, not even him.

I parked the car. Stella gasped as she took it all in—the house, the lake, the property as a whole. She immediately got out and made her way over toward the lake.

If there had been a scene here earlier, with cops and ambulances and flashing lights and people shouting and a dead body being hauled out of the house, you wouldn't have known it. The entire place was peaceful and calm, the house dark. It was about four in the afternoon, but the overcast skies made it feel more like eight. I sat in my car for a minute, saying the closest thing I knew to be a prayer, and watched Stella walk so close to the edge of the lake I thought she might fall in.

Her eyes were closed as I approached the lake and stood next to her. There was a string of rosary beads in one of her hands and a shiny black, round crystal in the other. She was whispering something, what I assumed, hoped, was an incantation to rid the lake of evil. She opened her eyes, put the beads and crystal back in her bag and pulled out a small bottle of holy water.

"I didn't know you were religious," I said.

"I'm a recovering Christian," she said. "But I'm also a Wiccan priestess. So rosary beads, a black jasper crystal, and holy water represent the best of both worlds!"

"It's a big lake, Stella. How far are you getting with that little bottle?" I was still nervous and on-edge, my claircognizance kicking in hardcore. And it was telling me this night would not end well.

"Don't you worry. There are ten more where this one came from." She slowly walked the whole perimeter of the lake, splashing the holy water onto its surface, repeating a blessing over and over until I thought I had it memorized. When she'd finished, she rejoined me and said, "Where to next?"

I led her onto the porch and was about to go inside when she paused to reach into her bag. She pulled out a green glass bottle of extra virgin olive oil. I gave her a funny look.

"Anointing oil," she said. "It's the best I could do in a pinch."

She poured some onto her finger and made the sign of the cross on the front door. "May your Holy Spirit flow through and fill this home up with your Spirit," she said. Then, "Smoke and air, fire and earth; cleanse and bless this home and hearth."

We stepped into the vestibule and she looked around, peeking into the parlor and the kitchen, contemplating. Stella started rooting around in her bag again.

"I'm going to cleanse the house," she said. "Then I'm going to perform a typical spiritual blessing." She pulled out a small battery-operated fan and handed it to me. "Hold this. Now do me a favor. Go around the house and open every window."

I did as I was told, and when I returned to the vestibule she was holding a lighter up to the end of a fat stick. The end glowed orange and she gently blew out the flame; the stick continued billowing out gray smoke.

"This is a white sage smudge stick, infused with palo santo, lavender, and juniper," she said. "It will cleanse and protect the house, and the smoke will blow away any negative energy."

I nodded and we were off. We went from room to room, with Stella waving the smoke from the burning stick into every open space, using the fan to get the smoke into corners, around window and door frames and up and down the walls. It was slow and time-consuming, but by the time she was done, there wasn't an inch of the house that hadn't been filled with that pure cleansing scent.

It was when we got back to the vestibule that the first twinge of a headache started. The house had been quiet before, but now it was so deathly still, like the calm before a storm. We glanced at each other and knew instantly we were sensing the same thing at the same time.

"Do you feel that?" Stella asked. "That shift in energy?"

I nodded and rubbed my temple. "It doesn't feel like a good shift."

"Quick," Stella said, putting the sage and fan back into her bag. She pulled out another bottle of holy water and the rosary beads, which she hastily put around her neck. She held the black jasper crystal in her other hand. "Follow me."

We started in the parlor. Stella sprinkled the room with holy water, saying, "In the name of Jesus Christ, I ask for Your peace and joy to inhabit this room. Smoke and air, fire and earth; cleanse and bless this home and hearth." She handed me the bottle of olive oil and told me to rub a sign of the cross on every window and door as we went from room to room, as high up as I could reach.

As we left the parlor, the door slammed shut behind us with a *bang*. It startled us and we both jumped and shrieked. We stopped momentarily, frozen in fear.

"Keep going!" Stella said, leading me into the kitchen.

My headache rocketed from a dull ache to a throb. I had goosebumps all over and a paranoid feeling of being watched. And was that a slight rumbling through the entire house, like the passing of an invisible freight train?

The house was coming alive, and it was pissed.

Stella yelled over the rumbling, spraying holy water as she went. "In the name of Jesus Christ, I ask for Your peace and joy to inhabit this room! Smoke and air, fire and earth; cleanse and bless this home and hearth!" I put my hands over my ears and prayed for the throbbing in my head and the rumbling in the house to stop.

She motioned for me to rub the olive oil on the kitchen windows. Then she pointed to her left, indicating she'd get a head start on the rest of the first floor while I anointed the kitchen windows.

When I found her a few minutes later in the dining room, the six-light brass chandelier—newly installed and a lucky find of Sam's at a local antique shop—was shaking so intensely that fine grains of plaster dust rained from the ceiling.

Stella looked undeterred, sprinkling more holy water, and more forcefully this time. "In the name of Jesus Christ, I ask for Your peace and joy to inhabit this room! Smoke and air, fire and earth; cleanse and bless this home and hearth." She turned to me. "Upstairs! Now, Lilian!"

I spun around too quickly and a wave of vertigo washed over me. I pushed forward and grabbed the handrail for support as we climbed the steps to the second floor. We went room to room, repeating each step: holy water, blessings, anointing oil. Wash, rinse, repeat, through each room. All the while my head throbbed and spun and the house convulsed. Through it all Stella remained a rock of stability. She was scared shitless, too, I could see it in the way her hands trembled, but her face was a mask of Fuck-You determination.

When we climbed the steps to the third floor, every window in the house started slamming shut on its own, one by one by one in rapid succession. We finished the third floor, raced down to the second, then down the steps to the first.

By then doors were slamming all around us, lights were flickering uncontrollably, power tools and equipment buzzed and vibrated, and the house still shook and rumbled over our heads and beneath our feet. It was hard to hear and even harder to think straight. And I felt it was no longer safe for us to be there. We had to go.

We reached the vestibule and Stella yelled, "The basement!"

"Fuck the basement! We need to get out of here!"

I grabbed her arm and tugged her toward the front door, but she resisted.

"Stella, we have to go. Now!"

"There's one more thing I need to do," she said. She reached into her bag and pulled out a palm-sized, black, shiny piece of jagged rock and held it to her chest. Eyes closed, she said, "With this black tourmaline, I dispel the powers of darkness that may be in this house!"

She kept her eyes closed as she whispered something over and over again, the tourmaline still held tightly to her. Suddenly her body loosened as if she were about to faint, and she wavered on her feet.

"Stella? Are you OK? We need to go!"

She opened her eyes, repeated the incantation one final time...and then passed out cold on the vestibule floor. The tourmaline crystal tumbled from her arms and rolled across the floor.

I rushed to her and cradled her head. Looking upwards, I screamed to the house, "Three more weeks, you son of a bitch! Just give me three more weeks and we'll be gone!"

Our senses were still under assault by thunderous noise and flashing lights. The house felt like it was about ready to cave in on itself. I gently tapped Stella's face several times. She awoke with a start, and I helped her to her feet. She grabbed the tourmaline and put it her bag. We rushed out the front door without bothering to lock up behind us, or even close the front door. Stella looked weak and was uneasy on her feet, so I helped her into the passenger side. Once we were buckled in, I slammed the car into drive.

And as I peeled out of the driveway with a screech, I silently wished the house would burn to the fucking ground.

CHAPTER TWENTY-NINE

I DIDN'T WANT TO GO back, but I had to make sure it was safe. It was the next morning, the day after all hell broke loose at The Property, and I had a couple of things on my to-do list that needed my immediate attention: one, see if there was any physical damage from the spiritual cleansing and blessing. Two, gauge morale after Bob's shocking death. Three, see if Eric would suddenly appear today, like he tended to do whenever I was there. Four, assess what kind of mood he was in, if and when he did show up.

Heart thumping, I pulled into the driveway. I didn't give myself time to talk myself out of going in; I marched up the porch steps, rushed through the front door—and nearly collided with Sam in the vestibule.

"Geez, Lil." He stumbled back a few steps. "Where's the fire?"

"Sorry, Sam. I was, uh, I was looking for you."

"Yeah, well. Here I am."

"Everything okay?" I looked into the kitchen and up the stairs to the second floor. The only comforting thing in that moment was the sound of banging and hammering and sawing, and the commands being given and taken.

Sam gave me a funny look. "Everything's good."

"How have you been feeling? Any more nightmares?"

Sam shrugged and shook his head.

"Any more shadows or apparitions?"

"Nothing like that. But I got to tell you." He looked around as if to make sure no one was within earshot. "Ever get that feeling that you aren't alone here? Like you're being watched? There are some mornings when I'm doing my walkthrough first thing, and I'm here by myself. I know there's no one else in the house, but it feels like there is. That's something new that's been happening."

"I know what you mean. I started feeling that recently, too."

His body shivered. "Creeps me out. And I still feel ... off ... especially when I'm here ..." he trailed off and looked around.

"I'm sorry."

"Not your fault."

"How's the house itself? Anything seem out of sorts?"

"Out of sorts...?"

I didn't want to alarm him more than I had to. At least not yet. He'd had enough drama yesterday with Bob's death, dealing with the authorities, keeping everyone calm. And he'd just about convinced himself the house was haunted, on account of his dreams and mood swings and a superstitious ex-employee, and now the feeling of being watched. I didn't want to put more shit on his plate. I didn't have the heart to be like: *Yeah, so, you know that little thing called the Becker curse? It's real. Last night, after everyone left, Stella and I performed a spiritual cleansing with sage sticks, olive oil, rosary beads, crystals, and the best of intentions. I'm here to see if it stuck. Because if it didn't stick? If the curse is still in effect, then I'm afraid we might all be fucked.*

If that was the case, he'd find out sooner or later. I think he was starting to believe it anyway, but I wanted to ease him into it.

"Out of sorts," I repeated. "You know, with what happened to Bob. I thought everyone might be a bit freaked out."

Sam sighed. "That was so awful. We watched a man drop to the floor and die in front of us."

"I know, Sam. I'm so sorry. I can't imagine."

"I called his widow this morning. Gave her our condolences. We should send flowers or something."

I chewed on a fingernail and stared off into space. If only Stella and I had performed the ritual sooner, Bob might still be alive. If only I'd taken Miguel's fear of the lake more seriously. If only I hadn't taken the project in the first place. If only I hadn't cheated on Kevin. So many fucking if-onlys ...

Not the time to unpack your stupid suitcase, Lilian, I told myself.

"Lil?" Sam said.

I snapped back. "Huh?"

"No need to be sorry."

"Yeah, I know. But I should've been here."

"There's no way you could know that was going to happen." He reached out to touch my hair, thought better of it, and withdrew. He cleared his throat and motioned with his head to the parlor. "Actually, there is one thing around here that's out of sorts."

I looked into the parlor and saw Eric standing with his hands behind his back, looking out the bay window at the lake. I hadn't noticed him when I came in.

"He's been standing there like that for a half hour," Sam said.

"I need to talk to him."

Sam looked in Eric's direction with disdain. "Yeah, you go do that. I have to get back to work anyway." He gave a muffled goodbye and walked outside.

I went into the parlor and stood next to Eric, who continued standing like a statue, overlooking the front property.

"Hello, Lilian," he said, still looking straight ahead. His voice was flat and his face unreadable.

"Eric," I said cautiously.

"Did you have a nice visit with Aunt Em at the cemetery?"

"She told you about that?"

Eric finally looked at me. "She did."

"What did she tell you we talked about?"

"Well, apparently you learned a lot about my life."

"I already knew about your childhood. Your parent's deaths. Your time in the German boarding school. You told me those things."

"I remember."

"She told me about your adulthood. Your travels around the country. Your periodic visits home." When Eric didn't respond I said, "Does that bother you?"

"No."

"That's good, because those years sound positive. The freedom and independence to travel and do what you want. Come and go as you please. That's the type of life many people would kill for."

"Kill for. Now there's an interesting phrase." He faced me and took a step forward so that he was nearly in my face. "Is there something *you* would kill for, Lilian?"

Kevin's doppelganger, I reminded myself. A demon in my view. I found him. And he was standing right in front of me. The gentle, tender man who'd kissed me a few days before was nowhere to be found. The person who had empathized with me, made me feel cared for and understood, was gone. What stood before me felt angry, malevolent and dangerous.

He knew that Stella and I had been here the other night. He knew what we had done. I could feel it. His energy was different. The energy in the house was different. The real Eric Becker was finally coming out to play.

I met his steely gaze. "I suppose I would kill to have my husband back."

"Is that so?"

There was a pulse of electricity between us, a sexual tension that crackled from his body to mine and back again. If anyone walked into the room right now and saw the way we were standing, how we glared at each other, it would be hard for them to discern whether we were about to fight or fuck.

"You met him," I said. "So you can understand how I would kill to have such a wonderful man back in my life, right?"

"You must be mistaken. I've never met Kevin."

"You met him three months ago at a town hall meeting."

"I don't think so, Lilian."

"Don't lie to me. I saw the CCTV footage."

Helen was certain she'd seen Eric talking to Kevin in the parking lot after the Community Day meeting at borough hall. But I needed more proof. I left the historical society, drove to the borough building and tried to convince the security guards to let me review the CCTV footage from that day. I got nowhere fast, so I invoked the Freedom of Information Act, and the two guards exchanged amused looks and burst out laughing. One of them told me that law was used for disclosure of information from federal government agencies, not the security footage of a parking lot in Small Town, USA.

In the end, though, I got my way—I saw the footage. It was my embarrassment and their amusement that sealed the deal: my reward, they'd said, for making their day.

And what I saw fit Helen's description of what happened to a T.

"What do you think you saw?" Eric asked.

I was growing weary of his stall tactics. "You and Kevin in the parking lot, near the front entrance, talking after the meeting."

Eric paused, then finally said, "Ah, yes. Now I remember. Tall fellow. Blonde hair, blue eyes. I recall chatting with him."

"What did you talk about?"

"You saw the footage, Lilian. You tell me."

"There was no sound. I saw the back of your hooded coat and the front of Kevin."

"Then how can you be sure it was me?"

"Eyewitnesses who identified you."

"Really? That's interesting..."

"Why?"

"No reason. Who are your so-called eyewitnesses?"

"That doesn't matter. The point is, Kevin looked agitated in the video. Disturbed. What did you say to him?"

"I honestly don't know what could've gotten him upset. We were just having a casual chat."

"Bullshit!"

We were both silent for a moment, staring each other down.

"Who are you?" I finally said, taking a huge gamble. "Is Eric even your name?"

"I am Eric Becker," he said, self-assuredly and without hesitation.

"You met my husband three months ago. You talked to him in the Borough Hall parking lot. Words were exchanged. Kevin was obviously upset. I'd like to know why."

Eric pushed a wayward strand of hair out of my face. I flinched but wasn't quick enough to deflect his hand.

"Are you afraid of me, Lilian?"

My answer was firm and resolute. "No."

Eric leaned in and whispered in my ear, "Perhaps you should be." Then he walked past me and glided out the front door.

I followed him, only because I was ready to leave, not because I was bruising for another confrontation. As I walked down the front porch steps in a huff, I saw Sam and Tyler taking a coffee break, leaning against Sam's pickup truck.

"Who wants overtime?" I yelled out to whoever could hear me. Three or four sets of eyes turned to look at me, and one of them raised their hand.

I made my way over to Sam. "Has anyone been asking about overtime?" I asked him.

"Sure, Lil. Couple guys."

"Give it to them. If fact, offer it to every goddamn person we got working on this house."

"I could use a couple extra hours," Tyler said.

"Awesome, Tyler," I said. "You got it."

Sam furrowed his brow. "That's gonna cut into our overhead."

"I don't give a shit. We need to button up this house sooner rather than later."

"What we need, Lil, is three more weeks."

"Finish it in two."

Sam opened his mouth to speak, but I cut him off. "No questions or objections, Sam. Just make it happen."

As I got into my car and drove away, I noticed Eric standing at the edge of the lake, watching me.

CHAPTER THIRTY

I SENSED THE STORM was coming. Three straight days of intense headaches and three straight nights of disturbing dreams. And I was stuck in a loop: I needed to sleep to get rid of the headaches, but every time I slept, I had nightmares. So those three days were spent mostly in bed, thinking and not sleeping.

Sam had promised me that the house would be done in two weeks. I don't know why I felt the need to move up our schedule. Call it that deeper inner knowing I'd been nurturing lately; that deep inner knowing was telling me shit was about ready to hit the fan, and that three weeks would be too damn late.

I trusted Sam to get the job done. In fact, he was the only one I trusted at this point. I didn't even trust myself. I'd allowed myself to be taken in emotionally by the ominous doppelganger of my deceased husband. I'd given him permission to push past my defenses. The resulting guilt and the shame made me angry, embarrassed and sleepless.

I didn't know what kind of shitstorm was coming, or when, but I felt it was inevitable. So when I wasn't in bed with a headache I was keeping busy, mostly on Property related business: paperwork, payroll, accounting. That way, if we had to bolt from the project before it was done, at least I could say my end of the bargain was finished to the best of my ability.

I took a three-day absence from The Property to do this. To focus, to strategize, to prepare. This is one of the few things I didn't feel guilty about. Sam was my foreman, he was handling things, and it was his job to be there every day.

He texted and called frequently, asking where I was, if I needed anything. He was worried, he said. Originally, I wanted him in the loop, to know everything I knew. So I told him about the Becker family history, about the deaths in the lake, about the Becker family curse. But when his personality started changing, when he started existing on a hair trigger, when I sensed his drinking was becoming a problem ... well then, all bets were off. From that point on, Sam was officially on a need-to-know basis. I couldn't afford for him to be distracted from getting The Property buttoned up in two weeks. So I sent him a few non-descript texts saying yes, I was fine and no, I didn't need anything. And that he'd be seeing me soon.

I also called Jake to see how the cash-out of Kevin's life insurance policy was going. If the shitstorm wound up being bigger than anticipated, I thought about skipping town entirely, selling my house and the business (maybe to Sam) and everything I owned and moving to Denver to live with my sister and her family with half a million in my pocket. Hell, even if there was no shitstorm at all, if we finished The Property and nothing came to fruition, maybe a change of pace was in order. A brand-new start somewhere else. Maybe I'd ask Sam to go with me ...

But I expected there to be fallout, which is why I also wanted to contact Stella, to fill her in, to get her feedback, to solicit her help for when Eric Becker released unholy hell. On the third day of my self-imposed exile, I reached out to her, but my multiple phones calls and texts went unanswered and unreturned. I had already reached out to Sam hours earlier, to let him know I was okay and didn't need anything and, by the way, is The Property almost done? But those calls and texts were similarly unanswered and unreturned.

I started getting concerned when, after six hours, I hadn't heard back from Sam. Stella, I could understand. I'd only reached out to her about two hours before. With four kids, a husband, and a business to run, the girl was busy. But Sam? Wasn't like him to let a text go unanswered. By now it was seven at night and my chores for the day were done and I wanted to unwind with a glass of wine and a good comedy, but I couldn't concentrate because my mind was racing. Where the hell was Sam? I checked my phone every few minutes, thinking I'd somehow missed a call or text.

And that's when the tingling started. On the top of my head, as usual, before spreading down my neck and across my shoulders, which was not normal. I shivered as an intense dread settled in the pit of my stomach. *Something is wrong. Very wrong.* With Sam, and possibly Stella. *They're both in danger, and you need to find them. Now.*

I raced upstairs, threw on some clothes and ran next door to Stella's. I tried to catch my breath before ringing the doorbell. Her husband Joe answered.

"Lilian, right?"

I nodded, still somewhat winded. He stepped out onto the porch, looking concerned. He left the front door slightly open.

"Is everything okay?"

"Fine, Joe. Is Stella here?"

"No. I thought she was with you."

"What made you think that?"

"Because when she left, she said she was going to meet *you.*"

"What time was that?" I asked.

"Around five."

"Did she say she'd be gone long?"

"She wasn't real clear on that." Joe sounded annoyed now.

We stood in silence for a moment, me chewing a fingernail, thinking, and Joe staring at me, looking for answers.

"So I take it you haven't seen her?" he asked, and I shook my head. "Did she tell you where she was going?"

"I haven't seen or talked to her. I called and texted her around the same time you said she left, but I haven't heard back from her. Do you have any idea where she might be?"

"Maybe. But I hope I'm wrong." He sighed, then murmured, "I can't go through this again ..."

"What do you mean?"

"Never mind, Lilian. Listen, I can't go looking for her right now. I'm in the middle of feeding the kids." He pointed over his shoulder, back inside the house. "Maybe in a half-hour or so ..."

If Stella was where I thought she was, I didn't have even thirty minutes to spare.

"It's fine, Joe. I have an idea where she might be, too."

His body stiffened, and he looked desperate and scared for his wife, but also, perhaps, a little annoyed that I would know where she was when he didn't. "Tell me where. I'll go with you. Just give me thirty minutes."

"No, let me go by myself. You stay put and take care of the kids. If I don't find her there, I'll call you."

Joe ran back into the house to grab his cell phone so we could exchange numbers. As he did, I peeked through the half-open door and saw the four Matthews children sitting at the kitchen island, each engaged in their own activity. The one girl looked up from her coloring book and said to Joe with a sad face, "Where's Mommy?" To which Joe said, "Don't worry, honey. She'll be home soon."

And as Joe came back out onto the porch, cell phone in hand, I thought to myself: I wish I knew that was true. But if she was where I thought she was, neither she, nor Sam—nor I, for that matter—would likely make it home anytime soon.

CHAPTER THIRTY-ONE

I SPED DOWN THE HIGHWAY with purpose, petal to the floor. I don't know how I knew where Sam and Stella were, I just knew. But just to be sure, I drove by Sam's house first. His pickup truck was gone, and I knew, then, with one-hundred percent clarity.

I pulled into the driveway of The Property and nearly screeched to a halt when I saw all the cars: Sam's pickup and Stella's VW Bug and Jake's SUV and Helen's Toyota. What were Jake and Helen doing here?

The house was dark, except for a light shining through the bay window of the parlor. I walked through the front door, cautiously stepped into the vestibule and stopped dead in the doorway of the parlor.

On the floor of the parlor was a pentagram drawn in white paint, encircled by five chairs. In four of the chairs sat Sam, Stella, Jake, and Helen. They were gagged, their arms zip-tied behind their backs. The fifth chair was empty.

In the middle of the circle stood Eric, pacing back and forth. Emma was there too, in a chair off to the side, looking weak and frail. When I gasped at the scene in front of me, six pairs of eyes looked at me simultaneously. Each of their faces wore a mask: terror, confusion, vulnerability, anger, determination, submission.

I turned to run, fumbling in my back pocket for my phone as I did. I wasn't sure how I was going to explain this to a 9-1-1 dispatcher, but it didn't matter. I just needed to make the call. I ran through the vestibule, trying to dial but Eric overcame me, grabbing my arm and holding me in place with a strength of what felt like forty men. He snatched my phone with his free hand and shoved it into his own back pocket.

"Where do you think you're going?" Eric said.

"Let me go!" I hissed, trying to break free.

"Soon. But first I need you to have a seat." He pointed to the empty fifth chair. He tried pulling me toward the parlor and I tried wrenching in the direction of the front door.

"This will go so much easier if you don't struggle," he said calmly.

I couldn't break free, so I had no choice but to go with him. As he walked me to the empty chair, my eyes went immediately to Sam. He was looking at me wide-eyed, and he subtly shook his head as if to say, *Don't do anything rash*. I shrugged at him, anguished.

Eric noticed our exchange and turned towards Sam.

"Samuel," he said. "Be a good boy, or else I'll have to blindfold you."

Sam struggled against the straps, his chair wobbling back and forth. "Fuck you," he said through the gag. As I was forced to sit in the fifth chair, I looked briefly at the other faces; most of them looked truly terrified, wholly ignorant of what was going on, why they were there.

And then there was Stella. Outwardly, she didn't appear to be afraid or confused. She just looked pissed. She stared Eric down, watching him pace in the middle of the circle. Our eyes connected and she motioned down to the side of her chair. I glanced down and saw the same bag of tricks she'd used for our cleansing and blessing of the house. I gave her a discreet thumbs up—though, unless she had a pair of snippers, I had no idea how any of her tools could possibly help.

Eric noticed this exchange too, but curiously he didn't say anything to Stella, or threaten to blindfold her. He actually looked at her warily and kept his distance. Something about Stella scared him. I would have to use that to my advantage.

I decided to play along, for now. Feel him out. Get a sense of his motives. I knew he had it in him to hurt every single one of those people in the circle, each one of them I loved in one way or another. So if I made a wrong move, angered him, there'd be no chance of saving them.

I glanced briefly at Emma, who looked at me with a wan, Mona-Lisa smile. Was she happy? Sad? Concealing something? I honestly couldn't tell.

"Don't hurt any of them," I said to Eric.

"I'm unarmed. Would you like to check?" He held up his arms in submission, inviting me to frisk him.

"No. Just let them go. This is between you and me. They're all innocent."

"None of you are innocent. You're all here for a reason."

"What are those reasons, Eric? What is this?"

"This is judgement day! Each of them, including you—" he motioned around the circle, his accusatory finger landing on me last—"will have a chance to repent for your sins."

At this, the four others moaned and gasped and cried.

"And then what?" I asked. "The good eggs get to keep on living, and the bad ones get dragged out to your little pond out front?"

Eric glided over to me, squatted down so he was inches from my face, and said, "You're all bad eggs. Your fates have probably already been sealed. But that's not up to me to decide." He seductively touched my cheek. I batted him away and he laughed.

"Leave her alone!" Emma croaked, interrupting Eric's laughing. She fell into a fit of coughing that left her out of breath and paler than I've ever seen her.

Eric stood up and turned toward Emma. "My dear Aunt Em, you know I can't do that."

Emma's voice was quivering but calm. "I wanted no part of this. You made me, Eric. You made me do this. You brought me here."

"I didn't make you do anything. It's the house. You and I both know that. The house is in charge, and it will always have its way. We are here to do its bidding. So we must both be here."

Emma's lip trembled, her blue eyes watery with defeat. She leaned back in her chair, gingerly and resignedly.

"What do you mean, the house is in charge?" I said. "Do you mean the spirits that reside in the house?"

Eric nodded and motioned around overhead. "So many ghosts of the past."

"And they want you to do what, exactly?"

"They want me to feed the lake. It's always so very hungry, constantly in need of new souls. And all of your souls will feel right at home there."

"Is that where you came from? The lake of fire?"

"Lake of fire..." Eric said slowly, seemingly impressed. "You are smarter than I gave you credit for, Lilian. "

"I've been doing my homework."

"Please, enlighten us."

"First things first," I said. "Shouldn't everyone know, doesn't everyone *deserve* to know, how the hell you look like my deceased husband, Kevin?"

All four of them looked up at Eric, then at me. I looked around the circle at each of them, bound and gagged, probably tired and hungry and in need of a bathroom, and silently implored each of them to trust me.

I intuitively knew I needed no such confirmation from Stella or Sam. They both knew exactly what I was doing. Stalling, biding my time, wearing him down ... one of those tactics was bound to work. And if my stalling plan didn't work? Well then, I'd find a way to burn the fucking house down.

"I'm pretty sure you know the answer to that," Eric said. "Go on, Lilian. Tell everybody."

"I'll start with the lake. It's a lake of fire. An abominable pit of hell where bad souls go when their human hosts die. As described in the Book of Revelation. A place of everlasting punishment for unfaithful, sinful people. That's what's in the front yard. A form of hell."

Stella was the only calm one in that moment. Jake, Helen, and Sam shifted in their chairs, cursing under their breaths and crying loud tears.

"You are correct. Hell is waiting for all of you, right out there." He pointed towards the bay window.

"And you are,,,what?" I continued. "Part of the recruitment team?"

Eric laughed. "Recruitment team ...I like that. And I like you, Lilian. You're smart and funny and beautiful. Quite the catch, right Sam?" Eric was standing in front of Sam, who started thrashing again, his chair rocking side to side. "But we'll get to that in due time." He turned away from Sam and back to me. "Please continue."

"Evil souls can rise up from the lake and take human form," I said. "But only if the human whose body they choose to inhabit was buried whole. This is where cremation comes into play. Cremated bodies are ashes and dust and therefore can't be inhabited by a soul. And your ugly soul inhabited my husband!"

There were gasps from around the circle.

"Becoming Kevin was essential," Eric said, "because I knew that would be the only way I'd be able to seduce you."

Suddenly four pairs of eyes were focused solely on me—shocked, surprised, disappointed, angry.

"You son of a bitch!" I said, rising from my chair and marching towards him.

Eric stepped forward and grabbed my arms hard to hold me in place. Sam pitched forward as if to stand, temporarily forgetting his legs were bound to the legs of his chair and nearly tipped over. He was talking furiously through his gag, a mumbled mess of garbled words that only he could understand. Eric ignored Sam's outburst and continued talking to me.

"Now, now, Lilian," he said. "I did you a favor by not tying you up and gagging you. Don't make me regret that decision."

"Let me go!" I said, thrashing against Eric's grasp until he had no choice but to release me. He motioned to my chair and silently bade me to sit.

I reluctantly sat. "You didn't seduce me. We kissed. That was it."

"But wasn't it magical, Lilian? The best kiss you've ever had?"

In that moment, I couldn't admit that it was, but I couldn't deny that it wasn't.

But memories of that kiss were the least of my worries.

My loved ones were being held hostage, for reasons that were still unclear to me. They had been captured, or lured to the house, by a man who was the devil incarnate, hell bent, it seemed, in harming us—or worse. There was a possibility that we could all die tonight.

And it was all my fault.

CHAPTER THIRTY-TWO

"CAN WE GET ON WITH this, please?" I said to Eric.

We were all still seated in our chairs, except for Eric, who continued lording over all of us. We'd all settled down after the revelation that I'd kissed my dead husband's evil doppelganger. I think everyone had been shocked into calm. Emma was quiet too, perhaps trying to preserve what little energy she had left, but perhaps because she knew her efforts were futile.

"Certainly, Lilian," Eric said. "Is there anything you'd like to add before we get started?"

"I'd like to ask, why me?"

"Because you were a stranger, unaware of the Becker legacy, and the so-called Becker curse. Therefore, you would be unafraid of us."

"So my ignorance and willingness to work with you made me an easy target?"

"In a manner of speaking. Although I wouldn't say you were *willing* to work with us. At least not in the beginning."

"I had my reservations."

"Plus, your tainted soul called out to the spirits in this house. And you, in turn, would lead us to Sam."

Sam had been staring at the floor, but at the mention of his name, he looked up and scowled.

"And Jake and Helen?" I asked, wondering what skeletons they had in their closets. What sins did they have to atone for?

"Patience, Lilian. We'll get to that."

Jake and Helen looked at each other, Jake looking pissed off and Helen sobbing. She'd been crying since I'd arrived. I recoiled at the thought of Eric treating us like puppets to be manipulated and controlled.

While everyone was quiet, I used the opportunity to speak to Emma. I felt awful involving her, but I knew if I could get through to her, get her to talk, she'd tell me the truth.

"Eric killed my husband, didn't he, Emma?" I said.

That very revelation, that Kevin had possibly been murdered and had not died from an accident, sent the room into a tizzy. Sam started grunting through his gag, fighting against the straps and ties. Jake bit at his gag and Helen squirmed in her chair. And Stella? She had her head bowed and was whispering to herself, as if deep in prayer.

Eric quickly strode over to me. "Leave her out of this!"

"What did he do?" I said to Emma, ignoring Eric. "I have a right to know."

"Lilian!" Eric said more forcefully, but I kept ignoring him. He looked at Emma. "Don't answer that."

I felt even more awful manipulating the emotions of a dying woman. But I had to try. I owed it to Kevin to try, to find out the truth. I approached Emma and knelt before her and placed a hand gently on her arm.

"Tell me, Emma. Please. You said I was like a daughter to you. If you cared for me at all, you'd tell me."

Emma wouldn't look at me. She kept her head bent, tears now wetting her thin face. "I'm sorry, Lilian," she said softly.

Suddenly I felt arms grabbing me around the waist as Eric dragged me back toward my chair. Sam yawped through his gag, his face red from straining. I struggled against his clutches, but it was no use. He was simply stronger than me. He thrust me down into the chair and we stared at each other, breathless from the struggle.

As he stood over me, I came at him with all my vitriol. "What did you do, you son of a bitch! What did you do to—?"

"I did what I had to do!" Eric yelled, and the room went quiet. His booming voice echoed through the room and slowly evaporated into the air until there was nothing but silence.

Sam looked at me, wide-eyed. Jake and Helen exchanged shocked glances. Stella lowered her head again.

"I did what I had to do," Eric repeated, calmer this time. "I did what was asked of me."

"You monster," I said. "Who the fuck are you?"

But I already knew the answer to that. He's the demon, Lilian. He's the demon in your view. Now how the hell are you going to get rid of him? And how on Earth are you going to save all these people...and yourself?

CHAPTER THIRTY-THREE

"IF YOU'RE GOING TO kill us, go ahead and do it already," I said to Eric, as he continued pacing across the pentagram.

"What makes you think I want to kill you?" he asked.

"Isn't that why we're here? To be judged and thrown into the lake of fire?"

"Yes, but *I* don't want to kill you. I don't want to kill any of you."

"Right. The spirits want us dead, to feed the lake. Well then, let's get on with it."

Jake, Helen and Sam gawked at me, as if appalled at my audacity, by my apparent lack of fear—and its potential to get us all killed. Stella, however, nodded at me with an encouraging look in her eye.

Make no mistake, I was terrified. We were about to die and it was all my fault. If I hadn't cheated on Kevin ... if I'd attempted to stay friends with Sam instead of abandoning him as his life was falling apart ... if I had said no to renovating The Property ... if I hadn't allowed myself to get close to Eric ...

If all those things hadn't happened, or if only *one* of those things hadn't happened, perhaps Kevin would still be alive. The domino effect of it all made me sick to my stomach. But I had to fight through it; I had to tap into my reservoir of fearlessness for all our sakes.

I got us into this mess, I was the one who had to get us out.

"Patience, Lilian," Eric said. "Your turn will come. I actually want to start with ... you." Eric pointed at Jake, who sat up in his chair.

Eric approached Jake and pulled the gag from his mouth. Jake coughed and stretched his mouth.

"What did I do?" he said, angrily. "What am I doing here?"

"Accounting fraud," Eric said matter-of-factly.

"What are you talking about?"

"Accounting fraud—the intentional manipulation of financial statements—"

"I know what it is, you psycho!" Jake interrupted. Being bound and gagged and kept against his will had obviously cracked his usual calm façade, because this was a side to Jake I'd never seen. Harsh and mean. I didn't know whether I should be impressed or scared.

"Then you'll remember that, in 2010, while operating as an independent financial accountant for one of your clients, you were accused of overstating revenue, failing to record expenses, and misstating assets and liabilities."

A pit suddenly appeared in my stomach. "Jake? Is that true?"

Jake looked briefly at me and back to Eric. "I'm paying my dues for that."

"Your actions were proven to violate Pennsylvania's state securities laws," Eric continued. "But the state Attorney General chose not to file a lawsuit, sparing you the possibility of jail time. You received a monetary fine instead."

"And?" Jake said.

"And, I'd say you got off easy. A monetary fine is hardly retribution for misleading investors and shareholders of the company you were supposed to be serving."

"It was a $500,000 fine. I maxed out all my credit cards, borrowed against my house, took out personal loans ... I'm still paying it back."

"Not to mention the damage it did to your personal life. Right, Jake?"

"My personal life has nothing to do with the poor choice I made *ten years ago.*"

"But it does, Jake. You lovely wife...Barbara, is it?"

"I'm done talking about this," Jake said.

"She threatened to leave you, didn't she? Served you divorce papers, if I'm not mistaken."

"Shut the hell up."

"But you talked her out of it. Went to couples therapy and after several months"—here Eric snapped his finger—"everything was back to normal. But not really. Nothing was ever the same between you two after that."

The room grew silent, as yet another shocking revelation was laid bare for all of us to hear.

"Jake, is all that true?" I said. "I've known you for thirty years. I never knew any of that ..."

"It wasn't your father's company, Lilian," Jake said. "You need to know that."

"I know. So why didn't you tell me? Maybe I could've helped you."

"It nearly ruined my professional reputation, and my life. I was embarrassed and ashamed. I thought I'd lose you and Kevin. As clients and friends."

I smiled at Jake sympathetically.

"So Jake hasn't received enough punishment for his crime?" I said to Eric. "You think he deserves to die for it?"

"Don't let him off the hook yet, Lilian," Eric said. "Jake, is there something else you'd like to confess?"

Jake looked both confused and irritated. "I don't know what you're talking about."

"Something about her half-million-dollar life insurance policy? Or should I say, her *million*-dollar life insurance policy?"

The top of my head started to tingle, and there was a slight throb in my right temple. I saw a vision of Jake standing at my front door, saying goodbye after our meeting. I remembered Jake had said Kevin's life-insurance policy was for a million, then backpedaled and corrected himself, saying he must've misspoken, confused me with another client.

I also recalled having a blinding headache in that moment, and wanting to say goodbye to him quickly so I could take something for it. Maybe I had been receiving a warning and didn't recognize it. Which didn't matter now, because the tingling and throbbing was telling me something was amiss. Jake was guilty of another crime.

"What did you do, Jake?" I said calmly.

Jake sat up and looked at me with wide eyes. "You'll get your money, Lilian. I promised you that."

"And you'll get yours, right Jake?" Eric said. "Half a million dollars?"

My back stiffened. "What does he mean? I don't understand."

"I believe it's called double indemnity," Eric said. "Jake, would you like to explain that to us?"

"No," Jake hissed.

"Then allow me. Double indemnity is a clause added to a life insurance policy that states the insurer will pay double the face amount of the contract in cases of accidental death. Did I get that right?"

Jake gave Eric a mean look, but said nothing.

"Did Kevin know about the double indemnity clause?" I asked Jake.

"Yes," he said. "He insisted on adding it."

"Why?"

"Because of the benefits. Accidental deaths are rare, ironically. But in his case, given your line of work, construction ... well, having an accident is more likely. Kevin knew that."

"He knew he was going to die," I whispered. It was a message that had been given to me previously, and here it was again. I wasn't sure of it then, but I was sure now.

Kevin O'Shea knew he was going to have a fatal accident.

"Plus, the premiums for these clauses are inexpensive," Jake said. "Double the payout for a very small investment. It was a no-brainer for Kevin."

The room went silent, and I felt six pairs of eyes on me.

"So you took Kevin's foresight and used it to your advantage," I said.

"I gave Kevin what he wanted," Jake said, his voice shaky. "You have to believe that."

"What Kevin wanted was for me to have a million dollars. Not have one of his best friends steal half a million dollars from his wife!" I was angry as hell, like I could easily drag Jake out to the lake and throw him in myself. "You lied to my husband. And you lied to me."

Out of the corner of my eye I could see Eric smirking, looking between Jake and me. He was enjoying this. Watching people confess and fight and fall apart...

"I'm so sorry, Lilian," Jake said. "I don't know what—"

"Have you no guilt about deceiving your *friends*?" I interrupted. "You didn't want to tell us about your other crime because you thought you might lose our friendship, but you were willing to *steal* from us?"

"I was desperate! I'm still in so much debt ..." His chest heaved and he looked on the verge of tears. "I knew you'd still be taken care of ..."

"And that made it acceptable?"

"Of course it didn't."

"You didn't think I'd ever find out? How were you expecting to get away with it? You thought I'd never read the policy that—?"

And I stopped, because I realized that I didn't have a copy of the policy. Jake had never given it to me, or to Helen, despite my repeated requests. Jake lowered his head.

"You thought I'd forget all about getting a copy of the policy," I said. "Or you were hoping I'd forget. I'd be too busy or grief-stricken to remember. And then I'd get a check for half a million, you'd get your half-million, and then neither of us would need the paperwork anymore. We'd move on and that would be that."

In that moment, the tingling and throbbing stopped. Like a light switch. *Click*, gone. I'd figured it out. The message had been delivered.

"I'm so sorry..." Jake said. "I don't know what to say."

"You make me sick," I said. It was all I could do to keep from lunging at him and strangling him with my bare hands.

The others had remained silent this whole time, but their emotions were written all over their faces. They all looked sad, and defeated, and very, very worried.

"Excellent," Eric said, walking back over to Jake and forcing the gag back into his mouth. "Who's next?"

CHAPTER THIRTY-FOUR

ERIC WALKED UP TO HELEN. Her eyes were red and puffy and smeared with eyeliner and mascara, but she'd finally stopped sobbing. He forced the soggy gag out of her mouth.

"Please let me go," she said. "I haven't done anything wrong. I don't belong here."

"Helen Whitman," he said. "You do belong here, right beside the rest of them."

"I don't know who you are, but you're not the Eric Becker I met three months ago."

"You're right. I don't look the same. I've had a pretty nice upgrade since then." Eric flashed me a wicked smile. I snarled at him and clenched my fists but remained seated, knowing full well I'd never be able to overpower him on my own.

"Lilian, the Beckers intentionally cremated everyone in the family," Helen said. "They wanted to prevent the evil souls like Eric from reincarnating or shapeshifting or whatever you call ... this." She motioned to Eric. "Frank knew it and Kevin knew it. It's...it's obvious now."

"I prefer the term... *reanimation*," Eric said.

"And I prefer evil doppelganger," I hissed.

"Who was he?" Helen asked. "Whose body were you inhabiting back then? I know everyone in this town, and I didn't recognize him."

"Does it matter? I'd much rather talk about you."

"I didn't do anything wrong."

"So you're saying nothing happened between you and Lilian's father in August 2003?"

Immediately my mind started racing. What was going on in our family in August 2003? Wait. My mother died in August 2003....

"I ... I don't remember," Helen said. "That was so long ago."

"Think, Helen. You were in love, weren't you? In love with a man you couldn't have."

Her eyes filled with tears again until finally her face caved into a mask of anguish. "No. Please, don't do this!"

"You were obsessed, weren't you, Helen? All the phone calls and emails that went unanswered. You just couldn't let him go, could you? Even though he was married, and he refused you time and time again. You couldn't leave him be."

Helen sobbed and said nothing.

"And when he refused you, refused to see you, refused to even talk to you," Eric continued, "you got angry, didn't you, Helen? You didn't like being ignored."

"I didn't do anything!" she said. Then she turned her wild eyes towards me. "I didn't do anything, Lilian! I put a stop to my behavior. I realized how ridiculous it was. It was wrong. And the pressure I was putting on your father ..."

I could only look at her, silent, waiting for the other shoe to drop.

"You didn't do anything right away," Eric said. "You bided your time. You knew Lilian's mother was sick. You knew she was dying of cancer. You thought that, maybe, towards the end, Lilian's father would be so distraught over his dying wife that he'd need consolation. A shoulder to cry on. Someone to help ease his pain. So you waited."

"I walked away. Left him alone. Told him I'd always be there if he needed to talk. I did the right thing. I loved him enough to walk away. Loving someone isn't a crime!"

"Of course it isn't. But maybe seducing a grieving, married man ought to be."

In that moment it felt like the wind had been knocked out of me. I was lightheaded, and found it hard to catch my breath. A wave of lightheadedness washed over me.

"Did you and my father ...?" I started. The thought of it, the vision of it in my mind, made me shiver with disgust.

My father. The man I admired and looked up to. The man who'd instructed me from a young age, until the day he died, that you don't shit where you eat. Work hard, play hard, and don't fuck around on your spouse. His words, his credo. I had broken his credo, and I just discovered that he had, too. While his wife was wasting away from cancer, he was having sex with another woman.

"It wasn't like that!" Helen was saying. "It just happened. He came to me. We both consented!"

My arms were dead weight in my lap, and I felt like my whole world had just caved in. I looked over at Sam, who watched me. I mouthed to him, "Did you know?" He solemnly shook his head.

Well, I thought, at least I wasn't the only one in the dark about my father's infidelity. That knowledge brought little comfort, but it was all I had at the moment, so I clung to it with what little energy I had left. I looked over at Stella and secretly wished she had a Men In Black-style neuralyzer in her bag of tricks.

Or, if nothing else, matches and lighter fluid.

CHAPTER THIRTY-FIVE

I DIDN'T THINK I, OR anyone else, could take much more. I was emotionally wrecked. I wanted to curl up in a ball and sleep for days. Weeks would be better.

"This is fun!" Eric said. "Who's next?"

He was actually excited about all this. He was grinning and rubbing his hands together in anticipation. I couldn't believe I'd fallen for him. He'd caught me at my most vulnerable, but I can't really be mad at him for that. I allowed it to happen.

And I knew better than to try and stop whatever he had planned, at least at the moment. Sickening as it all was, I had to let things play out. My intuition would tell me the right time to act.

"I think it's time," Eric said, spinning about, "we learn a little more about ... Stella."

Eric approached Stella, keeping a further distance from her. I'd noticed that when I first arrived; he avoided direct eye contact with her, and seemed hesitant to get too close. Did she possess some power that Eric knew could affect him, weaken him? If so, Stella knew it, because she was strong and confident, and didn't seem the least bit afraid of him.

He had to stretch his arm far to remove the gag from her mouth.

"I can't possibly imagine what beef you have with me, sweetheart," she said, once her gag had been removed.

"Ah, Stella! You're a practicing heathen."

"I prefer the term Neo-Pagan, thank you very much."

"Let's face it, Stella. You're a witch."

"Says the murderer," she said. "I'm a pagan priestess, actually. But witch works too."

"You practice magic and witchcraft."

"Guilty as charged!"

"Which means you worship Satan."

"We worship a Mother Goddess. And we worship animals and nature, too."

"You don't worship animals! You sacrifice them!"

"There's no animal sacrifice. Well, fried chicken and burgers on the grill. Does that count?"

Even though they were arguing, there was an ease with which they spoke. If you didn't know any better, you'd easily mistake them for siblings having a friendly spat. The rest of us could only sit back and watch the scene unfold, our heads ping-ponging back and forth between them.

It was about this time that I noticed Stella's shoulders and arms were moving up and down and back and forth. Her hands were still tied behind her back, so I couldn't see what they were doing, but I got the feeling she was trying to free herself. Sawing the zip ties back and forth and up and down against something—an exposed nail? A splintered piece of wood? Every time Eric faced her, she stopped, and when his back was turned, she frantically sawed away. I eyed her suspiciously and she winked, then discreetly lowered her eyes to her bag.

"Black magic!" Eric said, throwing his hands up into the air. "All of it!"

"Ain't nothing black about my magic, honey."

"But it's used to cast spells."

"Actually, we use the power of the Universe and the elements in nature for healing, protection, and to banish negative influences. Negative influences like you."

Eric was starting to look annoyed. He was scowling and his fists were clenched. He was trying to get a reaction out of her, get her to confess to something like he had the others, to leave them emotional puddles on the floor, begging for him to stop. Stella wasn't having any of it. In fact, she was starting to look bored. She exhaled loudly and tilted her head back and rolled her eyes. All the while sawing away every time Eric had his back turned.

"Then how do you explain the pentagram?" Eric said, motioning to the five-sided star painted on the floor.

That made me sit up in my chair. "Wait. Stella...*You* drew the pentagram?"

"Of course. An extra layer of protection never hurt anyone."

"How did you ...?" I said, dumbfounded. "When ...?"

Stella flashed me a smile.

"Well, Lilian," Eric said, "it appears your friend here used some of her human magic to ... see into the future."

"It's called clairvoyance, asshole," Stella said. "And it scares you, doesn't it? Because it means I can see what's coming, what you have planned."

Eric ignored her comment. "Well, I used my own power to summon all of you here, and Stella was nice enough to arrive first. She greeted me with cooking spray to the face."

"Best I could do in a pinch," she said, shrugging.

It was the first time I heard everyone make a sound other than a moan or a whimper or a sob. We were laughing. In the face of evil and uncertainly, we were laughing.

"I recoiled and ran into the kitchen to wash my face and that's when she did...this." Eric looked down in disgust at the pentagram.

"I knew what you had planned, Eric," Stella said. "The day after Lilian and I blessed this hell hole, I had a vision. And I knew."

"How did he summon you here, Stella?" I asked.

"Ready for this? He called my cell phone and pretended to be you. It was *your* voice. He sounded exactly like you. He, pretending to be you, asked me to meet him here at five today."

"*What*?" I said.

The other four in the circle started talking at once, mumbling through their gags, nodding their heads frantically. Stella and I looked at them, and she motioned to them all.

"Is that what he did to you, too?" she asked, and four heads nodded.

"You clever little devil," she said to Eric, and he bowed.

"How did you get all their numbers?" I asked, and he gave me a knowing look. Oh, of course. The internet. Anything and anyone can be found on the internet.

"Congratulations for figuring it all out, Stella," Eric said, still refusing to look her in the eye. "Now be a good girl and tell us why you would draw a pentagram if you didn't mean to invoke the devil? Not to mention ruin the hardwood flooring that Lilian and Sam spent good money refinishing."

"History isn't your strong suit, is it, sweetheart?" Stella said. "Do you know how old this symbol is? Cultures dating as far back as the ancient Egyptians and Babylonians used this symbol. The Christians, the Jews, the Taoists in China ... it was a positive symbol for all these cultures. Positivity and protection." Stella was still futzing around with her hands, trying to free herself. I decided to buy her some time.

"So how did it become negative?" I asked.

"That was Hollywood," Stella said. "An upright pentagram, with a single point upward, was essentially good. It has always been a positive sign. But the 19th century Romantics started questioning what the reverse meant. What if the symbol were flipped, and two points were upward? Well, that must denote the opposite of positivity. *Evil*. Hollywood, knowing evil sells, picked up on that and perpetuated the reverse pentagram."

"So you drew it to protect us?" I asked.

"Enough," Eric said, gruffly. "No more idle chit-chat."

"You started this conversation," I reminded him.

"He sure did," Stella said. "Besides, I don't know why you'd have such a problem with a pentagram. You *did* come from the lake of fire. You're accusing me of devil worship and witchcraft, yet you're evil incarnate. Not to mention a murderer. You, of all people, should identify with a reverse pentagram."

Eric didn't have a response for that. He simply said, "You're only delaying the inevitable."

Stella rolled her eyes. "So, anyway...pentagrams, or pentacles, represent the five elements: earth, air, fire, water, and spirit. If you want to get literal about it, then the symbol can also represent a human, the tip being the head, and two arms and two legs. Personally, I use pentagrams as a talisman, to remind me of my connection to the divine, to open and close circles...and to banish unwanted energies." She gave Eric a sidewise glance.

I was hoping that diversion, brief as it was, bought Stella a little more time. It must have, because Stella eyed me knowingly. But I still didn't know what she had up her sleeve; I just had to trust that I'd know when I knew.

"So do you want to tell me the real reason I'm here?" Stella said. "The shocking revelation you want me to confess to?"

"You belong to a coven of witches," Eric said.

Stella blanched at the word *coven*. "Please, we're simply a group of like-minded people who hang out and do positive incantations."

"And for those among us who don't know what an incantation is," Eric said, "enlighten us, please."

"Incantations are spells, charms, prayers. They're all the same thing. We speak them—sometimes we chant or sing. All depends. It's no different than going to church, really."

"You get together regularly, I assume?"

"Our ceremonial rituals take place monthly, usually. Sometimes more. All depends."

"Your little ... ceremonies," Eric said. "I assume there's alcohol involved?"

"Oh, goodness, yes. Usually wine. Lots and lots of wine."

"So is it fair to say that with adult men and women there, drinking so much wine, that things can sometimes get out of control?"

"Out of control? Like we get really silly and loud and have happy accidents where things get broken? Sure."

"No, Stella. I'm talking about things more deviant and perverse. Things like... drunken group sex orgies."

The room fell silent. I looked around the room to see everyone's reactions. Helen inhaled sharply. Sam and Jake glanced around the room as if embarrassed. Stella, ever rock steady, showed not a shred of embarrassment.

"Orgy has such a disgusting sound to it, doesn't it?" she said. "What we do is natural and beautiful. We celebrate the human body for the miracle that it is. In all its shapes and sizes. There's nothing deviant or perverse about that."

Stella seemed oddly proud. Then I remembered what her husband, Joe, had said. Something like, "I can't go through this again." He must have been referring to this. I could imagine that whatever Stella was participating in would cause friction in a marriage. Hell, I was unfaithful once and was never able to fully heal from the guilt. Stella was engaging in sexual acts with multiple people, consensually, perhaps men and women, on what appeared to be a regular basis.

I must have been spacing out, because when I came back to attention, Stella was staring at me, wide-eyed. For the brief second Eric had his back turned, she pulled both hands from behind her back quickly to show me that she was free. Then she bent over and reached into her bag of tricks with her right hand, while putting her left hand back behind her back.

She pulled out a small, round plastic bottle, palmed it in her hand, and returned her right hand behind her back just as Eric turned around again. I knew what she'd pulled out of her bag.

Holy water.

Helen was still crying, lost in her own pity party, while Jake stared wide-eyed off into space. Both were mentally gone. Sam, though...Sam must've watched my interaction with Stella, because when I glanced over at him he was shaking his head at me, his eyes pleading. *Whatever you got planned, don't do it.*

Sam had to know I had no choice. I was the only one who was free. I had to do whatever needed to be done. Stella was pitching me the ball, and I had to hit a homerun.

Eric approached Stella. As he did, Stella used the element of surprise to lean forward as far as she could, whipped her right hand from behind her back and squirted holy water in his face. Eric recoiled a few steps while frantically wiping water off his face.

With Eric distracted, Stella yelled my name and held up a coffee mug and a small, collapsible umbrella. I didn't understand what she meant at first, but then she made a stabbing motion with the pointy end of the umbrella and pretended to smash the mug. I knew then it was go time. Stella and I were going to double team him.

I ripped out of my seat and charged at Eric full bore as Stella threw the umbrella in my direction. I fumbled but caught it and immediately started jabbing Eric in the side, hard. He pulled his hands away from his face and tried to protect his middle. His face was wet with holy water and he blinked back tears. I couldn't tell if the holy water was affecting him somehow, or if his discomfort was merely from having water in his eyes.

Or perhaps he was crying from the pain I was inflicting to his stomach, his ribs, his sternum.

It was then that I realized Stella's leg weren't free. She'd only managed to free her hands. She shuffled forward frantically, each of her ankles tied to a chair leg, trying not to fall over. She pitched forward and as she did she managed to swing the coffee mug and connect with the left side of Eric's head. With a resounding *smash*, the mug splintered into several pieces. Eric screamed in pain and instinctively grabbed the side of his head, giving me the opportunity to continue striking his torso.

Eric shook his head as if shaking off the pain, blood streaming down one side of his face. Stella had fallen sideways onto the floor, and, with her one-time weapon now useless, she set about trying to free her legs.

It was pandemonium in the circle, too. Helen started screaming. Jake had awoken from his mental fog and was yelling through his gag at Sam to do something. And Sam—he was hopping forward in his chair, desperately yanking his hands and feet in all directions, hoping the ties would snap.

I'd underestimated Eric's strength. Despite a head wound and what had to be severe bruising, he still managed to wrestle me to the ground. After what felt like several minutes of struggle, but was probably only seconds, he managed to flip me over and pin my arms above my head with his hands and straddle me. We were both red-faced and breathless, and his head wound now dripped blood onto the floor. We stared into each other's eyes, both full of rage.

"Aunt Em!" Eric said, his chest heaving, eyes still locked with mine. "Bring me a gag and some zip ties."

"You get your kicks from tying people up, you sadistic fuck?" I said.

"I did warn you, Lilian. If you didn't play nice, I'd have to restrain you."

And as he hoisted me off the floor, dragged me to my chair and tied me down tight with the supplies Emma had pulled from her purse, I thought:

For fuck's sake, Lilian. Now what?

CHAPTER THIRTY-SIX

ERIC WAS PACING THE circle again, labored and limping. He had retrieved a handkerchief from Emma's purse, which he was holding to the side of his head to stop the bleeding. His other hand was stretched across his middle, clutching his ribs.

We were all back in the circle, Stella refastened to her chair and me newly fastened to mine. We were all exhausted, delirious, and crazy with fear. Except Stella, of course. Her hair was disheveled and her wrists bloody and bruised from freeing herself from the zip ties and she had a nasty-looking scratch on her face. Physically, she was a hot mess. But yet somehow she still appeared ... calm.

I did a quick assessment of my own body. My ankle was throbbing and I knew it must be sprained. But I didn't see any blood or bruising yet. For now, I was okay.

"Minor setback," Eric announced, wincing as he walked. "Let's continue. We have two left. And I believe I saved the best for last. Lilian, Sam—who would like to go first?"

I yelled through the gag and Eric came over and ripped it out of my mouth with one forceful hand gesture.

I swallowed and licked my lips to ease the dryness.

"What do you want to know?" I said.

"Well, I believe this is when you're supposed to admit your sin of adultery."

Nobody in the room flinched at that; it was an open secret that Sam and I had had an affair.

"Everybody knows that," I said. "The whole town of Pennsgrove knows. Kevin and I were able to move past it. Keep living our lives."

"Did you though, Lilian? Isn't it true that you secretly wanted to keep seeing Sam?"

I felt eyes on me. "What? No!"

Eric tilted his head at me, as if he knew I was lying. "You didn't want to end the affair, did you? You wanted to have your cake and eat it too."

Sam, who'd been fighting against his straps the whole time, fell still, looking at me. Eric noticed Sam's motionlessness.

"Oh, Sam. Did Lilian not tell you? Lilian never intended to stop the affair. It was Kevin who forced her hand."

"Shut up," I said calmly.

"Right, Lilian?"

"Shut the fuck up, Eric."

"Kevin threatened you with divorce, didn't he? Didn't he threaten to cut you out of the very business you had created? He was going to kick you out of the house and steal your company right out from under you."

"I hate you," I said. I hated him, but yet I was amazed at how he knew. How the fuck did he know? About me, and Helen and Stella and Jake?

"How would your life have ended up?" Eric continued. "Alone and homeless and no job."

The stillness in the room was palpable. Everyone in the room knew about my fling with Sam. But no one saw that coming. Not even Sam knew; I hadn't told him any of that.

"And all you had to do was stop sleeping with Sam," Eric said. "Didn't seem like such a large sacrifice for the sake of your livelihood, not to mention your marriage."

"I ended it. I did put an end to the affair."

"But not until it was almost too late. And what I can't fathom, is why it was so hard for you to give him up? It didn't have anything to do with love. You don't love Sam. You never did..."

Sam grunted and strained uselessly against the ties.

"Don't listen to him, Sam," I said. "He doesn't know what he's talking about."

"Oh, I think I do. And I think you do, too. And Kevin? He certainly knew you didn't love Sam."

"I loved Sam, in my own way. I still do. But yes, not the way I loved Kevin."

"That's how Kevin was able to move on, right?" Eric said. "Drop the divorce proceedings and let bygones be bygones. Because he knew that although you loved Sam, you were in love with your husband. As it should be."

Sam's shoulders dropped and he looked at the floor and I could only imagine what he must be thinking. So the next thing I said wasn't for anyone's benefit but his.

"Yes, I was in love with Kevin, but he wasn't in love with me. He loved me the best way he knew how, but he was never able to accept my true, authentic, flawed self. And that's not true love in my book ..."

To outsiders, Kevin and I had been the perfect couple. We had it all: a successful business, supportive friends and family, a steady, stable marriage, and love for one another. But that love was lopsided. I realized that now.

"True love is what Sam feels for me," I continued. We looked at each other, both starting to cry. "Sam makes me feel loved in a way that Kevin never could. Sam accepts me for me, flaws and all. He makes me feel needed and wanted and important. That's true love. And that's why I had a hard time ending the affair."

There was a moment of silence as the weight of all that sank in. Sam continued looking at me, and the rest of them looked like they'd just watched a romantic drama with an unhappy ending.

"How very special, Lilian," Eric said sarcastically. "Kevin knew he had you. You weren't going anywhere. You loved Kevin with all your heart. He knew that. But he had to test you. He did what he had to do, forced your hand by serving you divorce papers."

"Did Kevin tell you all that?" I said.

"Not directly, at first."

"What do you mean by that?"

"I overheard him talking to your lawyer about it."

"Liar," I snapped. "That's bullshit."

"I'm being honest, Lilian. You know that support group that Kevin belonged to? The one that, let's see ... Jake also belonged to?" He turned towards Jake, whose eyes darted open wide.

"How did you know about that group?" I asked.

"I'm a member of the YMCA, where their meetings are held," Eric said. "Sam calls it Fight Club. Which is so clever, Samuel." Sam glared at Eric and said "Fuck you" through his gag.

"Did you know this, Jake?" I asked.

Jake vehemently shook his head.

"I like the local Y. It's how I ... meet people," Eric explained.

"It's how you meet people you want to kill and throw into the lake?"

"Precisely. I didn't actually meet Kevin through the club. But I did find him there. And I overheard him talking to your lawyer. So, although I found Kevin first, this still all started with you."

I had to keep talking, to keep the conversation going, or else I was liable to lunge forward and attack him, chair and all.

"The first time you met Kevin was at the Borough Hall meeting?" I asked, and Eric nodded. "What did you say that got him so upset? Did you lay out your whole plan to him? How you were going to kill him and take over his body so that you could get to me and kill me...?"

"Of course not, Lilian. I just asked him to renovate the house."

"You ... you what?"

"It all started out so simply. I introduced myself, told him my ancestral home needed some TLC, and asked if he wanted the job. That's it."

"I don't believe you."

"I don't blame you. But that's what happened. Kevin said he was familiar with the Becker property ..."

"We drove by it once, years ago."

"... And then he said he wouldn't touch the place with a ten-foot pole. Seems he was familiar with the Becker house ... and the Becker curse, too. Never would've pegged your husband as the superstitious type." Eric shrugged. "Anyway, he turned me down."

"Then what?"

"Well, I tried to convince him, of course. Said it would be the perfect project for him and his wife, it would be profitable, keep you busy for months ... And he kept saying no. Perhaps I pushed a little too hard, came on a little too strong. Even so, I tried to keep the conversation civil. Honest I did. Kevin was the one who felt the need to escalate the conversation. Yelling and insulting my family ..."

"What did you do, Eric?"

"What did *I* do? Kevin is the one who angrily refused me *and* insulted my family's good name. Called them all rich, entitled bastards who deserved everything they got. So at that point I saw no other alternative in how I was going to get you involved, other than to get nasty. So that's when I told him I was going to kill him." He paused. "And then I said I was going to kill you."

I looked up at the ceiling, tears in my eyes. I didn't know Kevin had been familiar with the Becker family, let alone the curse. In twenty years of marriage, he'd never told me he knew anything about them. Maybe that's why he never wanted to renovate old homes; he associated them all with the Becker estate—haunted and cursed.

"I told Kevin that no matter his answer, the outcome would still be the same," Eric said. "That you would both die. And then I showed him alternate future scenarios: you renovating the house without him, you together romantically with Sam, you meeting your untimely death. He didn't like any of that. But he didn't need to see any of that, and he didn't need to know about my original plan, either. He could've remained blissfully unaware by just saying yes. But he forced my hand. So do you see how your decisions can sometimes come back to haunt you?"

"Kevin didn't do anything wrong," I said, feeling utterly defeated. "He was innocent."

"You're right. His only crime was loving you. But sometimes there has to be collateral damage. Kevin was it. Kevin was a victim of his own wife's sins."

The others grew more and more agitated: crying, biting at their gags, yanking and tugging at their bonds. They sensed, as I did, that time was drawing nigh.

We were very close to death.

I glanced over at Emma, at her almost lifeless body in the chair. She'd been silent this entire time. A silent witness to our pain, misery, and suffering. That was her role, that's why she was here. The spirits of the house proclaimed it.

I couldn't get through to Eric. His soul was black and corroded and there was no convincing him of anything. But Emma ... she was still human. She may've appeared lifeless, she may not have been watching everything, but she still had ears. She'd heard everything. And as long as her heart was still beating, there was a chance it contained some empathy.

"Please, Emma," I said. "Let us go."

She looked up at me, her face pale and gaunt and, I thought, full of death. "Lilian, dear, I can't."

"You can. You can let us go. No one needs to know. And we won't tell."

"The house will know," Emma said. "The house will know..."

There was a pause. A stillness descended, as if we were all listening for the house to respond. Like it was a living entity, listening, waiting. There was a collective holding of breath, synchronized heads looking around the room. And then ... nothing.

"You're a good person, Emma," I continued. "I know this is hurting you. You can end this."

"Oh, Lilian. I've grown so fond of you." She coughed several times and it took her a minute to recover. "I wish I could help you. I wish I could help all of you."

"We're good people," I said. "You know that. Flawed, yes. Irreparable, no."

"The spirits don't care about such things," Eric said, looking around the room as if speaking directly to the house. "They see only in black and white. There's no saving any of you. But if it's any consolation, your deaths will be quick. It won't be painless, but I promise it will be quick."

"You son of a bitch," I said. "Is that what you told Kevin, too?"

Eric just smiled.

"How did you know all those things about us? All our secrets?"

Eric stopped in the middle of the circle. "You and Stella aren't the only ones with psychic gifts."

I stole a glance at Sam, and when our eyes locked, he gave me a steely-eyed look of determination. He motioned subtly to his hands, which were still tied behind his back, but moving slowly and rhythmically. He was trying to free himself. He had a plan. I didn't know what it was, but I knew I needed to keep stalling as long as possible.

"You're a murderer *and* a psychic. Great," I said.

Emma held up a hand to silence us and get our attention. "I'm so very tired. Eric, please finish this."

"Wait!" I said. "Before we continue, there's one more thing that needs to be revealed." Eric gave me a quizzical look. "*Your* secret," I said. "You have to confess *your* sin. It's only fair. We told you all of ours. You said once that we're all afraid of the light. We want the truth to hide in the darkness, because we're afraid of what the light might reveal."

"Touché, Lilian. I did indeed say that."

"Seems to me the only one not being truthful tonight is you, Eric Becker. If that's even your name ..."

"That is my name. But I'm not who you think I am."

"Who are you?"

"Let me return the favor," Eric said. "Let me tell you who I am..."

CHAPTER THIRTY-SEVEN

"... BUT FIRST LET'S TALK about Sam," Eric said. "He's the only one left, and we can't continue until we finish the circle."

Eric's head had stopped bleeding. There was dried blood on his skull and some smeared down the left side of his face. He limped over to me, stuffed my gag back into my mouth, then walked over to Sam and removed his.

"You motherfucker!" Sam spat. He pulled against his restraints and rattled in his seat. "I swear to God when I get out of here I'm going to destroy you! You'll be wishing you were back in hell!"

"Now, now, Sam. This is a chance to talk about you, remember?"

"I'll make it quick," Sam said. "I'm an alcoholic and an adulterer. Got myself into a lot of trouble two years ago. Nearly drank myself to death. Had an affair with my best friend's wife. Lost my job, lost my wife and family, lost some of the most important relationships in my life." He paused and looked at me. "I got my shit together, or so I thought, until I started working in this hellhole, and all my demons resurfaced."

"Bravo, Sam. Very brave of you to be so honest. But you are missing one thing."

"Yeah? What's that?"

Eric smirked at Sam.

"If you're talking about my relationship with Lil," Sam said, "then yeah, okay, I'm in love with her. Loved her since we were kids. She made her choice though, and it broke my heart. My brain moved

263

on but my heart never did. So when she asked me to work on this project I jumped because I thought it would give us a chance to try again. Maybe we could be together this time. There, that's it. Happy now? Can we get on with it?"

"Oh, Sam," Eric said. "Thank you for that. But that's not what I was talking about."

"What the hell else do you mean?"

"Your youngest, Carly...."

Sam's face twisted into a mask of anger. "Don't you say her name! Don't you dare talk about anyone in my family!"

Eric ignored him. "You hurt her, didn't you?"

Sam's face was stern. "Shut the fuck up."

"How she cried and howled in pain...all the way to the hospital..."

This was a story I'd never heard. I looked around the room and it appeared that I wasn't the only one unaware of the incident. Everyone was wide-eyed and staring at Sam, waiting for an explanation.

I wish I could speak to him, but the gag made it impossible.

"It was an accident," Sam said.

"You were home with the girls and Debbie was at work," Eric said. "You'd had a few too many. Carly refused to go to bed when you told her to. You got angry at her continued disobedience."

"That's enough," Sam said.

Eric ignored him. "You raised your voice and grabbed her arms tightly. She got scared and started to cry. She said you were hurting her."

"I swear to God when I get free..." Sam said, but Eric continued.

"Becca tried to intervene as Carly tried to wriggle free. You pushed Becca out of the way and then forcibly threw Carly to the ground in a drunken rage."

There were a few gasps. I, too, was shocked.

"I didn't throw her to the ground!" Sam said, getting agitated. "She pulled free and fell backwards."

"Her right forearm fractured when it hit the tiled kitchen floor."

"It was an accident!" Sam repeated.

"Your sweet, innocent little girl was only four years old. Her arm was in a cast for a month."

Silence filled the air.

I tried to mumble through my gag at Sam. *Why didn't you tell me?* But it came out a garbled mess of words.

Eric looked over at me and then back at Sam. "I think Lilian is wondering why you didn't tell her, Sam."

Sam looked at me with pleading eyes. "I...I don't know, Lil. Maybe because I was embarrassed and ashamed and felt guilty. Even though it was an accident. It was a hard time then, you know..."

I did know. I nodded at Sam to let him know I understood.

Sam continued. "We dealt with it as best we could, Carly healed, and we moved on."

"*Carly* seemed to move on," Eric said. "But you couldn't. The 'accident' left you sleepless for months."

Sam hung his head.

"And Debbie? She never bought that it was an accident. She blamed you. She *still* blames you. And she still hasn't forgiven you for it."

"Tell me something I don't know," Sam said harshly. "I was embarrassed and ashamed and full of guilt. It was an accident but I took the blame, dealt with it all."

Eric eyed me, then turned his attention back to Sam. "So....it seems you and Lilian were keeping secrets from each other."

Sam and I looked at each other sheepishly yet apologetically.

"Don't expect this renovation project to change things between you, Sam," Eric said. "I know you were hoping to reunite with Lilian. Feel that spark with her again. But, well, if she didn't love you then, she certainly couldn't love you now. Especially now that this secret has been revealed."

"You asshole," Sam said.

I tried to scream through my gag. *That's not true! I believe you, Sam!*

But our words fell on deaf ears. Eric ignored us both. He appeared to be talking to himself, striding through the circle, deep in thought. "And honestly, why would Sam want her back? She disappeared from your life when you were at your lowest, right when you needed her most. And you loved her still, in spite of it. A woman, this woman" —he stopped in front of me and scowled— "who is an adulterer, just ... like ... my ... mother."

Everyone in the circle was newly confused. What's happening? They looked at each other for answers and came up empty. Eric is going to confess, I thought. That's what was happening. He was finally going to tell us who he was.

CHAPTER THIRTY-EIGHT

"MY NAME IS ERIC BECKER," he started. "I was born in 1912. Bastard son of Oskar Becker, Jr. and his tramp of a girlfriend, Geraldine. I never knew my mother. She abandoned me and my father when I was only a few months old. Dad loved Geraldine so much, and she claimed to loved him back. But she cheated on him again and again, and he continued to forgive her again and again. Because he loved her. Then, one day, she left. Dropped me on this front porch and took off, apparently with a new lover. Because of what she'd done to my father, the family cared so little for her they didn't even try to find her. She was never seen again. She was a dark soul, so I guess that's for the best."

Eric continued. "The family tried to do right by me. Especially my stepmother, Mary. God rest her soul. But I carried the bitterness and resentment of my mother's abandonment my entire life. She ruined my life, without having ever been in it.

"I fell in with the wrong crowd. They turned me. Made me even angrier than I already was. I took to the bottle and never looked back. I wrecked my life, I wrecked my liver, and I wrecked every relationship I ever had. I died a lonely, bitter, angry man. A young man. And that's who I was. That's who you see in front of you."

There were murmurs and quizzical glances. None of them understood.

But I understood. He was confessing to the real reason he'd chosen me to renovate his house. Why he singled me out personally, among all the other Pennsgrove residents. Sure, I'd been a stranger, so therefore more trusting. And I'd been ignorant of the Becker curse, which made me an easy target. But that reasoning had seemed flimsy to me. Now I knew the real reason.

I tried to speak through the gag. Eric came over and pulled it down from my mouth.

"What was that, Lilian? Something you'd like to say?"

"I said, I remind you of your mother. I cheated on my husband, a man I claimed to love, just like your mother cheated on your father."

"Yes, Lilian. I never got the opportunity to ask my mother why she did it. How she found it so easy to cheat on the man she supposedly loved. I needed to know. I thought you could make me understand how someone could do such a thing."

"Because we're human, Eric. And sometimes that means we hurt the ones we love."

"He was never human," Sam said. "He's evil. He's a devil inhabiting your husband's body. He doesn't know what it's like to be human. Before Kevin, he inhabited another body, the one he presented to Helen at the Borough Hall meeting. And who knows who the hell he was before that..."

"That's enough out of you," Eric said, and pulled Sam's gag back up and into his mouth. Sam started grunting, trying to spit the gag out.

Eric approached me as if to do the same and I said, "Wait!"

He halted and looked at me, as if to say *Now what?*

Sam had given me a signal before that he had something up his sleeve. I stalled to give him time—for what, I wasn't sure. But then we were distracted. Did Sam still want to move forward with his plan?"

"Sam?" I said. "Are you OK?" He gave me a look and I saw that his hands were still moving behind his back. And I could see that he needed more time. I had to keep stalling.

Eric looked at Sam and me quizzically, like he sensed we were up to something. He started to put my gag back in place.

"Wait!" I said. "I...uh...I have more questions. There's more about you we need to know."

"You heard Aunt Em," Eric said. "She's tired, and this has been dragging on way too long."

I stole a glance at Emma. Her head was bowed, and she was very still. If she hadn't recently spoken, I would've thought she had died peacefully right there in her chair.

"Only a few questions," I said, "Promise." Eric relented and told me to proceed.

"So your body was originally buried, then exhumed six months later and cremated," I said.

"Someone did their homework."

"I like to know who I'm dealing with. Same as you."

"We have that in common."

"That's about all we have in common."

Eric just smiled.

"Everyone in your family, in fact, was cremated," I said. "Was it to prevent what is currently happening to Kevin? Bodysnatching?"

"I wouldn't use so harsh a word. But, yes. No one in my family liked the idea of their bodies being ... re-used." Eric paused and looked at me curiously. "Do you have a point, Lilian? Because I don't think my family's burial preferences is what's really on your mind."

"What's on my mind is the fact that you lied to me and Sam about who you were. There never was another Eric Becker, born in 1974, named after his great-granduncle. There was only ever one. The one standing in front of us."

"Yes, that's right."

"The story about your life was a complete fabrication. Boarding school in Germany. Your parents dying in a car accident. Aunt Emma, who isn't even your aunt, becoming your guardian after they died. The friction caused between the two of you when she wouldn't allow you to come home for their funerals ..."

Eric continued my train of though. "... How I traveled around the world for decades. How I eventually came home to care for 'Aunt Emma' when she was diagnosed with cancer ..."

"All lies. The person you were pretending to be doesn't exist."

A thin voice arose next to me. It was Emma.

"There were two truths among the lies, Lilian," she said. "The people we told you were Eric's parents, my brother Thomas and his wife. They were real." She paused to cough. "They didn't die in a car accident decades ago. But they are dead. Both of them died several years ago of old age."

"And the second truth?" I asked.

"I really am dying of lung cancer. So I'm ready for this to be over."

"It's okay, sister," Eric said. His response caught me off-guard at first, until I realized they were truly related: older brother and younger sister. They shared the same father. "It'll all be over soon." He turned back to me.

"We had to lie, Lilian," Eric went on. "We needed a way to justify my sudden appearance. Me leaving home at a young age and not coming back for three decades made the most sense. I would become the black sheep no one talked about. That way, my friction with the family and long-term absence seemed believable. It did work, didn't it? Both you and Sam bought the whole story."

I wanted to punch the smugness off his face.

"There was one person who didn't believe a second Eric Becker existed," I said. Eric raised his eyebrows and I said, "Frank."

"Yes, he knew everything about everybody in this town."

"Did you kill him, too?" I said half-jokingly, not really wanting to know the answer.

"He knew all the Becker secrets. He had to go."

I balled my hands into fists and resisted the urge to scream at the top of my lungs.

Helen and Jake had been silent for awhile, each lost in their own world or scared into submission. On hearing about Frank, Helen began sobbing again and Jake hung his head.

Stella, though, had been alert the whole time, paying attention, listening. She didn't seem the least bit surprised by all the revelations.

I stole a glance at Sam and noticed his hands still moving behind his back. He kept trying to free himself. He nodded his head and smiled through the gag and I knew that meant it was almost go time. What *go* time entailed, I wasn't entirely sure. I'd have to wing it again like I did with Stella—and hope this one worked.

"Were you going to let me and Sam finish the house?" I asked Eric.

"Of course you were going to finish the house. I have plans for it."

"You want to turn it into a B&B for future victims."

There were a few gasps when I said that. Even Sam paused for a moment from freeing himself to look at Eric in disgust.

He ignored my comment. "You got too close to the truth, Lilian. You started sniffing around where you didn't belong. You could've bought yourself, and all these lovely people, some time had you just kept your mouth shut."

I ignored him in return. "I hate to be the bearer of bad news, but your guest house idea will never fly. The house doesn't like strangers. You know that. The house didn't like us being in here, sawing and hammering and making changes. The house hurts people when someone tries to make changes. So how on Earth are you going to finish this project?"

CHAPTER THIRTY-NINE

I LOOKED OVER AT SAM, who discreetly shrugged his shoulders at me and kept working his hands behind his back.

"So once Sam and I are dead," I remarked, "who's going to finish the house?"

"I'll find other contractors," Eric said. "I'll find some reason as to why you couldn't continue."

"The house will hurt or kill any contractors you bring in here. Innocent people."

"Small price to pay. Now, enough is enough. Let's get moving."

I looked over at Sam, who slowly pulled his right hand from behind his back. He was holding a small pocket knife. I silently laughed at Eric's mistake of not frisking any of them when they got here. And then I smiled at Sam's insistence on always having some sort of knife on him. You just never know when it'll come in handy, he liked to say. Like if you need to slice open a package, or cut a loose thread from your sweater...Or like when a murderous evil doppelganger has you strapped to a chair and you need to saw through some zip ties.

Sam slowly moved his feet to show me that not only were his hands free, but he'd also managed to cut the ties from his ankles. That's what took him so long, why he needed more time. How had I not seen him free his ankles? No matter. He was completely unencumbered, ready to dance. He fidgeted in his chair.

"What's your plan for us?" I asked Eric.

"One by one ought to work," Eric said, looking around the circle. "Down to the lake, one at a time."

I looked at Sam and he looked at me and we nodded at each other. Suddenly in one swift movement he was out of his chair, removing his gag, and rushing over to me to cut my hands free. Then he ran full-steam at Eric and charged him like a freight train.

"You first, motherfucker!" Sam said, slamming his full body weight into Eric. They both slammed to the ground with a huge thud, and the floor shook and vibrated from the impact.

Sam was slightly taller than Kevin, stockier, a little more solid, and a little bit stronger. So I wasn't worried initially when Sam was able to knock Eric to the ground. But I was concerned that Eric was stronger than I gave him credit for, so I could only hope Sam might pin Eric down long enough for the rest of us to make our escape.

I frantically started cutting my ankles free, periodically looking over at Eric and Sam. They were wrestling on the ground, punching and grunting. I had some time, but not much. My ankles free, I ran over to Helen to free her first.

I pulled the gag from her mouth, and she sobbed and coughed and sputtered. I started cutting the zip ties from her wrists, hoping my shaky hands wouldn't cut her. "When I free you, you run like hell, Helen. You get in your car and you keep driving and you don't look back. Do you understand?" She nodded and cried.

One down, three to go. Helen ran on shaky legs through the parlor and out the front door. Her car engine started, headlights flooding the room. I looked over at Sam and Eric, who were wrestling on the floor, punching and jabbing and grunting.

"How you doing, Sam?" I yelled, starting next on Stella.

"Just fucking fantastic," he said, breathless. "I could use the knife, though."

"Can't. I need it to cut everyone free."

"Let me kill this motherfucker with it, Lil, and *then* we'll cut everyone free."

I glanced back at Emma, who was calmly sitting in her chair, staring off into space as if completely oblivious to the sudden onslaught of violence. "No, Sam. How about Stella's umbrella? Could you use that?"

Sam sighed. "Fine."

I reached into Stella's bag, retrieved the umbrella and slid it across the floor to Sam. He grabbed it and started jabbing Eric in the ribs with it.

"You'll all burn in hell!" Eric cried, just as Sam stuffed his own gag into Eric's mouth. With every blow to his ribs, he screamed through the gag.

"Shut the fuck up!" Sam said.

"Emma?" I said, snapping Stella's wrists free and squatting in front of her to work on her ankles. I looked back quickly; Emma was still lost in her own thoughts. When she didn't respond I said to Stella, "You still got those matches and lighter fluid handy?"

She smirked at me. "What do you think?"

"When we're all free and clear," I said, "light the house up."

Her ankles free, Stella grabbed her bag and went to work. She gave the parlor a few squirts of lighter fluid, then left the room. I raced over to Jake, pulled the gag from his mouth and sawed away at the ties around his wrists.

"What can I do, Lilian?" he said. "How can I help?"

"When you're free, you escort Emma out of here. I don't know how she got here, but one of us might need to give her a ride somewhere. For now, just get her and yourself as far away from the house as possible."

Jake nodded and I kept hacking away until he was free. He stood and wobbled his way over to Emma, but she refused to go.

"Leave me be, young man," Emma said, shrinking away from him.

"Emma, ma'am," Jake said. "I'm pretty sure this house will be on fire in less than five minutes. We need to get you to safety."

"I'm not going anywhere. This is my home."

"But—"

"Run along, now," Emma interrupted, shooing him away with her cane.

Jake looked over at me. I glanced at Sam and Eric still rolling around on the floor; it looked like a sloppy wrestling tournament.

"Emma, if you don't leave in the next few minutes ..." I said.

"Lilian, dear. If the house is going to burn to the ground, then I'm going with it."

"But I thought you said you didn't want to die in this house. Because it had already bore witness to so much death."

She looked at me with tired eyes. "I know what I said, dear. A woman has a right to change her mind."

I nodded at Emma and held up a finger to Jake, signaling him to wait a minute. I ran through the vestibule into the kitchen, nearly colliding with Stella.

"All done," she said. "Ready when you are."

"Do you have rope?"

"I've got natural hemp rope in my bag."

"Why do you....? Never mind," I said, realizing that of course even the rope she used was organic and all-natural. And of course she'd thought to bring it along. "We might need to tie someone up!" I heard her voice in my head. Which is exactly what I needed it for.

"I'll be right back," I said. She nodded and I ran back into the parlor and rooted through her bag. I found the hemp rope and went to Sam's side, as close as I could get, anyway, without being knocked to the ground by an arm-sweep or leg-kick.

"Sam, let's drag him to a chair and tie him up." I helped Sam lift him off the ground, Eric swinging his arms and yelling and thrashing his head. I got an elbow to the ribs and knuckles to the face but figured at least I wouldn't burn to death. That would be Eric's fate. He was going down with the ship, and I'd make sure of it.

Eric had been weakened by the intense beating Sam had given him. So although his arms were still flailing, the rest of him was like dead weight. Sam and I thrust him down into a chair and Sam held him down as I tied him up as best I could. I wished in that moment I could remember the different types of knots my dad had showed me as a kid, but it didn't matter; the knots didn't need to stay tied for long.

Eric was breathless, his chest heaving and his face all red. He gave me the meanest glare. "You think you've won, haven't you? But this changes nothing. You may burn me alive, but my soul will survive."

"I'll worry about that later," I said.

"This is our fate, Eric," Emma said. "Don't fight it. It's easier that way."

"Jake, get the hell out of here," I said. He looked at me and Sam, and then at Eric and Emma, as if he was unsure. "Go. We'll be fine." I heard Jake say goodbye to Stella, then I heard his car start and saw the headlights spring on and he was gone.

"Last chance, Emma," I said. "Things don't have to end this way for you."

"Yes they do, dear."

And that was all she said.

At this, Sam and I really had nothing left to do but leave. I grabbed Stella's bag and stood in the parlor doorway, taking one last look at Emma and Eric Becker.

"Goodbye, Emma," I said.

"Goodbye, my dear Lilian."

"Eric," I said.

He sneered at me. "See you in hell."

I stood in the vestibule, taking one final look around at the beautiful home that Sam and I had almost finished renovating stem to stern. I wanted to cry.

"Let's get the fuck out of here," I said to Stella and Sam.

I handed Stella her bag. She struck a match and tossed it out in front of her. The three of us stood there, listening to the initial *whoosh* as fire hit fluid and ignited in our faces. Then we casually walked out the front door, across the porch, down the steps and onto the dirt driveway.

And there we stood, watching The Property burn.

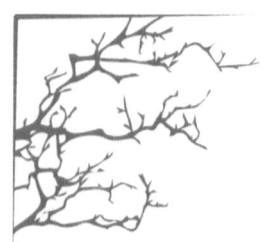

EPILOGUE

LOCAL HEIRESS DIES in House Fire

Emma Becker, 80, was found dead in her home early Wednesday morning after an overnight fire destroyed her ancestral mansion, located in the Lincoln Park area of Pennsgrove.

Becker was the oldest living heir to Becker Bakery, a family-owned retail and wholesale business of bread products. The Becker family established roots in the Pennsgrove area more than one hundred years ago.

Becker was found in the parlor of the home after firefighters contained the blaze and entered the home searching for survivors. No other bodies or survivors were found, so it is presumed Becker was alone in the home at the time.

The fire was reported around 11:30 Tuesday evening. First responders arrived to find smoke and flames completely engulfing the home. It took firefighters about an hour to put out the fire, which nearly razed the house to the ground.

The mansion recently underwent a $200K renovation that restored the Queen Anne style home, originally built in 1900, to its former glory. Lilian O'Shea, owner of LB Renovations, managed the restoration project. She could not be reached for comment.

The cause of the blaze remains under investigation by the county Fire Marshal's office, but it is presumed to be accidental.

Locals were quick to point to the Becker Curse as the cause of the fire, citing the many Becker family members over the years who'd died in the house or around the lake that sits on the property. The lake had even been dubbed the "lake of fire" for its association with these deaths.

None of those deaths were ever ruled suspicious so the Becker Curse remains, at least to authorities, a series of coincidental tragic accidents.

SAM AND I VISITED THE house—what was left of it—two days after the fire. I nearly cried when we pulled into the driveway and saw it all: a blackened shell of a house, piles of still-smoldering rubble, scorched earth where once there was grass. It was a devastated landscape, almost post-apocalyptic. But the lake—it remained intact, still and untouched. It bore witness to the events of that evening, but it wasn't giving up its secrets. Perhaps it never would.

I think I was saddest for Sam. After all, I'd wanted this project for him, to give him a karmic do-over, a new lease on life, something he could feel proud of. And now that was gone.

Neither Sam nor I wanted to be alone that night, the night of the fire, the night all hell broke loose. So I asked him to stay over. We laid on the couch in each other's arms until the sun came up, neither of us sleeping or talking.

Stella showed up on my doorstep that morning unannounced, stating that she was inviting herself over for brunch. She didn't blink an eye when she walked into the kitchen and saw Sam sitting at the island, nibbling toast and sipping coffee. She simply plopped herself next to him, said hello, and proceeded to close her eyes and place her hand on his forearm. Sam looked at me for confirmation of what was happening, and I put a finger to my lips.

After a few minutes of silence, Stella opened her eyes, grinned at Sam, grinned at me, and said, "Yep, that's what I thought."

I pulled together what food I had and made us a huge brunch of pancakes, scrambled eggs and turkey sandwiches. None of it was organic or free-range or non-GMO and Stella couldn't have cared less. She was too busy telling us how, the night before, she intentionally created a "bit of a mess" in the kitchen so that, if there was an in-depth investigation, the fire could look accidental in nature. Nobody would know all of us were there that night, she surmised, but still, she wanted to leave nothing to chance.

She'd turned one of the gas stove burners on high, dumped a bunch of extra virgin olive oil on it, and walked away to finish the task of squirting a little bit of lighter fluid, but mostly extra virgin olive oil, all around the first floor. She hoped authorities would come to the conclusion that the hot stove was left unattended, something started to smoke, then burn, then catch fire. And she hoped that the little bit of lighter fluid she used in the vestibule would be enough to start the fire, but not enough to be detected by fire investigators, and the olive oil would tell the rest of the story.

Which is exactly what the Fire Marshal reported: a week after the fire, authorities said there was no foul play or arson involved. No traces of flammable liquids were detected. The fire had been so intense, and the structural damage so extensive, in fact, that no suitable debris samples were recovered in order to even identify any flammable fluids at the scene. The fire was ruled an accident with undetermined cause and origin.

Case closed.

Slowly, everyone returned to their lives. Jake went back to his accounting business and Helen returned to her estate planning and Stella went back to her spiritual practice. But it hadn't been easy. We all needed time to digest everything that had happened and heal from the traumatic experience.

Stella had predicted correctly that Sam and I would start dating. Nothing serious. Neither of us were ready for any sort of long-term commitment. For starters, we each had our own demons to slay, baggage we didn't want to drag into our fresh start. Secondly, I didn't think I could ever love Sam the way I loved Kevin. So companionship was enough for me. We agreed to take it slow, see where things went.

About a month after the fire, I got the life insurance money from Kevin's policy. All one million dollars of it. My first thought was to travel the country for awhile, something Kevin and I had always wanted to do but never got the chance to because the business never allowed the time. Now I had the time *and* the money. I wrestled with the decision at first, but realized that Kevin would've wanted me to. So I left Sam in charge of the business (something he'd wanted all along anyway) and headed west—first to visit my sister in Denver, then San Francisco, LA, Seattle, Phoenix, Santa Fe, Salt Lake City.

I came home two months later and fell right back into my old life. The hoopla over the fire and the media coverage had given us good publicity and, upon my return, I found we had enough projects to keep us busy for months.

So I went through the day-to-day motions, all the while feeling that I didn't feel the same about the work I was doing. I had changed and grown so much; I was a different person, and now it felt like something was missing. The day-to-day wasn't enough anymore. There was a hole inside me I couldn't fill. I didn't feel complete. At the end of the day, I felt unfulfilled. There was something else I was supposed to be doing. I felt it in my bones, but I couldn't figure out what it was.

That knowledge of what I was supposed to be doing sat just outside my range of vision, on the periphery of my consciousness, and I couldn't bring it into focus. The more I tried, the further it slipped from my grasp.

I lived with that emptiness for several more months, while working side by side with Sam. And when the time was right, fate stepped in to fill that hole.

It wasn't what I was expecting, but it was exactly what I needed: a purpose, a mission, a higher calling.

And, ironically enough, I had The Property to thank for it.
THE END